C1

Even the blackest heart ... still beats.

QUENTIN COPE

MECURIAN BOOKS

https://www.mecurianbooks.com

COPYRIGHT & DISCLAIMER

The moral right of Quentin Cope to be identified as the author of this work has been assessed in accordance with the UK Copyright, Design and Patents Act, 1988 and all subsequent revisions and Copyright Law of the United States including related laws contained in Title 17 of the United States Code.

This book is a work of fiction. However, some real events and places may have been referred to or been described and unless otherwise noted, the author and the publisher make no explicit guarantees as to the accuracy of the information contained in this book and in some cases, names of people and places may have been altered to protect their privacy. Any other resemblance to actual persons, living or dead, events or locales is entirely coincidental.

No part of this book may be reproduced, stored in a retrieval system, or transmitted by any means without the written permission of the author.

Language – US English

Copyright © 2024 Quentin Cope
www.quentincope.co.uk

All rights reserved.

ISBN: 9798343838428

Also available in E-Book format

CONTENTS

Chapter 01	Page	... 001
Chapter 02	Page	... 013
Chapter 03	Page	... 027
Chapter 04	Page	... 043
Chapter 05	Page	... 058
Chapter 06	Page	... 069
Chapter 07	Page	... 080
Chapter 08	Page	... 093
Chapter 09	Page	... 103
Chapter 10	Page	... 116
Chapter 11	Page	... 127
Chapter 12	Page	... 140
Chapter 13	Page	... 151
Chapter 14	Page	... 164
Chapter 15	Page	... 180
Chapter 16	Page	... 193
Chapter 17	Page	... 208
Chapter 18	Page	... 226
Chapter 19	Page	... 234
Chapter 20	Page	... 249
Chapter 21	Page	... 259
Chapter 22	Page	... 271
Chapter 23	Page	... 284
Chapter 24	Page	... 296

CHAPTER ONE

A child is born ...

It began with a fumbling sexual encounter between two consenting adults. It took place on one unusually peaceful summer's day in 1945. The location would doubtless have been the tumbledown wreck of a stable building sited some distance to the rear of an 18th Century manor house; a property dominating the small Oxfordshire country estate of Farnborough. The individuals concerned were a young army officer; someone who had managed to survive the vagaries and ill fortunes of war in Europe ... and one Dorothy Beckett.

The conflict, described as World War Two, ended in Europe on May 8th, a day to be recognised henceforth as VE Day. Seemingly the Germans had lost ... and we, the Allies, had won. There was much to celebrate of course. This included the cruel continuance of food and fuel rationing and most would say of the time, if 'we' had just won a war ... it certainly didn't feel like it!

Both participants in the passionate physical activities taking place that day lived at the spacious manor house, known as Farnborough Hall. However the army officer claimed the elevated title of 'the honourable' in front of his name and the other carried the unflattering label of 'under housemaid' after hers.

This would not be a union blessed by God or any other individual living at the Hall, and so the regular 'coming together' of Captain the

Honourable Tarquin Ludlow and Dorothy Beckett, under housemaid, had to be carried out in secret.

During the early post war months, promises were easy to make but more difficult to fulfil and everything to support modern life appeared to be in short supply ... except the arrival of new babies. Unfortunately for Miss Becket, the birth of her child just happened to be one of them. This event however would not further her career below stairs, if indeed she ever actually had one, but it would definitely require her removal from Farnborough Hall.

When questioned, Tarquin Ludlow could not remember all, or indeed any of the pledges he had made to Dorothy during their ardent sexual encounters.

'The gal will have to go Tarquin ..!' pronounced his father, life peer Lord Avonsbury, once the news of Miss Beckett's pending arrival had been announced to all and sundry by a rather venomous head housekeeper.

Dorothy therefore had to leave the main house and, heavily pregnant, take up residence on one of the estate farms.

The whole process was to be supervised by the under housekeeper, a thirty-eight year old woman who had been with the Ludlow's all her working life. She had remained un-married, with her only family being the one she earnestly worked for. Mrs. Wyatt knew nothing about love but she knew what was right ... and what was most certainly wrong.

The birth proved uncomplicated and with a hoard of several white five pound notes pressed into Ms. Beckett's hands, she reluctantly gave her child over to a smartly dressed, unsmiling lady smelling of expensive perfume. She, in turn, whipped the boy child away to a grim looking stone built property on the edge of Oxford City.

The date was March 30th, 1946 ... and now the offspring of one Tarquin Ludlow and Dorothy Beckett belonged to the state.

The vile woman in charge of the facility revealed to all staff in the care home that the boy was 'spawned' of the devil and had his 'mark' to prove it.

This 'mark of evil' was in fact a small but decipherable 'S' shaped purple skin pigmentation defect on the right side of the child's neck. As he grew older and began to wear shirts with collars, a major part of the mark would be hidden from the casual observer. However, it would be at the centre of many a physical battle he would need to fight with other children as he grew sturdier and more self contained within the fledgling British Social Care system.

So, that's how this young boy's life began. Without doubt, it kicked off with all the promise of a shit deal and no-one looked to be planning for it to get any better ... anytime soon.

The earliest years of this orphan's life, say up to his sixth birthday, were a hazy, unclear memory of emotional distress, physical abuse and fear of the unexpected. Routine was to eventually become king and he would learn this through the heavy hand of several different masochists disguised as 'Home Supervisors'; psychopaths who moved their charge from one hellhole facility to another.

However, as the boy progressed in age and knowledge of the 'system' he quickly formed a view that the kind of institutions he had lived in held three types of inmate. First there was the bully; someone normally physically greater in stature than the average child ... and considerably dimmer. Then there were the emotionally disturbed; those boys who mainly suffered from some form of identity crisis, or other similar insecurity. Finally, there were youngsters like our young orphan; those who simply didn't give a fuck!

The boy learnt over a short period of time that being categorised as belonging to one of the second or third groups left him vulnerable to attack from the first; the bullies.

Up to the age of ten, he planned to face puberty with all his bones intact. To do this he kept himself to himself and concentrated on improving his physical fitness whilst quietly building up his self defence skills.

Good fortune provided a really positive start in this respect having discovered, quite by accident, a wartime self defence training manual at the bottom of a dusty basement cupboard.

This pocket sized gem of a manual had been designed for members of the wartime special-forces.

It was titled 'Get Tough' with script and illustrations by Major W.E. Fairburn and it took the reader through everything from a simple disablement to a quick and quiet death ... step by step!

After three years of study the boy learnt that the size and weight of one's opponent meant nothing to Major Fairburn and this fact alone was the one that fascinated him the most.

After such a long period of secretive training he became eager to stretch his wings and put his newly acquired skills to the test. He would need to 'pick his ground' of course. As the Major would confirm, time and again, at the end of each exercise, surprise would be his biggest ally and determination his secret weapon.

At the Park View Residential Care Home for Boys there lived one overriding bully. He was fourteen years old and tall for his age but dramatically overweight.

His nickname was 'Lardass' and he carried with him a team of three much skinnier individuals who were quick on their feet. These were runners and henchmen, tasked with capturing his selected victims and delivering them up for some heavyweight punishment.

The real name of 'Lardass' was Dominic Draker. He and his team would also be used on occasion by certain Home Supervisors to carry out specific disciplinary tasks, often in someone's dormitory and during the dead of night.

Draker controlled the ownership and distribution of cigarettes at Park View. The school accepted inmates up to the age of fifteen and literally everyone from nine or ten upwards smoked. It was illegal or course but the supervisors tended to ignore the activity as long as the cigarettes were bought from Draker.

So, it was time for the eager self defence student to pick his ground and he chose the first floor toilet block, a place where much of the cigarette dealing went on. Draker's boys would be constantly in and out, servicing their customers with cigarettes and maybe a quick peek at some particularly explicit pornography.

He didn't have to wait long. One of Draker's skinny associates appeared at the door to the toilet block with two young boys in tow, both looking a little nervous. All three entered the block and after waiting for half a minute, he followed.

The skinny Draker boy was named Tom ... and Tom, with a distinct scowl on his face, looked up as the uninvited boy walked in. The two young consumers held cigarettes in their hand, their eyes nervously flitting back and forth between Tom and the invading stranger.

"Fuck off!" Tom muttered turning his full attention back to his unsure customers.

"Are you talking to me?" the stranger asked, moving forward.

He moved just two paces further but would still be a pace short, according to the calculations of Major Fairburn.

Tom looked up once more. He was physically an inch or two taller than the intruder and now he appeared angry, red faced and feeling in his pocket. No doubt he would be looking for his flick knife. This was good. As soon as it appeared the

Fairburn student knew he would be in just about the right position; exactly one straight arm length away from his opponent's ugly, pock marked face.

Even he could not fail to be impressed with the speed of it all. As the skinny boy's hand left his pocket his self defence trained opponent leaned forward, raised and then straightened his arm with palm facing forwards and heel primed to lead the assault.

With the right hand now fully energised and heel travelling upward beneath the chin, Tom's head snapped back. His complete body then curled resulting in a fatal loss of balance as his attacker's right leg braced against him. Tom fell; head first, to the floor ... with a scream ... probably less an expression of pain and more a manifestation of surprise.

The knife dropped from his hand as he fell. The aggressor bent down and picked it up, pressing the spring activated blade release. With one swift movement he slashed Tom's shirt open from neck to waist, accidentally nicking him leaving a small cut above his groin.

The bulging, flickering eyes underlined the level of fear, perhaps not quite understanding what had just happened. However, once he saw the splashes of blood, he simply went berserk.

The knife wielding adversary turned to the two boys.

"There will be no cigs today. Better get going and as far as anyone else is concerned ... you were never here!"

They couldn't get away fast enough.

The 'Draker' boy, Tom, must have cracked his

head a little as he hit the hard tiled floor of the toilet block ... and that particular injury was now bleeding quite badly.

His lips quivered; eyes wide with fear.

"You bastard ... Draker will kill you for this ... and nobody will give a fuck ... do you hear me ...?"

The words, forced through tight lips, faded into a lengthy hiss as he lapsed back into a defiant silence.

"Well ... if I've not got long to live, I had better leave you something to remember me by ..!"

Turning quickly on his heel and raising his right leg as he went, he brought his foot down with extreme force on Tom's knee. The defiant boy shouted some obscenity or other but this was not the reaction expected. Indeed, it might not have been the reaction Major Fairburn could have looked for either.

Well, practice makes perfect. Raising his leg once more and mentally channelling all the energy he could muster, he brought it down hard on the Draker boy's knee once more.

This time he heard the satisfying 'crack' followed by the unearthly, echoing scream of pain.

With a quietly satisfied expression on his face, he considered that everything looked to be working well so far. One asshole down and disabled ... with just three more to go!

Closing the toilet block door after him, he left. Now he would need to make himself scarce; keep out of the way of Draker, his gang and his colluding Home Supervisors; let the events of today sink in and prepare for a late hour visit to his dorm.

The events of that dark, chilly night would be talked about at Park View and several other similar institutions in the local area for some time to come.

The manager of the home would have to explain, before an investigation board, how the hell a fourteen stone, five feet six inches tall child, in his care, somehow found his way out of a second story dormitory window, ending up with an un-enviable collection of possible life changing injuries.

That would not be all of course. Questions would be asked as to how one other boy ended up with a compound arm fracture and a curious back injury; one consisting of what appeared to be a single deep-cut knife strike stretching from the shoulder to the small of his back.

The final cause for concern would revolve around a third boy's injury consisting of an ear more or less completely ripped off and requiring some complex surgery to re-attach.

This nightmare of assaults and injuries also seemed to be linked to an incident earlier in the day when another boy's knee was left useless, treble its normal size and displaying signs of a smashed knee-cap and severely damaged ligaments.

None of the eighteen boys sleeping in the dorm saw or heard anything. There looked to be no concrete evidence against the suspected perpetrator of these crimes.

For the next few weeks, the boy who had

wreaked so much havoc on young Mr. Draker and his 'crew' knew he would need to be on his guard. He would therefore be deserting the comfort of a warm bed and grabbing as much sleep as he could in box cupboards, beneath stairwells and in the kitchen store-room. However, to his surprise, nothing happened. Everyone gave the boy a wide berth, including all staff, teachers and Home Supervisors. After his initial 'no comment' interview with the home manager he never saw Draker and his little gang ever again and no one at Park View mentioned the matter.

He knew he would be moved of course with the knowledge he would be too young to be placed within the Borstal regime. However there was a system of institutions known as Residential Homes for Vulnerable Children, and that was simply a name for some place like a Borstal ... but without the barbed wire.

At the age of thirteen, approaching fourteen, the boy ended up in a cold, bleak, heartless place called Denbigh House, located close to Newcastle. Some sort of mythical reputation arrived there before him. Everyone wanted to have a look at the latest 'hard-man' to enter the hallowed halls of Denbigh, an institution ruled with a rod of steel by its manager, Mr. Patton.

The boy was shepherded in front of the manager, flanked each side by a muscle bound, shaven headed Home Supervisor.

There would be no pleasantries.

"So, young man, open your ears and open them good. This is a tough gig. Denbigh House is packed to the ceiling with tough little shits like you ... but I give everyone here one chance; just one go at sticking the fucking tail on the donkey."

The two Supervisors smirked. He wondered what they might be like in a fight ... a real fight and not one beating up teenage children.

"There will be no trouble here ... do you understand? The first one we will always put down to a mistake, a misunderstanding perhaps between two testosterone pumped little boys claiming each of them had right on their side. However, the second one means you will leave here horizontally. Do you understand boy?"

"I do sir." he confirmed to the red cheeked, grey haired manager.

"Good. Now fuck off and remember I've got my eye on you!"

Denbigh House turned out to be far less intimidating than it first appeared. The inmates told stories of some gory going's-on and tales of boys simply disappearing from dormitories ... believe them or not ... but in general, everyone appeared to stick to the rules.

Mr. Patton was strict and in full control of everyone and everything that went on at Denbigh. The inmates and the staff all knew their responsibilities and, in particular, the lines that were not to be crossed.

Probably for the first time in his life, the boy

felt secure and able to take part in the learning environment. However, his time at Denbigh House was to be short lived. The maximum age for residency had been set at fifteen and as his birthday approached he was placed before Mr. Patton in order to discuss what opportunities might exist for him outside of this particular institution.

The choices appeared to be limited to a Borstal facility, somewhere in the South for two years and then released for civilian trade training, or join up voluntarily to Her Majesties Armed Services.

It took him less than a minute to decide. It would be the armed services!

"Good lad!" shouted Patton.

Now ... the big question ... which one?

For all the boys voting to join-up there would be some type of entrance examination followed by what was called a 'selection' process. For him, all of it was simply a breeze and twenty two days after his fifteenth birthday he passed through the gates of a well known RAF facility near Wolverhampton for the very first time.

He knew then, from that particular point, his life would change ... and change for the better. He looked around him at the shambolic assembly of civilians; boys sixteen or seventeen and their fussing rather nervous parents kissing foreheads and wiping lipstick marks from pale, hairless cheeks. Fancy hair-do's and slick suits were the order of the day for the many; for those who had been chosen to join the 'brylcreem boys'.

He smiled, wondering how many would be left after the first six weeks of what was commonly known as 'square bashing'.

CHAPTER TWO

A strangely secret business ...

I pulled my car up close to the barrier as a young military policeman stepped out of his guard room and gave me a wave. I flashed my security pass through the misted side window allowing him to lift the barrier.

'Good morning sir,' he mouthed and I waved once again in recognition of this regular early morning greeting. A brisk breeze blew landward from the sea carrying the rain near to horizontal and prompting the policeman to pull his weather proof jacket a little closer.

The sign above the guard room offered a greeting of its own: 'Welcome to CSOS Irton Moor. All visitors must report to security.' Beneath the warning an electronic display had been added showing the time as 06:40 and the date as April 6th, 1971.

Threading my way between three flat roofed brick buildings and a couple of dishevelled looking portable cabins, I parked my car at the rear of the nearby Nissen hut, a place occupied by civilian 'admin' staff. Feeling the effects of the chill breeze and driving rain, I walked the remaining fifty yards to 'the bunker' at a pace.

This was where it all happened and it really was a 'bunker', a bomb-proof, windowless shelter buried in the moor above Scarborough. New surface buildings were on the way I had been told but for now, the work of the Composite Signals

Organisation (CSO) took place in the crowded bunker buried many feet below ground and a place everyone working there had come to regard as home. With more than two hundred people pressed together in the rather claustrophobic space, the atmosphere could become a little 'crusty' at times.

I was one of the lucky ones having had a small secure space allocated to my team consisting of three technicians ... and me.

It was cramped; we needed to spread our wings a little, but so did everyone else and therefore we had been forced to 'make do' with a couple of workshop areas and a half glazed, soundproofed office space for me as the senior rank.

Ten years had passed since I first walked through the gates of a certain RAF training and education unit, a place that was destined to change my life forever. I was just a fifteen year old boy at the time; worried by nothing, frightened of no-one and with a brain like a sponge ... waiting to 'soak' it all up. Since that time I had never once looked back.

Using my pass key I opened the door to my unit. The sign on the door in barely readable, well rubbed letters spelled out; Number Three Communications Research Unit. (CRU3) Once inside, I could see right across the facility.

Someone sat in my office, at my desk; someone who must have had a pass key, not only to the office but the whole damn facility.

Once inside the workshop I stopped.

He looked up, eyes making tentative, hesitant contact. Did this look like a serving man to me? He could have been military or civilian and a good guess might be from the Secret Intelligence Service or our mother organisation, GCHQ Cheltenham.

My technicians would not arrive for their duties until around eight o'clock and it was now creeping up toward seven.

This was an unusual and possibly worrying event. I headed up a top secret unit and although I was still part of the Royal Air Force, I did not wear a uniform for work at Irton Moor. Most individuals I interacted with at the facility knew me as plain ordinary Gary Chase and not Flight Sergeant Chase.

Anyone wishing to meet with me outside of scheduled staff gatherings, military or civilian, were required to make an appointment and all such approved meetings would be held in the 'above ground' Admin Nissen Hut. Under no circumstances were meetings with strangers allowed inside the 'bunker' and so I naturally wondered what might be going on.

I entered my office, purposely blank faced and feeling tense. I waited a few seconds to see if he would be offering any explanation for being sat at my desk, in my chair, at seven o'clock in the morning.

I spoke; the irritation in my voice fairly obvious.

"I don't know who you are, or where you might have come from, but will you please remove yourself from my desk and then further remove yourself from this facility. This is currently a polite request but if you do not move within the next thirty seconds it will become less so. Do you understand?"

The dark grey haired individual looked possibly older than his true years. His suit appeared 'off the peg'; his tie obviously Marks and Sparks and my guess would be that his hands had come into contact with various 'blunt' objects over the period of an adventurous lifetime.

He felt inside his jacket for something which he eventually extracted and then threw on the desk top. It was a small folding leather wallet, similar to the one I owned.

"Open it!" he said quietly; his face still harbouring a darkness that remained unsettling for me. I moved toward him with caution; weighing up the possibility of successfully taking him out of the chair and on to the floor. It would not be a difficult task.

Perhaps he might have been thinking the same thing; moving the chair, on its castors, back away from the desk and up against the wall, limiting any room for manoeuvre.

I took the small wallet and opened it. On one side a metal rose centred Military Intelligence badge had been attached and on the other details of the badge holder, one Major Ewan-Magnus McAllister.

I guessed just from the name alone that Ewan-Magnus had never attended the state school system, therefore he might need to be treated with some delicacy.

I inspected the ID holder's details and the background security hologram carefully. It all appeared to be genuine. Now we would be having a conversation; that was obvious. But first, someone needed to be taking the high ground ... and that person would have to be me.

I threw the leather ID holder back on the desk.

"Very enlightening! Now, let us start again. Please remove your ass from behind my desk. You have thirty seconds to do so ... from NOW!"

I turned and walked to the office door. I opened it and rested my gaze on a confused looking Major McAllister.

"I really don't think you understand Sergeant ... I ... err ..."

"Yes Major. I understand completely. Now, this is the final time of asking. Remove yourself from this office. Military Intelligence has no jurisdiction here and how the fuck you got as far inside this building as you obviously have will be a matter for some level of investigation. Please leave immediately."

"It goes without saying ... I outrank you sergeant and you will live to regret this outburst of insolence ..."

He was now standing right next to me. I turned allowing him unimpeded passage through the door.

"You may outrank me if, for any inconceivable reason, we might both be in attendance at the same regimental garden party Major. However, down here, deep inside this GCHQ facility, I report to no officer or manager other than just one single person based in Cheltenham. You, my friend, are not him!"

I shut the door to the CRU3 facility as he finally passed through, and made my way back to my office. I was angry. Who on earth had given this rather rude army officer access to my facility? Whoever it was, heads would roll.

I sat at my desk for fifteen to twenty minutes attempting to rationalize what had just gone on.

Nothing like this had ever happened before.

The phone rang.

I answered it.

"Chase!"

"Brooking here Sergeant."

It was the boss ... my boss in particular; Air Vice-Marshall David Brooking.

"What can I do for you sir?" I asked cautiously.

"I think you know the score old chap. Some Major from Military Intelligence has been telling tales to Number Ten and in turn, certain people inside Number Ten have been telling tales to me."

"Oh dear! I'm very sorry to hear that sir."

"Well I can tell you straight away, no-one has ever approached me to discuss MI9 talking to you. This is all one more bloody screw-up generated by politicians and certain socially connected members of the armed forces; individuals who seem to think they are able to ignore protocol. He's quite irate I understand. What did you tell him?"

"I told him to 'fuck off' sir and I think he got the message."

"As a result, an official request for a meeting with you has now been made and is arriving on the tele-printer as we speak."

"What worries me sir is how the hell he got into my facility and then ... my damned office. Who generated a pass key for him? This is a serious matter and needs investigating."

"Staff here at Cheltenham will be on the case and whoever is responsible will be gone by teatime ... you have my assurance on that one. In the meanwhile, all your codes are being changed."

"What about my end? Do I have to do anything? Do I have to make some kind of report on the incident?"

"No. I really don't know what this is all about but you will receive an official request within the next half hour, approved by me, for a meeting with Major Ewan-Magnus McAllister. Maybe then we will find out what the mysterious army officer wants."

"Right you are sir." I offered. "Do you want any kind of paperwork from me after this meeting?"

"Let's just keep our 'powder dry' Chase ... politics are involved here and we will need to be careful where and upon whom we tread. The less paperwork to float around Whitehall desks the better! Goodbye Sergeant. Keep me posted."

"I will sir."

I put the phone down and made a diary note of the conversation. In my particular position, it paid to be careful.

The four meeting rooms in the Nissen Hut admin centre had been designed with comfort and security in mind. The furniture in each consisted of brown leather soft upholstered arm chairs, the kind found in the Officer's mess on many an RAF station.

All the necessary items to make tea or coffee were arranged on a table near to the single entry door. The temperature could be adjusted with a wall mounted thermostat and each room space was 'caged' or completely enclosed with an unbroken mesh of copper wire, known as a 'Faraday' shield. The four windowless rooms would be attended by explosives sniffer dogs before use and electronically swept for bugs and listening devices.

Three days after my disastrous first meeting with Major McAllister I settled myself into one of the 'comfy' leather chairs in meeting room two. I had in front of me a freshly made cup of coffee and a couple of tempting chocolate covered malted milk biscuits.

McAllister entered and looked around the room.

"Is it a 'help-yourself' refreshment service old chap?"

"Yes ... err ... I suppose it is ... 'old chap'!"

It was naughty of me to throw the 'old chap' back at him. However, he must have got the point because in all the conversations we had after that, he never ever used it to address me again.

I studied him carefully as he messed about, making himself some tea and eventually picking up a couple of fingers of Scottish shortbread.

He sat down opposite me, a brown leather briefcase resting on a chair next to him.

He spoke.

"Good morning Sergeant Chase. Firstly let me say thank you for agreeing to this meeting. We have a lot to get through, so I will try to be as swift as I possibly can within the boundaries of expediency."

I picked up on it straight away.

"Expediency? Who's expediency would that be Major ... yours or mine?"

McAllister looked up; the prepared opening speech now completely out the window.

"OK Sergeant ... let's cut through the crap and get straight to the point. I don't particularly like you and you obviously do not hold any special affection for me, BUT ... there is a job to be done and you and I have been chosen to work together to complete the task. Are you with me so far?"

I looked him straight in the eye. He offered a cold, determined and somewhat uneasy glare in return. From my point of view, the question did not require an answer. He searched his immaculate looking, officer issue leather document case and pulled out a pale blue file. It had my name typed into the top right corner, just above the stamped words 'MOST SECRET'.

The Major studied the file in silence for a minute or so; eventually looking up in order to attract my attention.

"You attended a meeting last month, in Chicago I understand; a very important meeting with representatives of a company named Inter-Tech. Is that correct Sergeant?"

"It might well be ... yes; myself and several others ... and please do not keep calling me Sergeant. My name is Gary and within any GCHQ facility, this is the name and only title I am known by. Do we understand one another?"

The Major coloured up; lips stretched tight indicating an uncontrollable level of frustration.

He did not take the rebuke lightly. He simply could not understand what the hell was going on. If a person was part of Her Majesties armed forces, then that person held rank of whatever level and should be addressed by that rank, especially in conversation with senior officers.

From his point of view, the sooner this most uncomfortable meeting came to a conclusion, the better!

"At that meeting ... Gary ... a very select number of people, all experts in their fields of electronics and communications, were introduced to something called a 'microchip', a very, very small 4bit data processing unit which will be marketed to the civilian world as the Inter-Tech 2112. This is already being talked about as a 'computer on a chip' and will most likely revolutionise the world of communications."

"That sounds about right to me ... Ewan."

The launch of the Inter-Tech chip was no great secret in the world of experimental electronics. However; the ability to manufacture the components at scale was not regarded as common knowledge. Now I hoped to find out what he actually knew; something a little less 'common knowledge' than just the launch itself.

"So, carry on. This cannot simply be the reason you have been chasing me down, just to get me to admit where I might have travelled to a few weeks ago."

"No Gary. I am much more interested in the unlisted and secure meetings that took place at the Chicago Plaza Hotel for two whole days after the launch event finished. You do remember that don't you? Do you want me to read out the names of everyone who was there?"

The glint in his eye indicated some level of victory.

"Well Ewan, I will be most pleased to hear from you about what went on during these meetings and ... what it has to do with Military Intelligence? By the way, when you say 'Military Intelligence' do you mean MI9 or some other such nebulous organisation?"

The officer leaned forward, ignoring the comment about his representation.

"You were being briefed on the capabilities of a military version of the 2112 microchip named 21M.

This model has sixteen times the calculating power of the standard chip and will bring military communications into a whole new world of accuracy and longevity.

Each of you attending that meeting received a pre-production model of the 21M to 'play with'. Arrangements were then made to ship to the UK a quantity of 300 'M' version chips for deep analysis by our most knowledgeable electronics and communications experts. One of those experts would of course ... be YOU!"

I smiled. The Major had the 'full nine yards', there could be no doubt about that. At this point I knew I would need to be careful.

"I can't comment on that Ewan. However, I

would ask that whatever your source, you check back with them."

"Are you denying the truth of what I have just told you Gary?"

"I am simply not confirming it Ewan. The whole thing seems to be a little above my pay grade."

I smiled once more, quite happy with the lie and wondering what his reaction might be.

The Major leaned back in his chair, obviously needing to take stock of the situation. Perhaps he might be thinking the man sitting in front of him was not the right man for the job ... whatever the 'job' might be.

I waited, maintaining eye contact.

"Can I ask when you expect this shipment to be delivered to you ... Gary?"

"You can ask Ewan, but I will not be telling you."

"I see. Well, as Shakespeare would have said ... 'here is the rub' my friend. You will not be seeing your microchips tomorrow, the day after or any day after that. They have been stolen ... Gary ... and I am here to encourage you to help me get them back!"

I couldn't quite believe what I was hearing.

"Stolen?"

"Yes Gary ... your wonderful world changing, top secret components have been fucking well stolen. Now, does that spark a little bit of energy within you because I'm hoping you will join me and my small team in the possibly arduous task of their recovery?"

I reached for a glass of water resting on the

coffee table beside my chair, sipping from it, using it as cover whilst my brain raced.

"Do you know who stole them?"

"No!"

"Do you know where they are?"

"No!"

"Do you know how much they are worth?

"No!"

"Hmm. Well that all sounds a little difficult then. When you say you have a team, who are they and how many are there?"

"You will find that out when you say 'yes' to the mission."

"The mission; so, this is a military operation then Ewan."

"Yes it is and you have only the time it takes to make one phone call, to whoever you like, and then tell me if you are in ... or out."

"There is no need to play the cloak and dagger with me Ewan. I'll not be ringing anyone until you tell me how this package, valued conservatively at half a billion dollars, went missing".

After a little huffing and puffing I eventually discovered the sealed and tagged item had been collected from the Santa Clara offices of Inter-Tech by a security checked employee of Maguire Logistics. At the point of collection his ID number was recorded and the shipment, measuring approximately a foot square and only weighing a few pounds, was handed over.

The parcel was to be driven, non-stop, to the 'Frisco' based Maguire Hub, in the van and by the driver who collected it.

"And ...?" I queried.

"After leaving the area limits of Santa Clara, the van, the driver ... and your bloody shipment of components disappeared!"

CHAPTER THREE

And so it begins ...

Air Vice-Marshall David Brooking remained silent as I explained, in some detail, the contents of my meeting with the Major.

"I can't influence you one way or another Sergeant. I am just reading the operational brief that hit my desk a minute or two before you rang. It all looks genuine; it's authorised at the highest level militarily and has been rubber stamped by Number Ten politically."

"Do you know who he will have on his so called 'team' and how safe I might feel being part of it?"

"From what I know of the Major, he moves in the shadows and is part of MI9 with direct links to the reserve 23 Special Air Service Regiment. That is a mean crowd Sergeant and the kind of guys you would only want on your side."

I listened carefully whilst 'the boss' read out the main part of the file he had been sent for the newly titled Operation Quick Capture. My job would be to test any recovered microchips purporting to be the 21M version, to ensure they were genuine.

The job of the Major and his team would be to find the damn consignment and then get me to wherever it might be. Having been in life threatening and dangerous territory operations before, I always felt it wise to remain physically fit and up to date with weapons training. Being wise was one thing; the need to be fully up to date was another.

My very first mission working with the darker side of intelligence operations involved searching the Hindu Kush mountain range in Afghanistan, a place alive with well armed revolutionary groups and tribes of outright bandits.

One of our PR9 spy planes had gone down somewhere in the northern region and it was my job to strip out some sensitive electronics on-board.

We lost two men out of a team of twelve, but the job needed to be done and when I returned to dear old 'Blighty' I found my role in the military had changed. I was now one of a small group of engineers and technicians on a 'go-to' list concerning all matters to do with the new world of solid-state communications.

Several so-called 'missions' later and here I was, looking to scour the world for a missing 'bag of chips' and I wasn't too sure that my luck would hold out for yet one more unnecessary adventure. Perhaps the AVM detected a note of reluctance in my voice.

"Listen to me Sergeant. You are the youngest of your full rank in the Royal Air Force. This is not just that due to some freak of nature you have an extraordinary mind capable of grasping the intricacies of many complex subjects. It is because you are able ... and willing ... to be a team player in some dangerous and irregular pursuits on behalf of your country. Do I make myself clear?"

"You do sir." I replied.

"Let me read it out to you; unmarried, no

children, no partner, handy in a fight, physically fit and up to date with arms training. You can see from our point of view how appealing you look as a candidate for this kind of operation.

No-one is twisting your arm here.

Either you do it ... or don't do it. However, if you agree to do it, then you will have to work with the Major. He will be running the show. If, for any reason you feel you won't be able to rely upon him to keep you safe, then simply tell him 'NO' and he will have to find another way of doing whatever it is he needs to do."

"I understand sir."

"One thing I can tell you. If you manage to recover those bloody chip things, you will very shortly find yourself the youngest WOII Warrant Officer in the Royal Air Force. OK?"

"OK sir. Leave it with me."

I re-entered the meeting room to face an expressionless Major Ewan-Magnus McAllister. He looked fidgety and possibly irritated to some degree.

"Well?" he questioned.

I ignored him and headed for the refreshments table to make a cup of tea. By the time I returned to my seat, the Major had become red faced and anxious.

"Well what?" I countered.

"What the fuck are going to do? I need to know and I need to know NOW!"

I sipped at my tea. Was this really the kind of

man I wanted to trust my life to in a possible set of strange and unhealthy circumstances?

"Before I give you my decision, I want to know who the other members of your 'team' will be. I need to have some comfort in knowing I will be as safe as is feasibly possible ... should the shit hit the fan."

"It's not going to be ..." began Ewan.

I interrupted.

"You understand my concern about the possibility I may end up in some ass-hole country where I might well be physically tortured for the sheer pleasure of the local police chief ... finally ending up with my head on a pole displayed outside the local city supermarket."

The army Major fell silent. He appeared to be holding an argument with himself; darting eyes, back and forth, nervous hand movements, signs of sweating palms.

Finally, prompted by a long drawn out capitulating sigh, he spoke.

"My team are a group of specially trained and trusted soldiers from 23 Special Air Service Regiment Reserve. They are experienced covert surveillance and capture specialists. The team will be made up of four SAS, you and me. Does that convince you? Do you think this team will be able to protect you when needed? If so, please give me your answer NOW and then we can damn well get on with it. Every hour we delay means the trail is getting colder."

"Having the SAS on my side does not provide me with any particular comfort, in fact I've always regarded them as a group of undisciplined, bloodthirsty bandits recruited from a collection of committed rogues and scoundrels ... but ... I would much rather have them on my side than the other."

I paused; a mountain of unanswered questions rotating around my brain.

"Well, someone has to do it. Count me in!"

With a fresh sigh ... probably one of relief, the Major stood and offered his hand.

I shook it. The grip was firm; the palms still damp and the smile infectious.

"Welcome on board Gary. Before we go anywhere, you will need to re-register on the Military Intelligence operational database for blood type, finger prints, latest weapons certification and medical etc.

There is a new thing the medics are experimenting with now called 'nuclein' or DNA testing and you will have to provide a new blood sample. It's some experimental form of irrefutable identity testing and eventually everyone in the military will need to have what they call a DNA profile. Will you be able to register with the quartermaster and get yourself signed off by the end of the day?"

There appeared to be no reason why I couldn't. I nodded my head.

OK ... Let's get this fucking job done!"

I quickly learnt from the Major two rather important pieces of information. Firstly, he had everything under control. I discovered, very early on in our forced association, the art of living with such claustrophobic management techniques would be to generally capitulate.

Secondly, I discovered, that even by pressing him hard on the matter, I would not meet any of the rest of the team; the SAS element. They would travel separately, accommodate themselves separately and manage their own communications separately.

I felt this to be a strange way of administering an undercover operation. One that may well be linked to god-knows-who in the murky world of espionage and government sponsored theft. However, I was assured this was a safe way of getting to where we wanted to go.

The first stop for us both would be the Inter-Tech headquarters in Santa Clara, California. This was to be mainly for my benefit; learning in some detail the technical differences between the 4 bit 2112 civilian chip and the 64 bit 21M.

If and when we find the missing shipment of components, it would be my responsibility to certify they were in fact 'the real deal'!

Seemingly, the other members of 'our team' had already left UK and would be checking out our accommodation before we arrived.

For me, the eleven hour flight to San Francisco was a restless, sleepless event although Ewan managed to snore his way through most of it.

We arrived at the Imperial Meridian Hotel just an hour after landing. It was late and I needed sleep, setting my room alarm for six o'clock in the morning. Ewan, on the other hand made no secret of the fact he was looking for something to eat and so I left him to it.

The following morning, fully rested and alert, I caught up with the Major at breakfast. He looked well and seemed to be enjoying a full American cooked feast with all the usual extras and 'sides'.

"Good morning Ewan." I offered as I sat down opposite the Major.

"Good morning Gary. I trust you slept well and find yourself recharged and ready to go."

"I am Ewan ... I really am."

He gave me a sideways look but made no further comment. I asked him what the plan was to be for today.

"We will be visiting the offices of Inter-Tech and meeting the owners of the company. You will spend an hour or two with their research crew who will hopefully be able to answer any questions you may have relating to the manufacture of these missing components.

I will be talking to their shipping guys ... the guys who packed and then handed over the shipment to their contractors Maguire Logistics. Then, I plan to visit Maguire to see what they have to say. I imagine it won't take long and then I'll meet you back at Inter-Tech. Is that OK with you?"

"Yep, that's fine with me Ewan." I confirmed and an hour and a half later we were sipping coffee in a rather untidy set of offices in Santa Clara.

I was particularly unprepared for what greeted me when we arrived at Inter-Tech. I perhaps expected something bright, shiny, big and very American. The truth of it was a small, nondescript, rather dishevelled looking factory style building with some brick built office space to one side and two portable timber office cabins taking up valuable space in a crowded car park.

I had met two of the three owners before, at the Chicago event a few weeks back. I introduced Ewan simply as a British intelligence officer in charge of investigating the disappearance of the valuable micro-chips.

With introductions, small chat and coffee over with, Ewan hurried off to the shipping department and I moved into a nearby reception room where two young engineers waited.

The car and the driver who picked us up from Inter-Tech to take us back to Frisco, turned out to be different from the car and driver who had collected us from the hotel. Were these two drivers, these two different individuals, part of the Major's surveillance team perhaps? Whoever they were, neither spoke a word on the way down to Santa Clara ... or the way back!

"Did you get what you needed today Gary?" asked Ewan.

"Yes I did. There are some pretty standard checks to be done at the point of finding the missing components and some more technical investigation when we get them back inside a property equipped laboratory. How about you? Did you get any clues from your meeting with the shippers?"

"Let's just say someone in the managerial team

at Maguire Logistics looked a little nervous when I questioned him ... so we won't be going too far from California anytime soon!"

With the remainder of the journey spent mostly in silence, when we arrived back at the Imperial Meridian I asked the burning question.

"So, what do we do now Ewan?"

"There are a few pieces of intelligence yet to mature before we leave California and I have some phone calls to make. So I'll meet you for dinner at say ... err ... seven o'clock and we should then be able to plan our next move. Is that OK with you?"

"That's fine by me ... until seven then."

Sat on my own in a busy hotel dining room, I fielded regular enquiries from smooth mannered waiters who wished to know if I might be ready to order yet. Three times I said 'No' and three times I checked my watch.

Now it was nearly seven twenty and I began to be worried.

Time to find out what the hell might be going on! Ewan's room number was 320, a junior suite consisting of a bedroom, bathroom and lounge. I occupied a similar room on the floor above.

Being about to knock on the door, arm raised and hand clenched, something made me stop.

I picked up on a noise from the other side of the door, a strange, indefinable noise but not so strange I hadn't heard something like it before.

It probably started out as a scream, a scream of pain perhaps; maybe a scream of torture, ending as a muffled animal-like noise, much muted to my ears by efficient sound insulation.

I paused, a moment trapped in time, hand raised and ready to bring attention to myself. What might be lurking behind this fucking door ... that was the question right now. 'Fight or flight' hovered over the decision making process.

Too late!

I banged loudly on the door with an open palm, the thumb of my free hand pressing down on the spy-hole. I pushed my body away from the door frame as much as possible in case someone might want to shoot through a closed door.

Thankfully I recognised the voice; it was Ewan.

"Who is it?"

"It's me ... Gary. Open the fucking door!"

I removed my thumb from the spy-hole as someone fiddled with the locks. Finally the door opened just enough for me to see the sweating face of Major Ewan Magnus McAllister.

I must have looked quite angry. I certainly felt so.

"What is it you want Gary?"

"I want you at the dinner table, a place you should have been over half an hour ago. Now, I don't know what is going on here, but open the damn door."

The determined eyes, processing the possible options gave it all away. I needed to do something now, something to take advantage of the initial surprise.

One unexpected but substantial push against the door and Ewan lost his balance resulting in an awkward fall backwards to the floor, his head eventually resting on what looked like a sheet of blue plastic. It took several seconds to take in everything that appeared to be happening in the room. The nearest comparable description would have to be a particularly gory scene from an excessively violent horror film.

The Major remained on the floor feeling the back of his head. All furniture in the lounge area had been moved back to the walls, creating a free floor space in the middle of the room. That floor space had been covered with a sheet of blue contractors plastic about ten feet square.

Laid out on the blood smeared sheet was the naked body of a man; a youngish man, probably in his late twenties. He looked to be unconscious.

Surrounding the unmoving body were four well built men, all dressed in dark clothing with features obscured by close fitting nylon ski-masks. One held a pistol in his hand ... and it appeared to be pointing at me!

In that split second I had the opportunity to consider my situation.

It did not look good.

When in doubt ... find a friend.

I extended an arm toward the Major and helped him to his feet.

"I'm sorry about that Ewan ... I hope you're OK?"

He muttered and swore on the way up, still feeling the back of his head.

The 'men in black' said nothing, the beaten man on the plastic sheeting breathed noisily and heavily. At least he was alive.

I felt pretty sure I would need to play this one very carefully. I didn't know who the hell the good guys and the bad guys were right now, so better to keep a tight lip and let Ewan explain.

"I suppose this looks quite bad to you Gary."

Was this a question or a statement, I didn't really know. I shrugged my shoulders, one eye on the man with the gun. The Major made the connection and, as a result of him giving out a loose sign with a bloodied hand, the man with the pistol lowered it to his side.

Ewan turned to me and smiled. I was quite taken aback. His mood appeared suddenly lifted, his eyes sparkling and focused. It was as if he had just come to some amazing conclusion allowing a cloak of concern and despair to be lifted from him.

A sudden mood change ...

Obviously welcome ... but not to be trusted!

"I'm sorry about the mess Gary. We have been doing some research here and ... err ... things became a little uncomfortable. I'm late for our dinner meeting. I do apologise. I'll just take a minute or two to clean up and then we can go."

He disappeared into the bathroom, leaving me with my mouth open and four pairs of hostile eyes focused in my direction, no doubt looking for any excuse to introduce me to the plastic sheeting ... face first.

I took my seat in the hotel restaurant next to Ewan, who remained chatty and in an outwardly ebullient mood. It was difficult to reconcile what might possibly have gone on in room 320 that day, supervised by Major Ewan Magnus McAllister, and his current buoyant, almost continuous chatter.

It was time for some answers.

"Ewan ... Ewan ... stop damn well talking for just one minute and tell me what the fuck has been going on in your room for the past several hours. Who is that man you look to have nearly beaten the life out of and who are those rather ugly characters with the ski masks. And don't tell me they are SAS because if you do ... I will not believe you. Do you understand me ... really understand me?"

The Major nodded his head.

The wine arrived and he sipped at his glass for a moment or two, perhaps in reflection or possibly more likely taking time to concoct some story or other to feed to me.

He lifted his head, avoiding direct eye contact.

"The guy on the floor is the driver of the disappearing courier truck belonging to Maguire Logistics, the one containing our missing shipment."

"And ...?"

"And ... as a result of his co-operation, we now have a name and address of someone who may not be directly connected to the robbery ... but knows someone who is."

"And ... the men in black?"

"You are correct. They are not part of our regular forces. This is quite simply because we feel actors from other governments may be involved in the theft and therefore we are using 'contractors' ... ones we know and trust."

"Civilians you mean ... criminal civilians; mercenaries and guns for hire. Is that what you mean Ewan?"

"Very possibly Gary ... very possibly!"

"You've put me in a spot here Ewan. If anything untoward happens on this so-called 'mission' of yours and a connection is made with a serving British military officer, then we will have a problem."

"What kind of problem Gary?" the Major asked, his face a blank, giving nothing away.

"Well, perhaps YOU can tell ME what kind of problem it might be to force Her Majesties Government to completely deny my existence ... or, on the other hand, be forced to do some kind of deal to get me back on British soil?"

Ewan sipped at his drink, his eyes focused on something in the distance, just for a second or two. He carefully placed his drinking glass on the table and moved forward, leaning on his elbows, his hands on his ears in some kind of conspiratorial pose.

"You seem to have forgotten about the third option ..."

"Oh ... and what might that be?" I asked.

"I just shoot you and then order my 'criminal civilians' to bury you deep in the fucking desert ...!"

His probing gaze never left me. I immediately became uncomfortable and wary at the same time. There was no answer to that. Did I think for one moment the Major had the guts to shoot me ... and then bury me in the damned desert?

Yes ... I did!

"So, is that what is going to happen to that poor bastard kissing the plastic on your hotel room floor Ewan?"

He fidgeted in his seat. Perhaps he was beginning to feel uneasy, although there might be another reason.

"He looks a lot worse than he really is. We are cleaning him up right now and taking him back to an address in Scotts Valley where his wife is patiently waiting under the protection of one of my men."

"Protection?" I hissed; "Don't you mean abducted and held against her will? I hope to God you can tell me these two human beings are now being kept well under your 'protection' ... and if not ... there will be consequences. Have you heard that expression before Major ... 'consequences' for your actions? This is not a 1945 bunker clearing exercise in Berlin. You can't go round beating the fuck out of people without there being CONSEQUENCES!"

I moved further back into my seat and picked up the menu card. I needed to break the spell, create a distraction of some kind and give me space in order to think.

"Time to order dinner I think Ewan ..."

"No ... I think it's time for you to piss or get off the pot Gary. You have a choice; join with me now and become part of this team ... or you can go upstairs and pack. I'll have you on the 11:30 flight to Heathrow and tomorrow you will be back in your top-secret office fucking about with screwdrivers and soldering irons. What is it to be my friend?"

I spotted the eager waiter making his approach and picked up the menu.

I looked him squarely in the face.

"Tell me the courier and his wife are both well!"

"To the best of my knowledge the driver will have been cleaned up and on his way down to the forest lodge address where we found him. I am not at liberty to tell you how we knew he was there ... but we did. An hour or so from now he'll be in the comforting embrace of his wife ... alive and well!"

I wondered about the truth of it all and found it very hard to believe. Perhaps there were other intelligence community assets involved? Who knows? One thing was for sure ... I needed a little more personal protection than a team of appearing and disappearing criminals acting the part of fully engaged bodyguards.

"Let us eat Ewan and if it looks like shots might have to be fired at any time during this little adventure of ours, then you had better get me a handgun; a very concealable Makarov 9mm preferably."

"Can I take your orders now gentlemen?" the waiter asked tentatively.

"You most certainly can." offered the Major through a broad smile.

I wondered if I was really doing the right thing. Probably by this time tomorrow I would have a much better idea.

CHAPTER FOUR

A bag of surprises ...

The following morning, after an early breakfast, I met Ewan in the hotel lobby. The relevant bills had been paid and I was told by a very helpful young lady at reception a car waited for us out front.

I now needed to know what 'the plan' might be; how we would be spending our day and at the end of it, did we think we would be any nearer to finding out what the hell happened to half a billion dollars worth of missing electronic components.

The light in his eye told me that without much doubt, Ewan wanted to get going. Explaining everything was such a bore to him.

"So ... where are we going today Ewan?" I asked.

"We are going to Sacramento, a couple of hours drive from here. We will be paying a visit to a Mr. James Wilson."

"And he is?"

"He is the person we understand to be the paymaster, the person who hovers one step back from the actual criminality but ensures everyone is paid the right amount at the right time. As you might have guessed Gary ... he is a lawyer and able to hide behind all sorts of nebulous legal structure. Let us hope he is in a co-operative mood this morning."

Ewan smiled one of his 'bright all over' smiles. As the days progressed I was to learn that this particular expression, exclusive to the Major, might well herald a series of painful episodes for someone ... somewhere!

"The car is waiting and on the back seat you will find a little package ... the item you asked me for last night. It's not loaded and there are four clips of 9mm ammunition to go with it. I have a lightweight shoulder holster in my brief case, if you need it. Make sure it's well concealed whenever you are carrying it."

"What if Wilson is not in a co-operative mood Ewan?" I asked.

"Then we will have to call in the 'persuaders' who have a safe-house on the edge of town. Whichever way it goes, I'm pretty confident we will have the information we need by this evening."

James Arnold Wilson, Attorney at Law, obviously enjoyed a good living. His house in Willow Creek, just north of the river, might be regarded as substantial by any measure. There were two high-end BMW's in the circular front drive along with a Range Rover 4x4.

We pulled up behind it. The Major went ahead and leaned on the door bell. A middle aged woman dressed in some sort of sleeveless tabard opened the door and Ewan quickly explained why we had come calling.

No: We were not police but we were registered as state licensed investigators. Did the lovely lady wish to see our credentials?

No: Mr Wilson was not expecting us.

No: There was no need for concern; we just wanted to ask him a couple of questions relating to a recent case of his.

No: We would not be taking up too much of his very valuable time.

Did we know it was Saturday ... not a working day?

I could see from the look on Ewan's face he might be beginning to lose patience with the woman.

Finally, after conjuring up some sort of relevant business card from his jacket pocket, Ewan waited, smiling politely as the 'tabard lady' shuffled off to relay all she had just learnt to Mr. Wilson.

Unfortunately for Mr Wilson, she made the simple mistake of leaving the front door open and that was our opportunity to enter. Ewan pulled a two way radio from his pocket, pressed the transmit button and spoke only two words; "All clear."

The middle aged woman suddenly appeared in the corridor, exiting a room on our left. She stood stock still, a surprised and worried look on her face.

"I'm afraid you can't ..." she started but then, without a sound, two men appeared directly behind her wearing dark coloured ski masks.

Ewan nodded his head in the direction of the door where he expected Wilson to be. One of the men grabbed the woman, hand over her mouth, and then, containing her protests, disappeared through a door on the right of the corridor.

The other silently entered the room where

Ewan obviously expected the 'target' to be. I watched everything going on around me from a rather detached viewpoint. There was not much for me to do. Ewan seemed to have everything under control.

I followed him into what turned out to be quite a splendid office cum library. The person assumed to be Wilson sat at his desk with the masked intruder holding a gun to his head. For someone in such a precarious position, he looked quite nonplussed.

"Mr. Wilson I assume." offered Ewan.

"You are correct." Wilson replied.

He avoided eye contact with either of us. There could be no doubt; Mr. Wilson was a cool customer ... a very cool customer indeed.

"Do you know why we are here?"

Wilson smiled. He knew why we 'were here' alright, but his answer to the question was to remain silent.

"I'm going to ask you some questions and if you give me the right answers, we can all be out of here ... done and dusted in half an hour. Does that sound OK to you?"

Wilson offered only stone faced silence in reply.

"Where are your wife and children?"

Still no interaction!

The Major let out a long sigh

"Or ... we can do it the hard way. We can transport you from here to a place no-one will hear your screams of pain or the begging for mercy. You may of course die during the interrogation process and then we will bury your body in a block of concrete eventually ending up on the floor of the Pacific Ocean.

You will simply disappear from this earth leaving your wife, your children and grandchildren to wonder what the hell happened to you ... for the rest of their fucking life!

Whichever way you choose to go, we will get what we came for ... do you understand?"

I understood the psychology; lay it all out on the ground first before the boot goes in. Make them feel guilty about family ... and finally ...

"They are on a school trek and orienteering day up in the north valley. They won't be home until this evening."

The lawyer gave out the information easily. It looked as if we might be getting somewhere.

Ewan pulled a stash of photographs from his pocket and threw them across the desk.

"These are images of the last moments, the last breath to be taken by a certain courier driver working for Maguire."

We exchanged glances. Had he lied to me? Was the person in these images actually dead? The look shouted ... don't interfere!

Wilson now displayed an amount of agitation, moving uneasily in his chair. He studied the pictures for a few seconds and then, still avoiding eye contact with either Ewan or myself, muttered:

"They will kill me ..."

"They may well do James ... do you mind if I call you James ... but it will depend upon how long it takes for them to do it? We can give you a head start from here; they will be bringing up the rear and so cannot make the obvious mistake of leaving you ... or any members of your direct family alive!"

That did it; expertly played. The family card finally broke the determination. Now we both understood that whatever he gave up might be believable to a high degree. That would be the best bet in this high stakes gamble. The big issue then remained; once drained of information, what would we do with him afterward?

James Arnold Wilson leaned back in his seat and opened a side drawer in his desk, the gun still pointing at him.

He withdrew a grey loose leaf file and threw it across the desk toward Ewan. It had a six figure number scrawled on the front face. Ewan poked at it and then opened it.

"What am I looking for here James?"

"The number on the file is an account number attached to a job. This particular number is, in effect, allocated to the exercise of liberating three hundred experimental electronic components ..."

"Liberating James ... liberating? Surely you mean 'stealing' don't you?"

"Whatever you want to call it ... someone wants those components, whatever they are, and that someone is prepared to pay lots of good money to get their hands on them."

Wilson's words had obviously struck a note with Ewan.

Are they still in the country?" he asked.

"Only just." replied the smiling law attorney.

"So James, where are they right now?"

"Your components are being handed over to the captain of a private charter jet in a locked and secure brief case ... err ... probably as we speak!"

That grabbed Ewan's attention. He immediately coloured up.

"Which airport, which plane and which ..?"

"The handover is taking place at Sutter County Airport, about forty five miles north of here. All the details are in this file.

I have already set up payment to everyone involved in the chain of events; the charter fees, a bonus for the aircrew, the courier carrying the shipment to the airport and the flight controller who will wipe the registered flight plan off the system once the plane gets airborne."

"What's the destination?"

"I don't know. The plan the aircraft must file with Air Traffic Control is contained in an envelope; an envelope to be handed to the aircrew, by the courier, when he receives a signature for the shipment.

Once the handover is complete I am to receive a phone call confirming the fact and then I will release all payments for immediate transfer to individual accounts. I have to tell you, I received that call approximately eight minutes ago! That's my bit of it all; you will need to read the file in detail."

James Wilson still held onto the beginnings of a smile but a whole different shade of worry now appeared behind the eyes.

'What would happen next?'

Ewan grabbed the collection of documents and began leafing through them.

He appeared to be satisfied.

He nodded to the masked captor.

"OK. Release the woman."

I think, at that particular moment in time, the Major might well have been tempted to do something quite permanent to the high flying lawyer. His left hand twitched for a second or two. I had noticed the phenomenon before, probably indicating his right brain to be in serious conflict with his left.

"You may be receiving a call from the FBI shortly. Once I have the microchips in my hands I will be telling them about the part you played in their theft. If you co-operate, you may have some useful years ahead of you. If you do not, I will personally come back here and shoot you. Do you understand?"

James Wilson became immediately ashen. The eyes told the story. The man standing in front of him held his life in his hands ... and now, for sure, he knew it!

Ewan turned to me.

"We need to get our skates on. We cannot afford to miss this opportunity."

We moved away from Willow Creek in two vehicles; the driver, Ewan and myself in one and the three remaining 'contractors' in the other.

The drive to the provincial airport at Sutter County became a little worrying at times; but as we made our approach to the General Aviation Terminal we could see the charter aircraft waiting with 'stairs down' ready to receive the crew.

Drawing to a halt outside the low single story building, Ewan flew out of the car and pushed through the terminal door with his hand inside his jacket.

I followed close behind with the security team stopping at the door.

Two guys in short sleeved white shirts carrying shoulder flashes, one with three bars and one with four, stood at a chest high counter filling in some paperwork.

They appeared to be aircrew and glanced up when we entered. However, they paid little notice. The two uniformed ladies sitting behind the desk focused their attention on Ewan, who remained with his hand inside his jacket.

He smiled. Then he spoke.

"Hi there ... I'm looking for the crew of that Falcon out on the apron ... I have ..."

The interruption came from the Captain, the man with four bars on his shoulder.

"That's my plane sir. We are crew for this trip. How can I help you?"

Ewan's left hand began twitching. Something might well explode here if I did not somehow interfere. I stepped forward, placing myself between the two flyers and the Major.

"Oh! I'm so glad we caught you. Can I ask if you have received a package from someone, a small package, probably small enough to fit into a briefcase?"

The two airmen looked slightly taken aback.

Reluctantly, the Captain admitted to having received the item and they were flying it to Calgary, over the border into Canada.

Ewan called the contractors in, glancing down toward the two uniformed receptionists.

"Don't touch any alarm bells ladies. If you do, someone may well end up dead."

At that point he drew his gun from inside his jacket and pointed it at the Captain.

"Where is it, the package, where is it now?"

"It's in the cockpit. We are ready to go. We have a fifteen minute window from start-up. Do you want to steal it... or what?" he exclaimed nervously.

Ewan turned to me.

"You and I will go to the plane with these two. The guys will stay here to make sure the ladies behave themselves, keeping all the doors locked until we know what we're dealing with."

I nodded my head along with our four man team of contracted minders. Hopefully, this whole damn business may well be close to an end and there will be no one more pleased than me to see it so.

The cockpit of the Falcon 10 executive jet showed as being a lot more cramped that I had expected. With just four normal sized persons it became difficult to manoeuvre.

The briefcase was a cheap looking affair with simple locks and a loose, moulded plastic handle.

"This is your bit now Gary." Ewan offered as he handed me the case.

"You open it and you tell me if this is what we are looking for."

"Anyone got a screwdriver?" I asked and the Captain conjured one up within seconds. I levered the two catches. They flew apart immediately. Opening the case carefully, I felt inside. There appeared to be a package and it felt about the right size. It also seemed to be secured within several layers of cling film. Taking out the one single item and using the screwdriver to score the wrapping, I emptied the contents back into the briefcase. It looked, at first glance, as if we had hit the jackpot.

"What on earth are they?" queried the Captain.

"This is what half a billion dollars worth of top of the line micro-electronic components look like my friend." I offered a confused looking Ewan.

However, in reality, I was not quite so sure.

I took a jewellers loupe, a very small magnifying glass, from my wallet; a useful item and one I had carried with me for a few years now.

It took exactly three seconds to come to the only sensible conclusion.

This was a complete box of tricks; a bag of fakes; a collection of molded resin strips, stamped with a few meaningless symbols in black and eight soldering tabs set in each side.

They were completely useless to anyone … for anything.

Giving out the bad news would not be easy. Everyone jammed into the limited cockpit space had become quite upbeat, with Ewan sporting a grin from ear to ear. He picked one up and played with it.

"I'm afraid I have some bad news gentlemen."

Ewan appeared not to have been listening so I carried on, focusing my attention on the aircrew.

"These are nothing but junk. Whoever gave them to you knew that. If he didn't, then he was being fooled also."

"Wait a minute here Gary."

Ewan now looked to be paying full attention to everything that was going on.

"Are you absolutely sure these are not the real thing ... I mean ... err .."

"There is no bloody substance to them Ewan ... no circuitry, nothing to make them work ... just a piece of smoked resin put in a mould, some tag connectors set in each side and a set of meaningless numbers stamped on the top. They have been carefully made to imitate the 'real thing' ... but in effect Ewan ... they are totally useless to you, me or anyone else. We have been HAD Ewan ... all of us here have been fucking well HAD!"

"Shit!" offered Ewan.

"Jesus Christ!" hailed the Captain.

The following silence lasted a long time; too damn long for me.

"Right then," I said, "What do we do next?"

"What are you going to do Captain?" asked a thoughtful looking Major.

"As far as I am concerned, we have been paid to collect a small parcel from here and fly it to Calgary ... and that is exactly what we are going to do ... that is if my crew agree?"

The young man with three bars on his shoulder nodded his head in agreement.

"Well, we can only wish you 'bon voyage' Captain. We thought we might be nearing the end of the exercise less than a few minutes ago, but it looks as if we haven't really begun yet." I confirmed.

"We both wish you a good trip." added Ewan as we all shook hands. Five minutes later we were all back in our vehicles.

"Where too?" asked the driver.

"Back to Willow Creek; someone has a lot of questions to answer, and this time we do not leave our high flying lawyer and gangster financier until we get something that resembles the truth."

Nearly an hour later we pulled up outside the broad fronted property in Willow Creek where we had been earlier. There was no sign of movement. Ewan and I walked up to the front door and rang the door bell.

No sign of life; no reaction.

I pushed at the door. It was unlocked and appeared undamaged. I shouted out for Wilson. No reply. All the hall furniture looked to be in the right place; no sign of a disturbance. I withdrew my handgun; Ewan had his drawn and was right behind me. The door to the office cum library was half open. I pushed it gently, allowing Ewan to leapfrog my position.

The words 'Oh shit' came back to me as I followed the Major and seconds later I knew the reason why.

The man we were looking for was dead, a cushion over his face and shot through with something the force of a .45 calibre weapon. There was very little mess.

The tabard cloaked woman, the housekeeper of sorts, lay on the floor behind Wilson's desk. Unfortunately, this looked to be a completely different method of despatch; very messy with half her head missing and pooling blood everywhere.

Ewan pulled the two way radio from his pocket and pressed the transmit button.

"You guys stay outside; we are leaving right away. It's a fucking nightmare in here. Wilson is no more ... and neither is his housekeeper. This is all less than an hour old and I'd bet next week's pay-packet whoever did this will be out there somewhere ... watching us."

We had a tentative reservation at the Hilton in Sacramento and being short on any other plan, decided to head there. If anyone might be following us, it certainly didn't look obvious. Perhaps Ewan's theory might have been a little wide of the mark.

The next day I woke earlier than usual and after a shower and a cup of tea settled down to watch the early morning local and International news. I didn't know what I might be expecting but the national news listed it as a headline of the day.

An executive jet with only a two man crew on board had been attacked with two rocket propelled grenades. The aircraft had exploded on the apron, outside the General Aviation Terminal at Calgary airport.

It had originally taken off from Sutter County Airport after filing a flight plan to Calgary. The circumstances of the explosion were alarming and would be under detailed investigation by the Air Accident Investigation Board and the Canadian security services.

However, the authorities did confirm the

identity of the aircrew, both killed as a result of the RPG explosions and one ground technician who received severe burn injuries. There would be no further bulletins issued to the press due to security considerations and terrorist activity was suspected.

CHAPTER FIVE

A few days earlier ...

Patrick O'Breian, Director of Intelligence, Irish Republican Army, was looking for a headline making operation to follow-up on the recent announcement. At the start of 1971, the IRA Army Council had sanctioned the planning of offensive operations against the British Army.

This would be the start of a long, bloody campaign and as a result, the first life of a British soldier claimed by the IRA had been taken in February. Now, in March, a rather surprising piece of intelligence had come Patrick's way.

The source was new to the IRA intelligence chief; a surprising source, a well connected source and, if true, the intelligence on offer might well turn out to be the coup of the decade.

However, it involved movements of men and materials and a manufacturing source ... within the USA. The IRA enjoyed the support of a strong base of sympathisers in the US. Mostly all were willing to make a sacrifice for the mother country, Ireland, so checking out the validity of the information passed to Patrick O'Breian would be an easy undertaking.

The operation revolved around a company in Santa-Clara, California. They had researched and now manufactured electronic components known as 'micro-chips', items about to completely revolutionise the electronics and communications industries, worldwide ... or so it was said!

Three hundred of these rare items, each taking many months to manufacture, were to be given to the UK military for experimental use and investigation. They would be shipped at the end of the month from Santa Clara to somewhere labelled, in military terms, as CSOS Irton Moor, believed to be part of the secret British communications operation known as GCHQ.

Patrick might well not have been that bothered about a few electronic components crossing the Atlantic, but the estimate of value attached to the shipment made his hair stand on end. If he could intercept the shipment, steal it and then sell it back to the British Government, the numbers involved would finance the whole of the homeland IRA operations for the next ten years. This was a once in a lifetime opportunity ... and now he must check it out.

The Olive Branch restaurant on Putney Bridge Road, South London had been chosen by Patrick O'Breian to meet with his UK head of intelligence. No doubt, his movements would be noted by British MI5 officers and the time, date and name of those enjoying a wonderfully healthy looking lunch would be on record.

What MI5 could not know of course was that as a result of this meeting the British Prime Minister, Ted Heath, would be putting himself and his near bankrupt government to the test. For O'Breian, this opportunity could not have come at a better time.

He had no need for hiding behind code names, although the person he would be meeting that day was known only to others by his operational code name which was 'Tommy'. Patrick knew his real name of course because he had recruited him in the early sixties.

Patrick O'Breian carried out a forward facing role as the Sinn Fein Public Relations Director and as such had no fear of travelling abroad or expressing his republican views.

Sinn Fein was unashamedly the political wing of the IRA and registered as such with all the relevant authorities. He wasn't exactly untouchable, but anyone wanting to arrest him for terrorist activities would need to have some pretty solid evidence to do so. Patrick was a careful man and he carried out his duties with professionalism and determination.

"So Tommy, what is all this fuss about? I hope I haven't come over to this shit-pit of a place to hear a load of nonsense from you my boy. I think you had better start from the beginning and work your way up."

Tommy smiled. He knew Patrick well and that behind the rebuke would lurk a smile of sorts. They were normally only able to enjoy each other's company for just a few times a year, and so this particular unplanned lunch together would be considered by both men as some sort of bonus.

"Well old pal, this one came completely out of the blue. Last Wednesday, I was standing at Whitechapel tube station and this 'fella' comes up to me, pushes a rolled newspaper into my hand and tells me he has read it and now maybe I would like it. He talked like a 'toff' Patrick ... and walked like a military man."

"So, it wasn't anyone we know Tommy. Did anyone follow you after the handover?"

"No. I did a three stop reverse loop on the trains and no-one followed me ... of that I am absolutely sure."

"And the message ...!"

Tommy passed a folded sheet of paper across the table. Patrick opened it out. One face appeared blank and the other contained a dozen lines of close typed script. They described the situation with the microchips but no detail. The message claimed the shipment to be worth several hundred million dollars ... and the anonymous writer wanted twenty percent. He assured the reader that the British Government would definitely pay over such a big ransom simply to recover the components and shut down any hint of a robbery ever having taken place.

"Money and politics! That really is a dangerous mixture and one that could easily explode in your face at any moment Tommy."

"But just think of what we could do with the money Patrick and then the leaked story of events that would probably sink this fucking government and bury that asshole Heath and all his upper class cronies."

O'Breian sipped at his wine. He remained thoughtful. Tommy knew not to disturb this process. If Patrick decided it would happen ... it would happen! If he decided it would not, then all the persuasive arguments in the world would fall on deaf ears

Patrick O'Breian read the note once more. This was a once in a life-time opportunity to score 'big' for the IRA. The instructions in the note were for 'Tommy' to be at Whitechapel tube that evening at six o'clock. A newspaper would be given to him with detailed information concerning the shipment of the highly valuable components and from then on ... they were on their own.

The delivery took place exactly as described and by six thirty Tommy and Patrick were chewing over the contents of the new note.

The contact confirmed that once the shipment was notified as secure and under O'Breian's control, he was to ask for a ransom of three hundred million US Dollars from the British. Twenty percent of that amount was to be lodged in a numbered Middle East based bank account.

Like all seemingly good deals, this one also came with a warning. Any attempt at a double cross would result in some very 'nasty' people coming to find them. Was this a bluff? The jury would need to stay out a little longer on that one.

Today was Friday, April second and the shipment was to leave a facility in Santa Clara on Monday, April fifth.

'Not a lot of time to do what needed to be done' thought Patrick. Fortunately, California, and San Jose in particular, was quite a stronghold for IRA sympathizers. This would be a simple high security robbery and something that could be managed from a distance. However, the man on the ground; the man doing all the planning and procurement would need to be good and fortunately Patrick had such a man in mind.

He looked up from examining the note and caught Tommy's eye. The words came out at exactly the same time driven by exactly the same thought.

"Liam Byrne ...!"

"That's yer man for this job alright Patrick." confirmed a beaming Tommy.

"I agree. Let's do it."

"There's not much time but our unknown friend has given us quite a bit of detail here; the name of the courier company, the route of the vehicle and the collection and delivery points. This is pretty damn good and we have successfully made clean, profitable hauls in the past with much less information than this."

Tommy nodded his head in agreement.

"We need a place with a secure phone line in order to get the wheels turning."

"I have a place in Lambeth Green. It's a clean safe house; it's got a phone and good parking about a hundred yards away. It's a lower ground floor apartment and we can come and go from the rear without being seen. There are no cameras and once we've done what we have to, I'll get rid of it."

"That sounds just right Tommy. So let's get going."

"Will you be telling anyone in Command Patrick? You really need their full blessing to carry out such an operation overseas?"

"What they don't know won't hurt them

Tommy. If it fails, then they will be none the wiser. If it succeeds, they will be fighting to see how much of it they can siphon off into their own damn pockets."

Tommy laughed out loud.

"Not 'till we've had our bit first though eh Patrick?"

"No – not 'till then Tommy ... not 'till then."

Liam Byrne had a smile on his face, sipping his early morning coffee in the comfort of his eighteenth floor San Franciso apartment. He enjoyed great views over the city and the kind of lifestyle any other thirty two year old bachelor might only dream about.

Liam, a successful Irish American businessman liked to be kept busy and Patrick O'Breian had just handed him a big one. There was a lot of detail to consider and not much time to rehearse anything. He only had the weekend, so needed to round up just three trustworthy souls who would take instructions without argument.

His first call would be to James Arnold Wilson, Attorney at Law, a well known defence lawyer operating out of Sacramento.

James Wilson managed money for the criminal world and managed it very well. He would be the Quartermaster for this operation and as far as Liam was concerned could be considered totally trustworthy.

Over the weekend, roster sheets would be photographed from the Maguire Logistics courier offices in San Jose. Knowing who would be picking up the goods from Inter-Tech would be key to a smooth and clean capture of the shipment.

From the roster sheet it could be seen there would be just a driver, someone who checked out as having a young wife but no children. On that busy Monday morning, the wife would be abducted as she left her house for work with little fuss and even less discussion.

As the Maguire courier driver arrived to collect the shipment, squeezing his vehicle into a tight spot in the car park of Inter-Tech, a note was to be pushed into his hand by someone in a dark jacket and rain hood pulled up around his face.

This would take him by surprise and before he could react, the messenger would have disappeared from view. The news delivered within the note would not be good and there would be no time for reflection. A decision to co-operate or not needed to be made ... wife or job!

The next bit would be a little tricky but if all went to plan, the driver would calmly head to the rear of the Inter-Tech building, collect the signed for consignment and return to his vehicle.

His instructions would be clear. He was to drive to a piece of waste ground some five miles south of Santa Clara. There a Chevrolet car would be waiting for him. At this point, his wife would be safe. On the front passenger seat he would find a set of instructions guiding him to an isolated woodland property near to Scotts Valley, south of San Jose. He was to follow the route exactly as they would be monitoring his movements on a tracker fitted to the car.

His wife would meet him at the property ... safe and unharmed. He was to stay there, with her and not communicate with anyone. Rent had been paid for a month and no one was expected to call at the address.

A telephone number linked to James Wilson had been scribbled on the back of the instructions in case help might be needed. This 'planting' of a telephone number was a key element in establishing a trail for anyone following behind. However, Wilson would be left unaware his phone number might very shortly be of relevance to someone who would not have his best interests at heart.

It was an audacious plan. There was a lot to take in. Liam now relied upon the driver remaining calm and co-operative. If, for any reason, the instruction to head for the waste land site was disregarded by the driver, then 'plan B' would be triggered and that would put his own people in danger ... unnecessarily.

By the evening of Monday April fifth, the valuable shipment was in Liam's hands. The whole operation to steal the microchips had worked seamlessly. Now, the dogs would be set loose and Liam wondered who the Brit's would send to get them back!

At ten o'clock a knock came at the door of Liam's apartment. He was expecting it. No words were spoken. Words were not necessary. Liam handed over a small bubble wrap package to the young messenger waiting at the door. Within seconds he was gone.

Liam locked the door and returned to his kitchen. Two small brief cases rested on the counter top and Liam was in the process of using a knife to cut some foam block packaging to size and then fit inside the cases.

The young boy would return the next day with three hundred copies of the microchip he had just entrusted to him. Liam would then package them up. One set would be the real McCoy. The second set, manufactured overnight by a very competent professional artist and forger on the other side of town, would be bogus.

Liam had a plan. It was a very expensive plan, a diversion of sorts, but considering the near priceless value of the package involved, Liam considered the risk to be worth taking.

By lunchtime on Friday, Liam had the two sets of items, the real set and the fake set, inserted securely inside the individual foam blocks and then into the brief cases. Viewing each package, inside and out and from all angles they looked to be the same. From this point on, a false trail of movements would be carefully constructed in the hope that whoever the British intelligence services sent looking for the components would find them ... but not necessarily the ones they wanted.

The next part of the plan would be to get the fake package over to James Wilson in Sacramento. He in turn, not knowing he might be handling a counterfeit version of the sought after components, would send it by direct courier to Sutter County Airport. This could only happen however once the charter flight had been organised and in place, with crew signed in and ready to go.

Liam now needed a way to get back to Ireland with the components intact. It would require careful planning and a route where border security might be considered lax. He also needed to carry the small case containing the components by hand during his journey and in full view of customs agents and all the normal airport authorities. It should not raise any suspicions and if questioned, Liam would need some paperwork to back up his reasons for travelling with the unusual items.

The risk of losing the package was not seen as being particularly high. The secret of holding on to them during the journey was to make sure they were valued correctly. Too little might raise the suspicions of border security staff; too much might prompt customs to seek a third party valuation and that could well blow the whole damn operation wide apart.

CHAPTER SIX

The luck of the Irish perhaps ...

Liam Byrne had become a successful businessman in America due, in general, to his careful eye for detail, and in part to his extensive IRA connections. His trip to Ireland from California, hand carrying the package of microchips, had been planned, checked and double checked. His professional artist and forger, the person responsible for manufacturing the fake chips, had produced some paperwork to Liam's specification. It consisted of a small pack of business cards linking him, as a senior executive, to a company named Dalton Electronics.

Along with the cards came a 'customs' invoice describing the items he carried as electrical link connectors for use in manufacturing electronic circuit boards ... or PCB's. They were samples to be demonstrated to a Dublin based company who manufactured PCB's.

It was stated in the descriptive paperwork these links would speed up the manufacturing process by nearly fifty per cent and Liam was hopeful of an order; but what about the cost of each component?

Well, the invoice would state sixty cents each for a bulk order minimum of five hundred units.

Liam had his story straight and rehearsed and now, before leaving for Ireland, he needed to make sure all the necessary house-cleaning had been completed.

O'Flaherty's bar was about a block and a half away from Liam's apartment. The owner, Jim O'Flaherty, was a supporter of the cause. As Liam walked in, the two exchanged a quick nod of the head and without stopping, Liam headed to the rear of the bar and the payphone on the wall.

Liam made his first call.

The voice at the other end confirmed the operation had been successful. The high flying lawyer James Wilson and his venerable housekeeper Mrs. Elizabeth Wyatt had both stopped a bullet in the cause of Irish Nationalism.

Liam felt genuinely concerned, but the trail had to go cold and it would do so with the death of gangster financier Wilson. Every piece of intelligence, every minute clue and every single hunch connected with the disappearance of the highly valuable micro-electronic components had now become worthless.

The crew of the aircraft making a delivery to Canada were now dead and whatever they knew or witnessed, died with them.

The paymaster in the plot to steal the original components was also dead and along with him went all the knowledge, the detail, the names and bank accounts of IRA loyalists on both sides of the Atlantic.

The second phone call was significantly shorter. The male voice at the other end confirmed the delivery driver and his wife were now dead. They had not suffered; a simple single shot with a .45 caliber to the back of the head.

The man involved, the delivery driver, looked to have been badly beaten by some third party, the voice advised, and he wondered if that might be an issue. Liam confirmed it would not and put down the receiver.

He wandered back into the bar and sat at the counter. His favourite drink was a cool refreshing Guinness and that was no secret in O'Flaherty's bar.

"If there's one there waiting Jim, I'll have it now like." he shouted.

Over his drink he mused on the success or otherwise of the operation so far; an operation ordered by Patrick O'Breian. It had worked well to date although perhaps some might have thought that six dead was too high a price to pay for a few items of metal and plastic. However, Liam was a business man. He was as up to date with technology as anyone could be living in a country thriving on it.

Patrick O'Breian was not a technical man by any standards. He was only interested in 'the cause' and the money needed to keep the flames burning, the rifles fed with bullets and the eventual re-uniting of the north of Ireland and the south.

After just one pint of a perfectly poured Guinness, Liam shouted 'Cheers' to Jim and left the bar. He had a journey ahead of him and he needed to be calm and collected as he passed through the various customs points on his journey back to Ireland.

The plain clothed customs officers were trained in spotting discomfort; excessive scanning of everything going on around them, sweating, changing hands frequently whilst pushing a luggage trolley, having too much luggage and maybe having not quite enough.

These were some of the signs they looked for and Liam, with one mid-sized suitcase and a small briefcase, hoped his luggage would be seen as just enough for a six day visit to Ireland. The route had now been confirmed and booked. Two flights would be necessary to get there; San Francisco to Toronto and then on to Dublin. The flights were booked on the same airline, Air Canada and a car rental had been confirmed for him in Dublin along with a hotel reservation at Jacobs Inn.

Early the following morning Liam received a call from reception. A taxi driver had arrived to take him to the airport. Liam closed his apartment door, taking the elevator from the eighteenth to the ground floor. Exiting the elevator he took a few seconds to visually check out the man in the dark grey jacket, blue loose fitting trousers and a baseball cap pulled a little further forward than perhaps it needed to be. The uniformed man on reception spotted him.

"Over here sir ... this is your driver ..."

He pointed to the man, who immediately turned his head. They made eye contact. There were only some split seconds available to make the choice ... go with him ... or hail a different cab outside.

The man in the grey jacket smiled. It was unassuming and open, perhaps even trustworthy.

"Thank you George." Liam offered to the receptionist as he allowed the grey jacketed stranger to lift and carry his suitcase. He was on his way!

Less than half an hour later, Liam found himself at Terminal Two, San Francisco Airport. He headed to the Air Canada check-in, alert and prepared. There would be several 'stress' points along the way on this particular journey and one of them would be moving from the entrance of the Terminal and up to the boarding desk. It was a place and time when anything might happen. A snatch from the side or behind; a knock on the back of the head; an injection covered up by an accidental collision of bodies or even a .45 bullet straight through the heart. He had no weapon, no way of fighting back. Finally he reached the desk unhindered.

So far ... so good!

He checked in his large suitcase, keeping hold of the smaller item.

"Do you want to check in your other case sir?" the helpful clerk offered.

"No thank you." confirmed Liam as he took another cautious glance around his space.

With boarding pass in one hand and the billion dollar consignment, costing six lives so far, in the other, Liam made his way to the business lounge.

He sat at the bar but would not be partaking of any alcohol today.

He must remain sober and vigilant, at least

until he delivered the shipment to Patrick O'Breian. The biggest test would be getting out of Canada. Entering Ireland should be less of an issue with a good sprinkling of cause sympathizers embedded within the customs section and airport management.

Flight time to Toronto would be just under six hours and the onward flight to Dublin a further seven hours. Liam had booked business class to give him more seat room. The case containing the shipment of micro-chips would be tucked as much as possible under the forward seat with his feet resting on it. So, even if he fell asleep, anyone attempting to remove the case would have to disturb him.

Once on board the aircraft and settled into his seat, Liam felt comfortable with the arrangement and would allow himself a nap on the way to Toronto.

Being 'in transit' from Frisco to Dublin, Liam had no need to pass through any form of customs checks. However, that did not mean the Canadian security services might not want to have a word with him ... or instruct customs to inspect his luggage.

The two hour wait at the bar in the departure lounge would be testing. Sipping at his second cup of coffee he spied two men in civilian dress, both wearing identity tags hanging from their neck. One talked into a hand held radio and both looked to have Liam in their sights.

They made their approach.

Liam buried his 'flight or fight' itch in order to remain calm and sweat free as it looked as if a conversation might well be necessary.

"Good evening sir." the taller of the two said.

"Can we have a look at your passport please?" the second guy asked.

"And you are?" questioned Liam.

"We are border security." said the tall one, lifting up his identity and security pass and nearly pushing it in Liam's face.

Liam pulled his Irish passport from inside his jacket and gave it to the second guy. He glanced at the passport and then down at the case with Liam's right foot resting on it. The tall one inspected the passport and then walked away for a pace or two and spoke for less than a minute into his 'walkie-talkie.'

He eventually called his partner over and they held a short conversation. The tall one came back and delivered Liam's passport.

"Thank you for that sir ... err ... just a random security check ... nothing to worry about. Thank you for your co-operation."

He smiled, at least the lips moved in an unusual coming together, but the eyes told a different, much darker story.

As they walked quickly away, Liam remained suspicious and nervous. Was this really a random security check by the authorities or ... an identity confirmation required by someone who might be out to do him harm?

The flight to Dublin was thankfully uneventful and Liam Byrne actually managed to grab a useful hour or so of sleep on the journey. Once on Irish soil, the veil of threat and insecurity lifted, he allowed himself a smile.

Just the last bit now!

Only one quick move through customs and then he should be free and clear.

"Where are you coming from today sir?" the uniformed officer asked.

"From Canada - Toronto in fact."

"Right sir ... can I ask did you pack your own luggage?"

"I did."

"And are these two cases the only ones you are carrying with you today?"

"They are."

"Could you place them on the bench to your left for inspection?"

Liam took a deep breath. It would now be essential for him to remain calm and so he lifted the cases onto the stainless steel counter top and unlocked both.

"Passport sir?"

Liam handed it over as the officer began to rummage through the big case.

Nothing to see there!

The small brief case however, was another matter. The officer opened it and inspected the parcel inside the foam block.

"And what is this sir?"

"Here is my business card and a customs invoice for these items. I am over here on behalf of my company, Dalton Electronics, for a meeting with our agent here in Ireland. As you can see from the invoice, these are sets of links used in the manufacture of printed circuit boards."

"Can you take them out of case and give them to me. I will need to check what you have there. From the information provided by this invoice, it looks as if whatever they are, there should be three hundred of them. Is that true sir?"

Liam was finding it difficult to hide his discomfort. What the hell was going on? The pathway through customs should have been clear for him. That's what Patrick O'Breian had said. He had the airport tied up ... he said. Nothing to worry about ... he said, but it looked as if someone had forgotten to tell the young officer standing in front of him, demanding that he hand over the package of components for a more detailed inspection.

This was not going to happen, but now he needed to come up with a good reason why he should not deliver up the multi-million dollar shipment of electronic components to the Irish customs.

At that very moment a tall gentleman appeared, a senior officer, shoulders laden with gold braid. He stopped behind the patiently waiting young man and tapped him on the shoulder. The two moved away from Liam and held a short conversation. The young officer returned.

"Thank you for your co-operation sir." offered the red faced customs official. "This paperwork all seems to be correct and you can go on your way sir. Have a nice day."

He turned and walked away. The more senior officer was nowhere to be seen.

With an obvious sigh of relief, Liam quickly closed the brief case, dropped his large suitcase to the floor and headed for the exit.

Once inside the arrivals concourse Liam was able to immediately relax. As he scanned the waiting crowd, his name came back at him in large letters written on a sheet of cardboard. It was being paraded by an attractive woman in a well fitted light grey uniform displaying the name of a car hire company; Eire Rental.

He moved toward her. She smiled.

"Mr Liam Byrne?"

"That's correct." he told the rather attractive lady through a broad smile. He felt inside his jacket pocket for the piece of paper with a reservation number written on it.

He read it out loud.

"ER-159-200 ... is that correct?"

"Yes it is sir." The young lady replied. If you would like to come with me, we have a bus outside and that will take yourself and another customer over to our off-site parking unit where your car is waiting."

The eye contact confirmed nothing but warmth and reassurance.

"Oh, and by the way, we have upgraded you to a BMW Five Series ... and we hope you will find this vehicle a little more comfortable than the small Ford we originally had reserved for you."

She smiled once more.

Liam was a happy man. Ireland was a country

where the IRA held influence at all levels of society such as a heavy hand at a customs station to the upgrade of a small family car to a top-of-the-range luxury vehicle. These were small but obvious positives as far as Liam was concerned and made him proud to part of the 'cause'.

In the ferry bus waiting outside the terminal sat someone who looked to be a fellow traveller and a male car rental rep. Both carried a welcoming smile but said nothing. Liam held onto the brief case but was quite happy for the large suitcase to be stored in the back of the bus with two others.

Liam became instantly relaxed and therefore possibly off his guard. The bus driver turned left to exit the airport road network and make his way onto a perimeter road leading to several acres of ground where most national car rental companies were based.

The first shot could barely be heard; the suppressed muzzle of the firearm pushed hard into Liam's back. The second shot, above his right ear, was also reduced to a mere hiss by the silencer ... and then, Liam Byrne, successful businessman, IRA sympathizer and International traveller was no more.

The driver shouted.

"Is it done?"

"Yes!" confirmed the attractive young lady.

Taking the next turn right the driver confirmed they would be heading toward Dundalk to dispose of the body and the vehicle.

CHAPTER SEVEN

An untimely double cross ...

I sat in silence as the Major released expletive after expletive. We had not only been following a false trail, carefully constructed by whoever was behind the microchip robbery, but it now materialized that six people had been put to death in order for the perpetrator to remain concealed.

It was a hell of a price to pay and confirmed to both Ewan and to me this team of thieves had adopted a no-holds-barred policy in protecting their highly valuable haul of microchips.

Not only was the robbery itself well planned and audacious, it appeared the cover-up had been equally ruthless and unhesitant. This looked to have the finger print of the IRA all over it. The Major was fuming.

The eleven hour flight from San Francisco to Heathrow had not put him in any better mood and having rooms booked at a Bayswater Hotel, I was desperate to get rid of the Major and catch up on some restful sleep.

Eventually I managed to convince Ewan he might be due some rest and relaxation as well and still swearing to 'cut the balls' off whoever planned such a well executed operation, he left me to my devices.

I ordered a light meal through room service and a chilled bottle of Chardonnay. Having consumed half the bottle of wine, I lay back on the bed and closed my eyes.

There were lots of different scenarios playing in my head. Perhaps Ewan was right. The IRA was certainly a lot more than a rag-tag army with ambitions above their capabilities. They were well trained, vicious in applying discipline, relatively well funded; dedicated to the cause of re-uniting Ireland and about to launch a war on the British, the like of which had never been seen before.

The trail had definitely gone cold and only a simple guess might reveal the current location of the microchips. For sure, the starting point had to be 'where are they now?'

Ewan voted for Ireland but I was not so sure. Perhaps they were still in America and the current movement intelligence was yet another bluff in this complex series of events. He had all the military and civilian intelligence authorities scraping their informants for leads and demanded something positive by breakfast the following morning. I expected a ransom request to have appeared by now, but Ewan assured me no such contact had been made.

So, if whoever stole the microchips either didn't know how much they might be worth or were not looking to sell them, then the only other motive for the theft would be an attempt to capture the technology. Now, I wondered, who might want to do that?

Over breakfast, Ewan and I discussed the situation.

"Have you learnt anything new since last night?" I asked.

"Yes Gary. There is more detail to come but another body has come to light. Identity is still unsure as both the body and a vehicle it was found in had been torched."

I tried to make eye contact with him. He looked tired and probably still needed sleep.

"So, tell me what you know."

"We believe ... and when I say 'we' I mean the British Security Services 'en masse' and not just Military Intelligence: we believe Gary that this deceased person could well be someone known as Liam Byrne. He has travelled under several different aliases over the years, but this well known US based businessman and dedicated IRA sympathiser arrived in Ireland yesterday, under his own name and guess what he was carrying?"

He raised his head; his lips moved.

"Here is a photograph taken in the customs hall at Dublin Airport. Look at this man and what he is carrying."

Ewan pulled a colour photograph from the inside pocket of his jacket.

Although the image might have been considered a little grainy, it contained enough detail to match the small brief case with the one they had opened in the Falcon jet at Sutter County Airfield. A sharp intake of breath underlined my surprise. It wasn't just a likeness; it was bloody well identical.

I sat back in my chair.

"OK Ewan, what the fuck does this tell us. I assume the man in the photo is Liam Byrne ... is that correct?"

"It is Gary."

"So, from what you've just told me, this guy was some sort of high-up honcho in the IRA ... he looks to be carrying the case of microchips ... and now he's fucking well dead!"

"That just about sums it up Gary. Now he is well and truly dead ... so who the fuck has the microchips?"

I poured more coffee.

"Does this mean this crazy venture we are on has come to an end?"

"No it has not Gary. It's really only just beginning."

"Well, let me tell you this my friend, unless you can come up with a plan to recover the damned micro-chips that requires my immediate input ... then I have to tell you I have a job to do and I need to get the hell back to Irton Moor. Don't worry about processing my expenses, I feel sure my boss will sign off on them."

Now, Major Ewan Magnus McAllister, rising star of the Special Operations department at Military Intelligence, MI9 looked completely deflated.

"I have to go after them; you see that don't you Gary. Too many lives have been lost and the murder of Byrne will make everyone on both sides of the Irish Sea very uncomfortable.

If one of the loyalist groups in the north claim responsibility, it will be the only match required to set the petrol soaked, dry tinder of Irish politics alight.

You see that don't you?"

"I see a lot of things Ewan, nearly all of them involve you and I want no part of them. I will pack now and make my way back to Scarborough.

I can't tell you it's been a pleasure ... because

it's not! And if you ever do actually find these fucking micro-chips ... do NOT ring me!"

After checking out of my Bayswater hotel, I took a taxi to Kings Cross railway station. The journey to Scarborough would be about three hours and I calculated I would be home by dinner time.

Three hours on a half empty train provided a great opportunity to be awake; disengaged with my surroundings and simply ... think!

The Major obviously felt distressed about not having tracked down the missing micro-chips. However, it was not the end of the damn world. Inter-Tech confirmed their manufacturing process continued at the best possible pace and probably, within a year would have another batch of several hundred new components ready for us to use. Many wise heads had been put together when the first hint came from the Americans that the secret to manufacturing a reliable, low energy consuming multi-function transistor set had been discovered.

We had tried and failed, along with the French and the Germans, so given the opportunity to experiment with such an advanced component might well turn out to be the pinnacle of my career.

I could see the motive behind the original robbery; a well planned and well executed event. However, the ultimate method used to silence everyone involved in the process was shocking and frightening at the same time.

Were all the actors who played a part in getting

the shipment of micro-chips to Ireland now dead? That would be a question for the Major. Would it be possible to now rule out the IRA as the current owner of the components?

From what Ewan had told me, a mix of differing factions operated under the 'freedom fighter' flag. One thing was for sure, if what they wanted was money, then they would be crawling out of the woodwork quite soon with their demands. What would the Major and MI9 do then?

If any other motive lay behind this curiously well managed criminal activity, then it was my guess the intelligence authorities of a mix of cash rich countries might well be involved.

With the cold war at its height and international relationships at their most sensitive, my best guess would be to look to the east for an answer.

After the adventure and tension of the past day or two, I was not looking forward to returning to my rather compact two bed apartment in Scarborough. It commanded great sea views but caught all the easterlies and could be as cold as hell in the winter.

The flashing light on my telephone instrument warned of a message in waiting. It was from the boss, Air Vice-Marshall David Brooking, and the delivery sounded a little tense.

'Get down to Cheltenham to see me when you get back. Give Dorothy a ring to let her know when you expect to arrive. We have things to discuss.'

The arrangement, finally confirmed with Dorothy, chief assistant to the AVM, was for us both to meet for lunch – midday in one of the private dining rooms at the White Horse Hotel – no uniforms.

David Brooking appeared fifteen minutes late. He looked flustered as he sat down, offering his apologies.

"Before we start … are we drinking or not drinking?"

"That's up to you sir. I'll not be driving back to Scarborough today. They've managed to find me a room here, so I'll go back tomorrow."

"Good. Well I have a driver; so on such a rare occasion where we meet face to face outside of the 'big office', we might as well celebrate the fact with a glass or two or wine."

The Royal Air Force Command Officer smiled and I joined him. Brooking had a plan. Order the food; choose the wine and then spill the beans … in other words tell him every minute detail of what happened in America so that we might just get a small handle on what to do next.

In describing to Brooking what had taken place, I tried hard to keep the events in sequence and provide as much detail as I could remember.

Two hours, one and a half bottles of fine wine and a couple of coffees later I was done. Brooking had only interrupted on a couple of occasions, looking for clarification here and there, but other than that, he sat quietly absorbing every single word.

At the end and after a minute or two of complete silence, he eventually spoke.

"So let's get this absolutely straight Gary; as of this moment in time, we have no idea where these blood microchip thingies are … or who might have them. Is that correct?"

"So it appears sir."

"Well, as you can imagine every pompous, short tempered, 'I told you so' asshole in the security services, on both sides of the Atlantic, are going fucking mad. There are bodies everywhere Gary with the IRA loving every minute of the limelight being focused firmly on them. If we are not careful, some mad bastard is going to leak all this to the damned press and then the shit will really hit the fan!"

It was unlike David Brooking to use so many descriptive swear words, but he looked to be pretty well wound up.

"I think getting Military Intelligence involved might have been a mistake." I offered.

"How do you think McAllister performed? Did he have his finger on the pulse from the start and who do you think he was using as crew for the operation?"

"Look sir, I don't care who might have been instructed to get to grips with this problem, McAllister did his best. The crew he employed did what he told them to do, but the robbers were always one step ahead. We were being played by the bad guys sir ... well played and one thing was for sure, when they wanted to shut down the trail of evidence, they did so ruthlessly."

"So, no matter what they find in Ireland …"

"The trail and all the evidence showing 'who did what' has now disappeared sir ... and if anyone says they have some 'intel' to give, whoever receives it will not live long enough to enjoy any possible reward. That's what I think sir."

Brooking sipped at his coffee.

"How dangerous is this for you right now?" Brooking asked, lifting his head to make full eye contact.

"Well, that depends upon who now holds the micro-chips, what their motive is to have stolen them in the first place, and what they feel they need to do with them. There are only two 'non-political' options. The first is simply to trade them for a lot of money with us or another European country. The second is to use them as part of a weapons development programme for some Middle Eastern or Far Eastern country."

"Hmm ..." Brooking muttered, putting down his coffee. "... and where does that leave you and McAllister?"

"The Major from MI9 will know no difference as he appears to play such deadly hunting games all the time. With the Irish situation about to explode any minute, he will be in his element working undercover and beating the living daylights out of everyone he reckons to be an informant."

"From what I understand, Military Intelligence Nine have now been removed from the scenario and MI6 have taken over on the basis this has become an International investigation. I have told them you will no longer be part of any active operations and that 'if and when' the components we seek are recovered they are to be returned to me."

I wondered if that was actually true. I felt pretty sure Brooking would not tell me lies but others may be telling lies to him.

"What about your personal security. Do you have a weapon, because if not I can authorise an issue to you and a warrant to carry it?" Brooking confirmed.

"McAllister found a Makarov 9mm for me in California, but obviously I couldn't bring it with me."

"That's not a problem. When you get back to Irton Moor the RAF Regiment guys will issue you with the weapon and anything else you need. The concealed firearm warrant will be signed by me and issued to you in a couple of days."

"Thank you sir."

"Look Gary, I want you to be careful over the next couple of weeks. Whatever you may become involved in, we know for sure the IRA have been part of it. They have lost one of their best recruiters in the US and one of their best fund raisers. They will not be happy, and no matter how many reassuring political statements are made, there are rogue elements within the high command that may see things differently."

To be frank, having the venomous IRA on my back was not something I particularly looked forward to. That's why a Makarov would offer me an amount of comfort, or at least some small way of fighting back.

David Brooking finished his coffee and raised his hand for a refill.

"So Gary, if you were forced to take a guess, who do think has the Micro-chips now?"

The question needed some thought and was obviously playing on both our minds.

"All I can say is that the 'Provos' or the IRA itself, must be first in the frame for ransom demands and coming a close second would be the Arab terrorist organisation Black September. They're both seeking International attention, have a scary agenda to promote and look toward armed revolution rather than political dialogue. Then of course there is the Red Brigades, probably seen as second rank to the other two but nevertheless more than capable of carrying out an operation such as the Irish intercept. So, from my viewpoint, top of the list for needing the money ... would be the Irish ... in one form or another!"

I could see the Air Vice-Marshall was struggling somewhat with my answer.

"As for the technology motive ... stealing the components to de-engineer them and get a head start with microelectronic technology, there are many in the frame. It can't be the Americans ... they already have it. It can't be us ... the Americans are giving it to us free! It can't be the Russians because they are probably several steps ahead of the Yanks as we speak. You can't put a space station into orbit, as the Ruskies are about to do, using valves and capacitors.

My top two candidates for the 'technology' option are the Iranians; the Shah himself alongside his notorious SAVAK, his so-called Bureau for Intelligence and Security.

These bastards are mean and heartless, and although we and the Yanks support him, and more or less manage his armed forces for him, his ambitions for Iran are difficult to define.

Finally, I would be happy to put money on the Israelis. The Mossad intelligence and security operation is sophisticated and tough. They do not normally take prisoners and are more than capable of carrying out such a murderous operation as we witnessed in the States and in Dublin.

They are desperate to climb aboard the technology wagon. Every step they take might well be one more step ahead of the west. They are betting the future of the whole damn world is going to be micro-electronics in one form or another, whether that is applied to military or civilian projects.

In order to finance any kind of future for a nation plonked in the middle of an arid desert surrounded and outnumbered by aggressive neighbours, they need to be able to trade in order to survive. They have set their sights on technology sir and would be desperate to get their hands on our set of micro-chips!"

Brooking studied his third cup of freshly made coffee for some time. He looked to be genuinely concerned about the situation and the number of actors that were becoming increasingly involved.

"So, what do we do now sir?" I asked.

Brooking looked up, swiftly returning from the world he had temporarily habited during the past couple of minutes. A decision had been made.

"What do we do Gary? Well firstly we should separate ourselves from any more involvement with people getting them-selves murdered. Secondly, you need to take a step back from offering any form of assistance to MI9 and if MI6 want to talk to you, they will need to come through me. Is that clear?"

"It is sir ... very clear!

"Lastly, until these bloody components are found, or at least someone owns up to having them, I want you to have a round the clock body guard, a car and a driver."

I thought about the last bit. A full-on body guard would become very claustrophobic, very quickly.

"Could we just settle for a car and driver and rely on everything else to be covered by the Makarov?"

The Air Vice-Marshall smiled.

"OK ... but stay out of the spotlight ... and whatever you do ... do not speak to that damn McAllister in MI9. Trouble follows him around and seeks him out. Is that clear Sergeant?"

"It is sir ... perfectly clear!"

CHAPTER EIGHT

Cometh the day and the opportunity ...

The Honourable Colonel Sir Tarquin Ludlow, purchasing and procurement, Section Three, Technology Group One, at the Ministry of Defence could not shake what others called 'that disgusting habit' of smoking.

He drew heavily on his fifth Benson and Hedges of the morning. His surroundings appeared bleak, the only view from the stinking, un-swept smoking shelter being that of irregular rooftop shapes protecting the Ministry of Defence Whitehall building.

Dark angry clouds pressed down from above adding even more dispiriting texture to a singularly depressing skyline

The year 1971 would be pivotal and life changing for the Colonel, although he didn't know it yet. Tarquin sat behind his quite moderately sized desk in an office needing a detailed map of the Whitehall labyrinth to find.

He travelled down to London and his office at the MoD by train from his family estate at Farnborough, located a few miles north of Banbury in Oxfordshire. He would travel 'down' on Monday and back 'up' on Friday. This routine would make him late for work on the Monday and early to leave work on the Friday ... but no-one seemed to care. It was the Colonel's routine and for the many years he had been working there, staff at all levels had become used to it.

Tarquin Ludlow was forty eight years old and very shortly would be promoted to Briagadier. A year later he would be saying goodbye to his regular commute and retire from the Army. He had been a disappointment to his superiors especially those who expected him to step easily into the shoes of his father, Lord Avonsbury; observed by most as being a 'splendid chap', a life peer and decorated General officer.

The work Tarquin undertook at the MoD was ill-defined and spectacularly routine. He chased an order or two here and there and even took part in various briefings ranging from the introduction of new re-styled shirts for 'the men' to upgrading of the nation's main battle tanks.

He held little well defined responsibilities at the MoD, which suited him without doubt. However, he did have his worries and the one that concerned him most was ... money!

Tarquin Ludlow was no gambler; never considering himself to be a lucky man. However, it was not luck he needed to take a careful post-war look at the revolution taking place in the relatively neglected world of agriculture.

The several rent paying farms on his estate employed too many people and too little modern machinery. As such, over the years, the income from each had become less and less and once he lost his army salary, he feared the consequences for the overall estate would be fatal.

Many pieces of paper passed across the Colonel's

desk in the course of a normal working day, most not being worthy of a second glance. His job would be to either stamp them with a 'Section Three' approval or pass them on to 'Logistics' for transport arrangements or 'Finance' for payment procedures. The letters, notes, chits and memos did not often contain any information other than that relating to a specific item or particular coded reference.

The job was boring, but the pay and allowances were good; good enough to keep him and his estate intact. It also paid the mortgage on the one bed London apartment he used during the week, a comfortable place with a view of Waterloo Bridge.

The eighteenth of March was a Thursday. It was also the day that the 'Finance' request form 118A/71 landed on Tarquin's desk. It was an unusual piece of paper requiring a payment to be made to a source in the United States.

This source, named Maguire Logistics, had been tasked with collecting a shipment of goods from a company described as Inter-Tech, based in Santa Clara California. The consignment was to be collected in a secure manner then shipped by RAF aircraft across 'the pond'. Delivery would be made to a certain Flight Sergeant G. Chase at a GCHQ facility posted as Irton Moor, near Scarborough.

It caught the Colonel's attention; especially the paperwork attached to the request marked Top Secret. This was a single 'flimsy', a word used in the military to describe carbon copies of original orders and original signatures of those who raised them.

The 'flimsy' contained a description of the goods, the package size and the insurance value.

Description of Goods: Electronic components, prototype Class IV, Microchip Base, Model 21M, Military Grade, 6Volt with Internal Distribution Bus and Common Earth.
Number of Items: 300
Package Dims: Approx 12 inches x 12 inches x 4 inches.
Weight: 25 Ounces.
Value for Insurance Purposes: 620M.

Colonel Ludlow read the movement order carbon copy sheet twice more. Something did not make sense. Firstly the 'flimsy' should not have been attached to the finance request, especially as it was marked Top Secret. Secondly, the value appeared to be wrong. The script '620M' meant nothing to him as it was obviously a typing error.

The signature at the bottom of the carbon copy was that of Tarquin's boss, General Sir Peter Hawthorn and his office was a short walk away on the floor above. A quick phone call confirmed the General would see him right away if he would care to come up to the seventh floor. But first he felt an unexplainable need to take a copy of the documentation, a personal copy for his eyes only. Call it instinct or precaution, something prompted him to take the illegal copy and lock it away in his desk drawer.

"Come in my boy." the General offered as Tarquin tapped lightly in the door to his office.

"Thank you sir ... and ... err ... thank you for seeing me as short notice."

Both men smiled, heading for the red leather sofa suite that filled the space in one corner of the rather grand timber panelled office suite.

They sat down. Tarqin had the finance request and 'flimsy' attachment in hand. He extended his arm toward the General.

"I've come to show you this sir. It's rather an unusual directive and it has the 'flimsy' attached, which you will know sir is highly irregular. However, it has landed on my desk; it has your signature on the bottom and I was wondering what you wanted me to do with it."

More polite smiles appeared probably masking some insecurity on behalf of the General and a particular curiosity on behalf of the Colonel.

"Let me have a look at it."

Peter Hawthorn took the paperwork and read it through in detail ... twice.

"This should not have gone to you old chap. There has been an administrative error here I'm afraid and that's why the 'flimsy' is still attached."

"Oh ... well ... if that is the case sir, what should we do about it now? The 118/A reference has already been posted in my action log ... so ... I have to put something in there!"

The General tilted his head toward the ceiling creating a suitable pause in the conversation.

"There is another small thing I noticed sir.

There has been a typing error on the value of goods for insurance purposes. It won't pass any of our procedures unless a real and proper value is noted for the goods sir ... so what should it be?"

The General reddened slightly and dropped his eyes from the ceiling to lock on to the questioning administrator.

"It all looks quite correct to me Tarquin old chap. Although you might be right in one way as I can't see whether the valuation figure is in US Dollars or Pounds Sterling."

The Colonel looked confused.

"Correct sir? What is correct about 620M. It simply doesn't mean anything to me whether one reads it in Dollars or Sterling?"

"Yes Tarquin. I think the figure is more or less right ... approximately six hundred and twenty million ... err ... Pounds!"

The Colonel became awkwardly speechless. Surely that could not be right. Something weighing twenty five ounces being valued at several hundred million pounds could not be right ... could it?

"So, thank you for bringing this to my attention Tarquin. I'll take this matter off your hands and deal with it if that's OK with you?"

"But surely sir, no company in the damn world is going to insure this. What on earth is contained in one tiny package that can be valued at such a ridiculously high level? Are you sure that this is all above-board and completely correct sir?"

"I am Tarquin!" said the General firmly as he raised himself from the sofa; an indication the meeting must now be considered over. He offered a hand toward Tarquin.

"How is everything with the family old chap? Martha and the children well and prospering I hope?"

"Oh yes sir, they are in fine spirits."

"Good ... err ... good. Well ... we really must get together again socially Tarquin. It's been a long time and I'm sure our two wives will have much to talk about ... especially considering your pending promotion."

"Yes sir ... that would be much appreciated. I will wait for your call General."

"Excellent old chap ... and ... err ... a word to the wise. If I were you, I would destroy any and all details or information relating to this matter. As far as you are concerned this meeting never took place and you never saw this document."

The General waved the paperwork in front of him.

"So, I can leave this all in your hands sir?" the Colonel asked cautiously.

"You most certainly can Tarquin ... you most certainly can!"

The Honourable Colonel Sir Tarquin Ludlow returned to his office to consider what had just gone down. Something was not right. An amount of research needed to be undertaken. The Colonel smelt money ... lots and lots of money!

Within twenty four hours he had un-earthed the bones of the matter; the history behind what were being called micro-chips; the involvement of the American electronics business Inter-Tech and their arrangement to allow the British Government to experiment with a programme of hi-tech applications research.

There would be no charge for the supply of these early production components but their value on the open market might well be considered inestimable. So, having got to the bottom of that particular mystery, Tarquin Ludlow saw this top secret transfer of technology from the United States to Britain as an opportunity to make a substantial amount of money. However, there would not be much time to put together a plan.

The Colonel had made many connections over the years in his role within the Whitehall military purchasing machine; connections which, in the past, had often supported his urgent need for hard cash. However, a few thousand here and there as bribes provided by manufacturers, eager to move up the list of suppliers to the Ministry, only just kept the wolf from the door.

Keeping a twenty six bedroom mansion maintained and watertight and substantial grounds trim and managed cost money; money his father, the rather extravagant Lord Avonsbury, had already spent on summer balls, lavish parties, fast cars and slippery women.

The overall estate, and the farms servicing it being near to bankruptcy, needed urgent financial support and Tarquin was the person responsible for providing it. The extraordinary figure of six hundred and twenty million pounds represented a prospect that would definitely never pass across his desk again. He needed to make a decision and he needed to make it NOW!

Unlocking his desk drawer, Tarquin pulled out a grey manila file. It was headed 'IRA' and appeared quite bulky. He flicked through the pages of data until he arrived at one titled 'Conner Sullivan – Code Name: Tommy. Nationality: Irish. Function: IRA Military Intelligence Group. Cover: Bar Manager – O'Mally's Pub and Restaurant – Peckham.

This would be his man.

This kind of character made things happen and was known to be well connected within the IRA senior command. Being regularly tracked by MI5, it would not be difficult to find him and then conjure up a way of drawing him and his IRA chums into a plan; a plan for an audacious robbery followed by an even more audacious ransom operation.

The Colonel smiled. What should he look for here ... ten percent; maybe even twenty percent? If the ransom value was put at around half the commercial value ... say three hundred million, then twenty per cent would represent a cool sixty million. With that kind of money, all of the Ludlow family's problems would be over.

A quick visit to the rooftop smoking shelter and a few long draws on a Benson and Hedges cigarette would calm the excitement of the moment.

General Sir Peter Hawthorn studied the form 118A/71 and the flimsy attached to it provided by Tarquin Ludlow. Eventually, he folded it carefully and placed it in the secure drawer of his desk. He was puzzled slightly but also quite angry that such a document, with a Top Secret flimsy attached, had somehow broken out of 'the system' and ended up on Ludlow's desk.

He had decided to walk down to the Accounts Department three floors below and personally approve payment for secure transport and courier services as billed directly by Maguire in the States. This ensured that the paper trail for this 118A order would be closed down within the ministry and all 'backsides' would then be completely covered ... especially his own!

CHAPTER NINE

A dangerous piece of luggage arrives ...

Patrick O'Breian sat in O'Keef's Bar in Dundalk sipping on his third Guinness of the afternoon. The town was a popular place for IRA sympathisers to gather, being close to the border with Northern Ireland. It was a place where there was much cross-border activity, being a sorting house of rumour and real intelligence in equal measure.

Patrick was in mourning for a good friend lost over the past forty-eight hours, Liam Byrne. He was also lamenting the plan that allowed the highly valuable consignment of microchips to be stolen from him.

At this moment in time, IRA command did not appear to be aware of Patrick's activities relating to the capture of the electronic components. However, with the murder of Liam Byrne, there was little chance they might be left in the dark for much longer. When it all came out, Patrick would need to have a good story to tell or else he might end up being short of two kneecaps ... or worse!

Several things needed to be done. Firstly the missing components must be recovered and the individuals involved in Liam's murder brought to book.

The big question had to be were the microchips still in the damn country? If so Patrick was confident he would know before the end of the day. Half the Garda, the Irish Republican police force, were strong supporters of 'the cause' and as soon as they knew something, then Patrick would know it also.

So far, it looked as if whoever might have been involved in the hi-jack of the priceless components had covered their tracks well. The smoothness of the whole operation suggested whoever it was had been trained for the job and this suggested the involvement of an established terrorist organisation. It also pointed in the direction of another country with a well trained and organised external security service. But who could it be?

Every two hours Patrick entered the public telephone box about a hundred yards or so south of O'Keef's. He made a phone call to a Dublin number. It was a clearing house for information flowing into the organisation. The 'cloaked' number was changed every twenty four hours and the British MI5 hadn't cottoned onto the arrangement so far.

He listened intently to what the 'Protector' on the other end of the phone line was telling him. It would be fair to say that Patrick O'Breian was shocked.

The story so far was that word had come from Belfast. A young man named Murphy Conner had sat that very lunchtime in a certain pub, drinking heavily and flashing cash. He took great pleasure in telling anyone who would listen he had been the driver in a snatch and murder where a top IRA officer had been 'done'.

At around two o'clock, he had been grabbed by 'soldiers' from the Belfast Brigade and taken to a deserted farm property a mile or two west of the border. There, the 'truth apparatus' was revealed to

Mr. Conner and he quickly gave up everything he knew and perhaps even one or two pieces of intelligence he had made up.

It turned out that the loose mouthed individual was a paid member of the recently formed Ulster Defence Association, a paramilitary operation, unofficially backed by British MI5 to counter the activities of the fast growing IRA.

So, the big question now was where were the components? Were they still in Ireland, Northern Ireland, and secreted somewhere within the UDA Command or in London ... under the protection of MI5.

The Protector' wanted to know if the informant Conner was to be kept alive or his body dumped in a ditch somewhere. Patrick thought it better to keep the lad alive ... for now!

He checked his watch, the time approached twenty minutes past six o'clock in the evening. He needed to get to Dublin as quickly as he could. A meeting was required; a meeting with a small group of individuals; individuals making up the IRA high command. He needed to 'come clean' about the microchip operation, the disaster that had overtaken events and the new information indicating the UDA had become involved.

If they were to recover the stolen components and capture the smiling young lady, her fellow male rep and the innocent looking passenger aboard Liam's bus, then they would need to get a plan together to carry out a major operation in Belfast. It would have to be done tonight.

Patrick O'Breian expected more than a rebuke from the General Officer's making up the IRA Senior Command. However, they all appeared quick to offer praise and support when they heard the figures involved.

One in particular was finding it difficult to visualise three hundred million dollars in paper money and asked Patrick to tell him how many large suitcases it would need to transport it.

From the intelligence provided by Patrick they knew who was involved and where they would be sleeping that night. If the abduction of Conner had been carried out without fuss, then the three further individuals they planned on 'lifting' would have no idea anyone might be coming for them.

That would be the key to a smooth capture; no shots fired and no one in the immediate area disturbed from a healthy sleep.

The operation to kidnap the 'names' provided by the 'Protector' could not have gone smoother. They were all contained within one address, a place they had obviously regarded as a safe house. They had all been drinking, probably to excess, guaranteeing heavy eyes and dulled senses during the break-in.

Safe house or no safe house, Patrick O'Breian's specialists quickly and efficiently abducted the two men and one woman. There was no sound, no shots fired; no curious neighbours writing down licence plates of visiting vehicles. By the time everyone had caught their breath they were half way to the west coastal town of Ballyshannon and the farm at Tirconeen. This was an IRA interrogation site, a place where people would visit if they had fallen foul of 'the rules' or been labelled an enemy of the Irish republican cause.

When the silent 'soldiers of the UDA' had their blindfolds removed, each scanned the gloomy interior of the high roofed farm building; a floor of cold concrete and a scattering of dried straw. There was a smell attached to the building, a smell of death; the stink of the many murders and episodes of torture that had been carried out here during recent months.

The pale faced but silent woman looked up. Above her, suspended from a roof beam was a body, a naked body; a silent, possibly dead body dripping blood to the floor. She let out a gasp. The man hanging there was unrecognisable but she knew damn well who it was.

"Conner ...!" she muttered breathlessly.

O'Breian sat on a straw bale, smoking a cigarette and studying the three protestant members of the Ulster Defence Association laying, unmoving on the rough concrete and stone floor.

He stood and bent down to whisper in the ear of the terrified woman.

"So me darlin'... who's going to be first?"

At this she burst into tears and one of the two young men captured with her shouted out a warning.

O'Breian moved over to the defiant looking youngster.

"Well then ... it'll have to be you!"

Six pairs of eyes focused on him from behind black ski-masks. These three men; these three practiced criminals and trained IRA intelligence officers were highly proficient in the black art of delivering pain.

"Strip him and string him up ..." O'Breian said to the 'eyes' ... "... and strip the other two. It'll be the woman next ..."

By seven o'clock that morning O'Breian ordered the interrogation activities to stop. He and his team needed refreshment. They had yet to discover who held the valuable electronic components and what they intended to do with them.

The young man hanging next to the dead body of Conner looked a mess, but he was still alive. He had admitted to taking the micro-chips and killing Liam Byrne but insisted that once at the 'safe house' in Belfast, someone they didn't know armed with a password took the briefcase and its contents away. Where to? They didn't know.

After a breakfast of sorts, prepared and eaten in the deserted farm house, Patrick O'Breian began to feel quite agitated. He was no fan of senseless violence but the use of it had got him this far and now he simply needed to know where the fuck these elusive bloody components were. He wanted them back and he wanted them back ...TODAY!

This whole damn business was wrapped up tight. Patrick began to fill with growing frustration following intelligence that never once seemed to be ahead of the game and pointing in a direction much more focused than that of a few dumb-assed protestant gunmen.

Something was going on here. He cast his mind back to what kicked all this bloody mayhem off; his meeting with 'Tommy' at the Olive Branch Restaurant in Putney. What was it he said?

'He talked like a 'toff' Patrick ... and walked like a military man.'

Was there something in that revelation he had missed? Tommy was right of course. Military men did have a particular walk; a walk and a posture drilled into them during those very first six weeks of training. It was a time looked back upon with affection by some and known to everyone who had suffered the indignities of it as 'square bashing'.

Patrick had made a decision. They were wasting their time here. He needed to get hold of 'Tommy' and to do that he would need to go through the Protector. The nearest 'clean' phone was a public call box in nearby Ballyshannon. He turned to his three mask carrying intelligence officers. It was time to put this to an end.

"I'm going in to Ballyshannon. I should be back fairly soon. Finish these three; a bullet in the back of the head. Take the digger tractor and bury all of them at the back of the hillside overlooking the lower field. Make sure you put them down deep; we don't want any fucking dog walkers making headline grabbing discoveries ... do we?"

All three men nodded in agreement, each carrying a half-smile, pulling the ski-masks up over their heads once more. There was murderous work to be done at the isolated farm and then a substantial clean-up operation to be undertaken. They would probably be there for the rest of the day.

Patrick jumped into his car and headed off to town and the single telephone box located on the south side of College Street. He hoped to Christ the box had not been vandalised. Time was slipping away from him. It had been nine hours since the abduction of the UDA soldiers and by now, every fucking protestant in Belfast with an air rifle would be on full alert.

The Protector had good news and bad news. He had just been speaking to 'Tommy' in London and there was some surprise news.

His phone number was changed every two weeks. This was standard procedure as approved by Patrick and went unrecorded in the BPO billing and finance section. The IRA had many sympathizers embedded within the British Post Office engineering department, nationwide. They had influence over all telephone exchange switching operations and used it in the fight against the enemy.

"Tommy had another message pushed into his hand again this morning ... at the Tube station. He only caught a glimpse of the rear of the guy who gave it to him, but he was sure it was the same character."

"What did it say?"

"I've written it down. Wait a minute. Right, here it is.

Do NOT lose the shipment again. I have had to use valuable resources to get it back. It is now in

Ireland at the location below.
Left luggage locker number 29, departures area, Dublin Airport.

The key will delivered in a magnetic key box attached under the rear wheel arch of your car. You will find it there after six o'clock this evening. Do NOT lose this package again! Make the ransom demand on Friday. The PM will be back in No. 10 and he will get first sight of it. From then on, be careful. You don't want the SAS knocking at your door in the middle of the night do you?"

"How was it written?"

"Close typed on a fingerprint-free piece of clean paper, concealed in yesterday's newspaper."

"Hmm ..." offered Patrick. "Someone is playing a fucking dangerous game here and if we are not careful, at the end of the trail there might well be a few more dead bodies.

Don't talk to Tommy. When I have the shipment back in my hands, I'll go over to England and shut Tommy down ... keep him out of danger whilst all this shit is going on."

"I'll get my number changed more frequently." confirmed the Protector, "... and I'll move location to-morrow. This guy ... whoever he is ... seems to have a handle on how we do things and may be holding a pile of data on us."

"I agree. If I can get these bloody components back, I'll keep a low profile myself and make sure the intelligence unit is tight but more importantly ... safe!"

At five thirty that evening, Patrick O'Breian sat

in O'Keef's Bar in Dundalk sipping on his first Guinness of the day. He was not nervous about the planned delivery of the left luggage key and had no interest in attempting to capture whoever was prepared to deliver it.

He had mixed feelings about the person who might be orchestrating the disappearance and then the appearance of these bloody micro-chips. He didn't know for sure if he was facilitating access to this valuable package because he was a sympathizer to the cause or because he saw an opportunity to make what would turn out to be a fair sized lump of money. Sixty million was not to be sneezed at.

Whatever the motive, whoever he was appeared to have his finger on the pulse and remarkable access to military intelligence matters.

After his second pint, Patrick checked the time; 6:30 ... was it too early to check? No! The message said six o'clock.

Time to go!

Feeling under the nearside wheel arch of the Ford Cortina, Patrick felt for the metal key box. As promised, it was there and appeared to be free of wires or any other attached items. He removed it carefully. The box contained only one key, a small, flat shiny key with a chrome finish. It looked just like the kind of key he expected.

Patrick O'Breian breathed a sigh of relief. It would take just over an hour and a half to get to Dublin Airport. He would do a few circuits first as he left Dundalk, just to be sure, and then he headed for the R132, a route that would take him south to Dublin Airport.

Leaving the car in the short term parking area, Patrick walked toward the arrivals terminal. It was a cautious journey. Was he being led into some kind of trap? Was this the fucking MI5 playing with him again? He checked around him as each step carried him nearer to the terminal entrance.

He carried his personal 9mm automatic concealed in a shoulder holster. If anyone looked to be approaching him with malice, they would be faced with a choice; a live or die kind of choice.

After circling them twice, Patrick established that no one looked to be attending to any business at the luggage lockers. Patrick produced the key and tried it in the lock of number 29. What would happen when he turned it? Would it explode in his face, perhaps killing him and others nearby? Would it ...?

This was not the time to think, this was the time for action. He turned the key to the left, heard the click and then the door swung silently open. Inside was a small briefcase. His heart pounded. This looked to be the 'prize' he had been looking for. He checked for any exposed wiring; anything at all attached to the case that should not be there. Everything appeared to be OK.

Patrick lifted the case carefully out of the locker, taking another long look around him for any suspicious eyes, bulging jackets or men reading newspapers.

Everything seemed to be clear but he was not out of the damn woods yet. He had to get back to the car and away from the bloody airport. Several minutes later, with the case in the trunk of the Cortina, Patrick O'Breian pulled out of the car park and headed into Dublin City. He would not be going home. He would be going to a 'safe house' in the east of the city, a place where his car could be concealed in a nearby private garage.

The job was done ... or was it. Once inside the un-loved, compact two story property, he would check the contents of the brief case and then he would know for sure whether or not he was being played.

He placed the case carefully on the kitchen counter top. He remained nervous. If ... whoever it was ... wanted to kill him, would they do it with a bomb activated by opening the locker door? Or maybe when he removed the case from the damn locker? Whatever arrangements might have been made, these options would possibly kill or maim innocent bystanders.

So, having some type of explosion rigged to the opening of the case would be more likely; an exercise that would be carried out by one person only and no others nearby.

Patrick inspected the case, checked for any ticking, any loose items inside any signs of holes having been drilled from the outside and any scratches or lever marks on the catches.

Sweat appeared in lines across his forehead, hands trembling noticeably. The decision had been made. He lifted the catches with the thumb and finger of each hand. The lid sprung open. He flinched.

To his complete relief, a set of protective

packaging was revealed surrounding a number of strange looking components.

'So ...' thought Patrick. 'This is what all the fuss is about!'

He smiled. Whatever game might be in play with the 'toff of military bearing' ... he held the ace card and all the substantial resources of the Irish Republican Army will now need to be drawn in to make sure it stayed that way.

By this time next week, the IRA coffers could be considerably richer to the tune of several hundred million pounds ... and Patrick O'Breian would become an Irish Republican hero!

CHAPTER TEN

Lost and found ... the chase continues...

The phone call was an annoyance; the time far too damn early and the hangover I appeared to be suffering from incompatible with any form of polite response.

"Yes ... do you know what bloody time it is?" I shouted at the dangling instrument.

A smooth unflustered voice answered my aggressive tone. Dorothy, chief assistant to the AVM purred the words, lowering the temperature of what was to be a short conversation.

"If you would care to put your phone on scramble please ...'

This caught my attention. I reached for the button on top of the telephone base unit and sat up on the bed.

"The boss wants to see you at Number Ten, today at twelve o'clock. So, you had better get your skates on Gary. No uniform please, but bring a weekend case, your passport and your military ID. A car will be at your apartment at seven-thirty. This is a secure journey and the password is 'dogfight', single use only. There will be just one person in the car, the driver. If anyone appears inside or hovering outside the car ... don't get in. Oh ... err ... and by the way, bring your handgun with you ... and surrender it when inside Number Ten. Is that all clear Gary?"

"It is my wonderful Dorothy, but has anyone told the boss it's Saturday for God's sake and ..."

"No use complaining. This is what you signed up for. Be alert and be polite whilst inside Downing Street. Much depends upon the outcome of everything that happens today.

Bye, bye Gary."

The line disconnected, the flashing red function light on the telephone died, indicating the line was truly disconnected from any other device.

I fell out of bed and checked the time with clearly focusing eyes; a quarter past five.

'Too fucking early' I muttered to myself as I headed in the direction of the bathroom.

An hour later, being fully refreshed, headache all but gone and stomach working gratefully on a larger than normal portion of bacon and eggs, I switched on the radio and the BBC world news service. Perhaps I was hoping to gain a clue as to why I was wanted at the PM's office ... and on a Saturday to boot!

The news however was pretty bland; no new international incidents, although there were plenty of politicians spouting unscripted opinions, hoping possibly to start one.

Wearing what I considered to be my 'country outfit', I tucked the Makarov 9mm tight into the concealed shoulder hung holster; covered adequately within the roomy Harris Tweed jacket. There was time for yet one more cup of tea. I switched off the radio and sat in silence, eyes closed, sipping my tea, clearing my mind, focusing on what might be ahead.

When the doorbell rang I moved quickly to the window giving out a full view of the street below. The car was there, a black Five Series BMW. By the look of how it sat on its springs, I guessed it was one the armoured versions. Someone, somewhere seemed to be taking whatever this was, completely seriously.

I checked the street, left and right. It all looked good. Time to go!

I opened the front door to my apartment to find a smartly suited gentleman, clean shaven and holding a pair of black leather gloves in his hand. My eyes were immediately drawn to them. What might they be concealing?

"Password ...?" I demanded as our eyes locked.

"Dogfight!" he replied without hesitation.

My attention returned to the gloves. He opened them out and put them on. I felt immediately relieved and withdrew my hand from inside my jacket.

"OK ... let's go my friend ... or do you have a name?"

"You can call me Jackson sir." ... came the quick reply, accompanied by a quite genuine smile.

As we both settled into the black shiny executive government transport, Jackson informed me the journey would take about five hours. I voted to stay awake and alert. Anything could happen in five hours.

〰️

My arrival at Number Ten turned out to be an

unspectacular quick-step through the rear entrance on Horse Guards Road, where I was searched by a rather tough looking policeman ... and my Makarov removed.

I was then guided politely through a labyrinth of odd spaces and corridors and eventually shown into a small conference room. Dorothy and Air Vice-Marshall Brooking greeted me.

"It's good to see you sir and you also Dorothy." I said. "Did you come up this morning or ...?"

"No ..." David Brooking interrupted. "We've been here all bloody night. The AVM did not look to be in a particularly buoyant mood. I sat down next to him. He pulled the sleeve of my jacket and leaned in to whisper in my ear.

"Whatever the hell goes down here today Gary, you do not HAVE to do anything ... do you understand?"

I must have looked confused. He picked up on it immediately. As a result, he moved in closer.

"Take your lead from me and whatever happens with any assignment you agree to, the army and the active intelligence services MUST be kept out of it. You'll understand more later; more when we have had time to talk, but let me tell you there is a bad smell circling around here somewhere, so keep your bloody powder dry!"

"Can I guess what this might be about sir?" I asked.

All I received in return was a dark look. Brooking definitely appeared to be wound up about something ... and my best guess as to the cause would be those damned micro-chips again.

Fortunately we would not have to wait long as within minutes the PM entered, followed by his Private Secretary and none other than Major Ewan Magnus McAllister.

Polite greetings and introductions having been made, we all sat down at the conference table. Brooking focused in on the Prime Minister and I opened the thin paper file distributed to each one of us by the Secretary.

The PM began.

"Everyone here ... in this room ... has at one time or another signed the Official Secrets Act and so I would remind you that what is said in this room is protected by the act. Does everyone understand?"

A murmur of agreement rattled round the table and the PM allowed his lips to form something representing a smile.

"I will cut to the meat of the matter. You are all aware of the debacle surrounding the shipment of a large quantity of electronic components from America to us here in Britain. Lives have been lost as a result and despite having one of our best and most senior intelligence officers on the case, we have not been able to recover them."

The Major moved uncomfortably in his seat, his fingers trembling imperceptibly; keeping them occupied by drawing invisible shapes on the polished hardwood table top. He opened his mouth as if to speak but then the movement died. He obviously thought better of it and the PM continued his briefing.

"The Americans are not happy but that, unfortunately, is the least of our worries. Simply put, the Irish Republican Army ... the IRA ... have confirmed they are in possession of these very, very valuable components and have offered to 'sell' them to us for a ... for a ... ridiculously unrealistic figure."

I suddenly became connected and in a suspicious enough mood to pay attention. Now I could see what the boss was on about, making sure I carried a weapon of some type and to be vigilant when getting in and out of vehicles.

We exchanged glances. Brooking raised his eyebrows as if to say 'I told you so'.

The PM looked round the table, perhaps expecting some level of response. There was none.

"Would anyone like to comment?"

"Yes sir." offered Brooking.

"I see from the file you have given us that you suspect certain individuals of being involved. You have included detailed descriptions of their activities et cetera, but nowhere can I find any information about possible demands from the IRA in relation to the recovery of the items"

The Prime Minister sat up straight in his chair and looked the Air Vice-Marshall in the eye.

"They value this complete consignment of three hundred items, described as 'micro-chips', to be around six hundred million pounds sterling."

"And ... how much of that do they want?"

"Half!"

"How much?" shouted David Brooking.

"That is ridiculous sir ... do they really think they can hold the British Government to ransom over a few bloody electronic components?"

"It appears so!" interjected the Major who

quickly turned his attention to me.

"We have an expert in this particular field of research sitting with us in this very room, so let's ask him. What do you think Gary?"

All eyes swivelled in my direction. Dear oh dear. This was a point at which I might unknowingly talk myself into a large pot of burning shit ... or say something that would release me from any involvement with what was going down here ... leaving this nest of political vipers in enough time to catch the last bloody train of the day ... back to Scarborough.

I spoke, reluctantly.

"I'm afraid I'm not qualified to place a value on these items, but I can tell you that if we, as a nation, intend keeping up with the Yanks, in terms of military technology, we need these bloody microchips ... and we need them NOW!"

The following silence grabbed everyone. Who might be prepared to do what?

"OK Sergeant Chase, here's the situation. We are paying the ransom but there is no way we are exchanging one single penny unless the individual components are verified first. Whether you like it or not, you are the most qualified person we know able to carry out such a task. Are you with me so far?"

"I am sir." I replied cautiously.

"You will be backed up by the Major here and his ..."

"I'm sorry sir, but I would be quite nervous going into such a tense situation with a load of violent religiously driven political fanatics on one side and a set of trigger happy British soldiers on the other. Operation 'Quick Capture ... as allocated by the Major here to what has gone on so far, must now be assumed as closed, shut down or somehow not being financed by the MoD anymore. Is that correct?"

"That is correct." confirmed the Major.

"Good ... then no-one, including me, is bound any further by the brief of that operation, so that means I am no longer committed or under operational orders and I can hopefully get back to work."

That did it. Brooking gave me a dark and unflattering look, the secretary scribbled on his pad with some vigour; the Prime Minister looked shocked and concerned, and Dorothy just smiled.

"I can of course give one of the Major's soldiers a quick course on how to interrogate the chips and confirm they are genuine ... and that might solve more than one or two security issues."

"You seem to forget Mr. Chase, although you live in a quite special kind of environment, carrying all sorts of privileges that would not normally be made available to most serving airmen of your rank, you are still in her Majesties Royal Air Force. Therefore you will do as you are damn well told."

The PM delivered the words calmly and I received them with an equal level of 'cool', making sure I retained the major part of a smile.

Brooking was not happy ... and he said so.

"I'm sorry to say this sir but what started out as a 'help and assist' project for my Sergeant here is now turning into a military farce. If you want Gary to simply check each of the components for validity, then he ... and I are most eager to co-operate. However, if an uninvited British soldier is discovered creeping about in the bloody Irish undergrowth somewhere, then you can say goodbye to Gary and probably goodbye to your bloody components."

I should have kept my mouth firmly shut of course, but I didn't and as a result I found myself a reluctant volunteer to face a bunch of fanatical terrorists inside their own headquarters ... with no escape clause of any kind ... and do so with a smile!

The plan was to fly me in a private aeroplane from RAF Northolt to a small airstrip at Abbeyshrule in County Longford. I would leave for Ireland the following morning and the aeroplane would stay at the airstrip until ordered to come back.

Major Ewan Magnus McAllister remained remarkably quiet during the remainder of the meeting except for one telling question.

'How long will it take to check every single one of these components?' he had asked.

My reply was based upon some quick math of three hundred items at about three minutes each with no breaks totaling up at around fifteen hours.

They all seemed a tad surprised.

A sensible guess then, including breaks, sleep and eating would be a full twenty four hours needing to be put aside before the job could be declared complete. I wondered if the IRA officers in charge of what was going down there had thought it might take this long.

I watched Ewan. He had that strange half smile hanging on his face and to me that spelt trouble. Little did I know what kind of trouble that might eventually turn into?

Booked in to the Dorchester Hotel, both Brooking and I felt a dire need for a large whiskey or two. I checked the time; six-thirty. I was on my first sip when the 'boss' arrived.

He picked up the other half full whiskey glass on the bar and took a slug. He looked worried ... and I told him so.

"I've a lot to think about here."

"Such as ...?" I asked.

"Well, as you are asking, your safety for one thing. The possible interference of that bloody devious Major for another and I also have my suspicions that something does not sit right in terms of events and who knew what and when?"

"I'm not following you sir."

"What I am trying to tell you Gary is that I fear there is a third party involved here ... someone pushing all the buttons, someone in 'the know' and therefore by default, possibly being a senior member of our armed forces ... a traitor of sorts!"

It was a theory obviously, but one worth considering.

"The IRA are just too well informed Gary. They have been one step ahead of everyone right from the beginning. They knew every detail of the physical shipment of the components from the Inter-Tech offices. When they unfortunately 'lost' them upon arriving back in Ireland, they suddenly re-appeared from somewhere.

The team of UDA operatives had to have been

given up by someone, somewhere. So, whoever the individual is, the one who actually has a handle on all this is able to scrape intelligence from both sides. This is either a very lucky or a very well protected operator ... and I'm still trying to work out which."

I mulled over the AVM's words.

"So, sir, is there anything you feel I should know ... before stepping into the lions lair?"

"Just keep your eye open for any connections, any links back to the UK from anyone you come into contact with. I think you will be looked after by their intelligence chief a guy called Patrick O'Breian.

Don't be fooled by him.

He is a trained killer and will drop you without hesitation if he feels you are a threat to the organisation. Tread carefully with him but he is the most likely connection with any senior figure, military or political, on this side of the Irish Sea."

CHAPTER ELEVEN

A lucky escape perhaps ...

The trip to Abbeyshrule, across the Irish Sea, in the uncomfortably narrow-seated air taxi turned out to be a bumpy one. I hoped it was not a sign of 'things to come'.

It would therefore be safe to say I was not in the best of moods when I arrived in Ireland; small weekend suitcase in one hand and tool bag in the other. A car waited outside the General Aviation hanger and as the aeroplane drew up on the apron, a mid-sized man in jeans and a leather bomber jacket exited the car and waited.

He shouted across to me as the engines died.

"Is it Gary Chase?"

"It is." I shouted back. "I think you might be expecting me."

"I am for sure. We have a car waiting for you."

A quick rub-down and a close inspection of luggage and tool bag by the driver left me clear to enter the rear of the black Mercedes. The man in jeans introduced himself as Patrick O'Breian. We shook hands and then we were off. Where to? I did not know but it would take just over an hour to get there.

The farm at Ballyshannon could not be considered suitable for a long stay, but just a night or two would be fine. That was what I had been told by Patrick ... and when we arrived there I immediately saw what he meant.

The IRA Intelligence Officer showed me to a

room where I was told I could sleep. The bed appeared comfortable; the sheets and floor clean and dusted. Downstairs, the kitchen looked to be 'cosy' and fitted with all the necessary appliances.

"This is the warmest part of the house and you can do all your jiggery-pokery on the kitchen table here. Is that OK with you Gary?"

"It is Patrick. It's fine." I confirmed.

Half an hour later, someone arrived with a couple of giant pizza's and then there were four of us; Patrick, the driver, the pizza delivery man and ... me! No one so far had mentioned the microchips and the reason for me being there. I thought that to be quite strange. Over our pizza the banter between the three Irishmen travelled back and forth and by the end of the makeshift meal, I felt quite relaxed.

Eventually, I asked the question ... but I was unprepared for the answer.

"Right Patrick, if you don't mind, I would really like to start work on the microchips, so if we could clear the table, I'll get straight at it; the sooner I start ... the sooner I finish."

I looked at him expectantly. The three exchanged glances.

"The items you need are not here yet ... but they will be!" offered O'Breian, a dry smile accompanying the delivery.

A shiver ran down my spine.

"What the fuck do you mean; they are not here yet!"

"I mean exactly what I say. I have not met you before; I don't know who the fuck you really are and what kind of science fiction trackers you might have planted about you ... somewhere."

"Do you think I am going to lead you by the hand straight to a shipment of goods worth hundreds of millions of pounds so the SAS can simply descend on us all, steal the components and put a bullet in the back of the head of all of us ... YES, all of us Gary ... you included.?"

Time to be wary: the last thing I wanted to would be to turn a stable situation into an unstable and therefore unpredictable situation. Behind the smiles, these men were killers and there might be some truth in what he said about the SAS. It was a tense moment and it showed on every face in the room.

"I'm sorry Patrick." I countered. "I see where you are coming from and I ..." He cut me off.

"I have sixty of my men surrounding this property Gary, all waiting for the first sign of any unusual activity, any unauthorised movement and any smoke signal that may well indicate the 'Indians' are coming over the fucking hill. At the first sign of any unusual activity anywhere near this farm, you will be dead. Do I make myself clear?"

"You do Patrick ... you most certainly do. So, with no components to work with ... what's the plan?"

The IRA Intelligence Chief gave me a cold look leaving me fidgeting in my seat.

"You should get some sleep. The components will be here overnight and we will all be up early to enable you to start work. Do you have any more questions?"

"None thank you Patrick. I'll be ready to go in

the morning. I really would like to be gone from here by tomorrow night."

"So would I Gary!"

The next morning; up, washed and ready to go at five thirty I found the others cooking up breakfast. A plate had been set for me and everyone appeared to be in good spirits.

Should I ask the question or not; Patrick could see it was on the tip of my tongue.

"The components are here in exactly the same condition as we ... err ... found them. After your breakfast you can get straight to work. Is that OK with you Gary?" he queried.

"It is Patrick." I confirmed.

He nodded to the one who delivered the pizza the night before. Pizza-man left the room and returned seconds later with a small brief case. I had seen it, or one very much like it, at Sutter County Airport some days before. It looked promising.

I pushed my finished plate away and slipped the catches of the case. The contents were as I expected. Perhaps Patrick could tell that from the look on my face.

"Is that the real McCoy there Gary?" he asked.

"It certainly looks like it. Yes, this does look promising. So, I'll get my tools and start right now."

I carried a pad of lined paper in my tool bag along with a free standing backlit magnifying glass, a nine volt battery, some bell wire and a small, hand-held multi-meter; an electrical voltage and current measuring instrument. On the first sheet of paper on the pad I scored five columns with headings showing serial number, volts in and then volts out from three different pins. I wrote underneath the voltage headings the figure I expected to see. One extra empty column on the right of the page would note the result of the test ... pass or fail.

I showed Patrick the test sheet and briefly explained what was what. He looked concerned.

"Are you expecting failures then Gary?"

"No. However, it is possible. The manufacturing techniques used to put these chips together involve all kinds of heat and cooling processes and things can go wrong. This is why the Americans sent over three hundred and not just thirty. I expect any failures to be less than ten percent of the whole shipment."

Patrick smiled.

"Well, you seem to know what you are doing, so we will all leave you to get on with it."

By nine o'clock that evening, I had finished. The exercise had been a gruelling one and to give Patrick and his crew due praise, they had kept me fed with sandwiches and tea throughout the day. Other than that, they had all stayed out of my way.

I sat down with Patrick and reviewed the score sheet. There were less failures than expected; only eleven in total.

I explained what all this meant and he seemed to take it all on board. The 'score' sheet was to go with the re-wrapped and packaged shipment.

I had been instructed to telephone a number in Whitehall to let them know the checks had been done and the results. I was to phone immediately after the checks had been completed, no matter what the time of day or night.

This I did, with Patrick listening in.

Whoever might have been on the other end, they appeared not to be part of the decision making process. The phone line installed at the farm could not be used for incoming calls.

This was for the obvious security of the IRA group who worked the safe house. But this meant no-one on the end of the line in Whitehall would be able to ring me back. They knew that of course and so an arrangement was made for me to ring the Whitehall number again at nine o'clock the following morning.

The voice of Whitehall asked if I was 'safe'. Patrick and I both smiled.

"Yes, I am quite safe thank you but I really do want to be back at work ... I have a lot to do ... so make sure I am out of here tomorrow!"

The evening passed slowly with games of cards, packets of crisps and the odd tot or two of smooth tasting Irish whiskey, a substance appearing to be in plentiful supply.

With daylight breaking through the dusty, cobwebbed windows around six o'clock, I shook myself together in the shower and prepared for another day.

Patrick and 'the boys' were ready for me at the breakfast table. Three eggs, toast and five bacon rashers would no doubt set me up for the day. However, it had not passed me by the possibility this feast could be my last. If just one small thing went wrong now, someone might well start shooting.

We all watched the hands of the wall mounted kitchen clock gradually swing toward nine o'clock in silence. There would be several hundred million pounds sterling depending upon the outcome of this call. I picked up the phone and rang the Whitehall number hoping to God no-one did anything silly.

The fresh authoritative voice at the other end answered immediately stating I was to be transferred to Number Ten. Several clicks could be heard during this process telling me that other actors were now in the game. This was no surprise to me, however, the next voice I heard was.

"Can you tell us Sergeant, do the goods you currently hold pass technical inspection?"

'Jesus Christ.' I muttered to myself, 'Is this who I think it is?'

Patrick interrupted my train of thought.

"Why on earth is that man calling you Sergeant?" he asked. "Are you in the fucking military? No-body told us that Gary. I think you have some explaining to do if you want to leave here in one bloody piece!"

His face had turned a dark red, his hands trembling as he reached into the rear band of his trousers.

His two henchmen looked quite startled.

Patrick produced his personal weapon and levelled it in my direction.

I shouted down the telephone at the gruff voice with a Scottish accent.

"Is this Ewan McAllister?" I demanded.

"It is Gary ... and now we need to stay focused because ..."

"I received a promise that you were to be nowhere near this fucking exercise ... and yet ... here you are. What the fuck is going on?

Pizza-man began to move up behind Patrick. He was no doubt manoeuvring to get closer to me.

The sound of a single small calibre, high velocity bullet going through the kitchen window and burying itself in Pizza-man's neck re-focused everyone's attention.

I grabbed the closed brief case and hit the floor.

Six more shots entered the kitchen and then there was silence. Something told me this was an opportunity. I picked myself up, still holding the case tightly and whilst the other two were still thinking about it, I moved off ... through the half open kitchen door, out into the yard and diving behind an old mud covered, parked up Range Rover.

Gunfire began again but it all appeared to be directed toward the farm house. I peered up into the driver's seat. The keys were in it. Time to take a risk!

I carefully pulled the door open, slid up into the driving seat, started the vehicle at the very first effort, slammed it into gear and headed for the track leading from the farm buildings to what passed for a public road here in Ireland.

Without warning or expectation, a gun waving Patrick O'Breian appeared in the middle of the track. I pulled up; leaning heavily on the brakes.

He wrenched the passenger door open and threw himself into the cab.

"Go ... go ... go...!" he shouted and with only a second or two of hesitation, I floored it.

"What the fuck is going on?" I shouted, fighting for control of the ancient Rover.

"I was hoping you would be able to tell me!" he offered angrily.

He still had a gun in his hand and therefore held my full attention.

"Have the other two managed to escape?"

"They're both dead Gary ... dead as fucking Do-Do's ... sliced in two with explosive rounds from automatic weapons. These are professionals Gary. The only thing I need to figure out is which fucking side they are supposed to be on?"

"Jesus Christ." I muttered. This was all turning into a shit storm.

"I hope this is nothing to do with you Gary ... because if it is ... you're a dead man ... you know that don't you!"

An awkward pause ... a discomforting silence ... a particularly pertinent question.

"Where do you think you're going?" he asked.

"To the airstrip at Abbeyshrule ..."

"Do you know how to get there?"

"No ..." I yelled in reply.

"Turn right at the bottom of the track where it meets the tarmac road and then left when you hit the crossroads ... and be a bit bloody quick.

Whoever is on our case might well be trying to

stop us getting there." I glanced in his direction, wondering why, with everything that was going on, he seemed to be helping me.

"You still have the components I assume?" he asked.

I indicated the seat behind me. He turned and nodded his head.

"Don't forget Garry. Wherever they go ... I go!"

The words did not sound necessarily menacing, but they were not particularly re-assuring either.

"What the hell do you think might be about to happen now Patrick? We appear to be in the brown stuff ... or to be more accurate, I appear to be in the brown stuff. We will need to ring someone when we get to the airstrip."

"Why didn't you ... or anyone else, tell me you are somehow connected to the military. I thought you were a civilian working at GCHQ. I'm a bit disappointed you didn't tell me Gary."

"That's because I am a pretty unusual animal in the British military. I live my life as a civilian but I am paid by the Air Force and give my loyalties to the Air Force.

The only reason they sent me to do this job is that these 'chips' are so new and so revolutionary, I am the only one who can do the job of verification that Number Ten insists upon before handing you any money.

We have already seen one set of very good fakes ... and no-one wants to go down that road again. Does that make the situation clearer Patrick?"

He mulled over the words for a minute. Then he turned to me.

"OK Gary ... let's leave it there and concentrate on getting to Abbeyshrulen ... and arriving in one damn piece."

An hour later, as the Land Rover topped a rise in the road, the airstrip appeared laid out below us. Patrick and I both let out an involuntary sigh of relief. I steered the vehicle to the small collection of buildings at the end of the runway. The twin engine air taxi sat on the apron outside the general aviation hanger.

Pulling up in front of the GA office, I touched Patrick's sleeve, interrupting his movement to leave the Land Rover.

"Can I ask you something Patrick?"

He turned to face me squarely and nodded.

"Do you really think they will pay you three hundred million pounds for these damned microchips? Before we risk God knows what dealing with these smooth talking political liars, I just want to know if you really feel you will be able to trust one single word they say."

The IRA Intelligence Chief smiled.

"I don't have to trust anything they say Gary ... you do. It's you who will be doing the talking. What I have to trust is everything that YOU say Gary ... and when I find I can't do that any more ... I shall kill you!"

He left the vehicle, opened the rear passenger door and pulled out the brief case.

He turned in my direction ... still smiling; the outline of a handgun just about detectible sticking out the rear of his trousers. In the GA Office, the employee on duty received Patrick's message loud and clear when he told him to 'fuck off', leaving just the two of us alone in the small administrative space.

I picked up the phone and rang a Whitehall number. Someone answered immediately.

"Are you safe?" the voice queried.

"No particularly." I replied.

"Can you expand?" the voice said.

"Not to you ... whoever you are. I think you will need to transfer me to someone ... so let's just fucking well get on with it!"

The silence went unexplained and then, thankfully, a friendly voice came on the line.

"Gary ... is that you?"

"It is sir and it's good to hear your voice."

Air Vice-Marshall Brooking sounded in good spirits.

"Where are you Gary?"

"I'm at the Abbeyshrule airstrip. I have the components with me; they are all safe and in good condition. I also have with me Patrick O'Breian and to be frank, we are both lucky to be alive."

Brooking sounded alarmed.

"What happened? Are there now even more actors muddying the waters in this bloody game of 'catch me if you can' Gary?"

"There certainly are. We were attacked early this morning by someone using 5.56mm amour piercing ammunition. This ammunition has a very special sound effect as it travels. It's a sound I've heard many times before. It's quite distinctive; a titanium tipped bullet passing close by your ear at over three thousand feet every single bloody second ... and I heard it again this morning. This is SAS territory sir and I hope that bastard McAllister is not involved in any way."

The silence became telling. Patrick, listening in on the conversation, became fidgety.

The Air Vice-Marshall spoke. He sounded tense.

"I need to speak to someone. I have this number and I'll ring you back. It may take some minutes, but please don't do anything ... or go anywhere until I have spoken to you again. Keep an eye open. Any sign of unwelcome activity, you ring the Whitehall number."

The line went dead leaving both Patrick and I to ponder the situation.

CHAPTER TWELVE

Out of the frying pan ... into the fire!

Brooking did not feel he was somehow putting forward a request to the private secretary sitting outside the PM's office. His words had been chosen carefully. They constituted an instruction, a clear and unambiguous instruction.

"I need to see the Prime Minister." he muttered as he walked with some determination past the secretarial desk.

The young man behind it, someone who took his 'guarding' duties quite seriously protested, but it was too late. The Air Vice-Marshall was in.

There were two individuals with the Prime Minister and as Brooking entered, they all three looked up.

"I'm sorry to interrupt Prime Minister, but something rather urgent has just cropped up and I need to consult with you ... in private ...!"

The PM, now carrying a confused and slightly annoyed look, waved a hand to the other two.

"I hope this is worth my time David."

"It is sir. You have my complete assurance on that. You might even say it's a rather 'life or death' sort of matter!"

The senior Air Force Officer remained straight faced and fixed to the spot. A minute later, Brooking and the PM were alone.

"What can I do for you David?" the Prime Minister enquired. Outwardly he appeared calm and collected. Beneath the surface however, he was annoyed at the rudeness of the interruption to his normal working routine.

"Did you authorise the use of Special Forces, in Ireland to somehow hi-jack the plan we have all agreed upon to pay a ransom for the recovery of these dam micro-chips?"

"I ... err ... I spoke with ..."

"Spoke with Prime Minster? Who did you speak with ...?"

"Major McAllister came to us after our meeting and he had a plan which I think has some merit and will turn out much less costly to her Majesties Government than the current ..."

Brooking had no intention of letting him finish.

"Less costly?" Brooking shouted "Less fucking costly? What the hell do you think you are doing? You have already sanctioned the killing of two people and if your Major has his way ... there will be two more very shortly ... one of which is my man Chase!"

The PM turned pale, his pulse beating in his ears.

"Two men did you say ... but these are terrorists aren't they; they go round torturing people and executing them ... and the Major told me that ..."

"Don't you understand that Major fucking McAllister is a psychopath and he has now set the British SAS against the Irish Republican Army. They are probably surrounding the airfield in Abbeyshrule as we speak.

If this SAS troop ... under YOUR orders, manage to somehow murder the IRA's most senior Intelligence Officer currently taking refuge there,

THEY will then be coming for you. If they end up killing my man Gary Chase, also taking refuge there ... then 'I' will damn well be coming for you. So listen to me ... get hold of that bloody lunatic Major and end this NOW."

Air Vice-Marshall Brooking left the room at a pace, ignoring the continuing protests of the secretary. The PM buzzed the confused and embarrassed aide.

'Get me Major McAllister on the phone ... NOW!'

Ten minutes later, the Major found himself locked in conversation with the PM. It was a short one.

The first part simply required confirmation from the Major that the SAS had been used in a black operation to recover the Micro-chips and that at least two people were now dead as a result.

The second part required confirmation that this SAS troop now had the airfield at Abbeyshrule surrounded and were awaiting a final order from the Major to move in.

"Get them out of there McAllister; not only out of Abbeyshrule but out of the bloody country. What about any bodies left at the farm?"

"They're taken care of sir." offered the Major.

"What do you mean ... taken care of?"

"Well ... they have been ... err ... incinerated sir. That leaves them unidentifiable by a third party sir ... standard procedure after we've identified and photographed them for our records ... sir."

The PM had been left speechless, but finally words came.

"Incinerated Major ... incinerated? I simply cannot believe it. The IRA high command will go mad ... mad I tell you. What a complete fuck-up this is. I authorised a quick 'snatch' operation to grab the components before transferring the money. No-one was supposed to raid property and no-one was supposed to get killed. Shut it down Major ... and shut it down NOW!"

Brooking moved quickly after his meeting with the PM, hurrying back to his Whitehall office, a small cramped space but a convenient space to work from when in London. Picking up the phone, he dialled the number on the piece of paper in front of him.

Chase answered more or less immediately.

"What's happening sir? My Irish friend here is becoming a little agitated."

"Well, firstly the perceived threat to your safety has been neutralized ... and ..."

"I'm sorry to interrupt sir, but what does 'neutralized' mean. Those fuckers who attacked the farmhouse meant business. It looked to me like an SAS job for sure ... so who the hell was behind it. Trust has been completely eroded at this end and O'Breian is now as likely to put a bullet in the back of my neck as he is to shoot the next person who walks through the damn door!"

"I'm sorry to hear that Gary ... but I'm afraid that McAllister somehow got himself involved ...

and you are right ... it was a troop of SAS who attacked you. However, they have now been called off and should be on a helicopter taking them back to the north as we speak."

"What about the two men left behind?"

"I'm afraid those two poor souls have been burnt and bagged ... and any remains will no doubt end up at the bottom of some lake or other before the day is out."

The short silence that followed spoke volumes. Patrick stood right next to Gary, listening to what was being said. He didn't flinch as he heard the news.

"Jesus Christ sir, this is beginning to read like a damned horror story and wherever a dead body appears, it seems that somehow McAllister is involved with it."

"When all this is over Gary, we will be having some sort of investigation into our friend 'the Major' but right now the important thing is to keep this bloody operation on track."

Patrick whispered ... "Put the phone down. Someone is outside ..."

Before he could finish, a shot rang out. It appeared to come from the rear of the hanger where the maintenance office and crew room were located. Pulling a Glock 9mm from his trouser waistband, Patrick pushed at the door connecting the office to the open hanger space. He did so with caution. Another shot came from somewhere to his left. He fired his weapon twice. Gary heard a clatter as the intruder dropped what may have been his rifle.

"I'm really sorry Patrick ..." Gary shouted,

"My boss told me these SAS bastards had been withdrawn ... and he's never fed me bullshit before ... I don't understand what the fuck is going on here ...!"

"Don't worry Gary. See that rifle on the floor. It's a British Lee Enfield .303, a second world-war vintage weapon available in hundreds of thousands. It's solid, it's powerful; it's accurate and reliable ... and very cheap to buy!

This is the work of the Provo's, the Provisional IRA, the traitors who split from our central command.

There will be more. We need to get the hell out of here ... they will have somehow heard about the micro-chips. They desperately need funds. Flogging them back to your lot, or perhaps a more sinister operator, would see them set up for a long time ahead."

"You obviously know these gunmen and how they operate a lot better than me Patrick, so do you have a plan to get us to-fuck out of here?"

"The airplane is the best bet. Where's the pilot?"

"He's in the crew room. I'll go and fetch him and explain what's going on."

"Be careful but be quick. I'll take the .303 and cover the entrance to the hanger."

There would be no time for niceties.

The three technicians and the pilot of Gary's air taxi had hit the floor with the noise of the second shot.

Gary pushed open the door and pointed at the pale faced pilot.

"Is it full of fuel?"

"Yes ... it is ... and I hope you are here to tell me we are leaving!"

"I am ... let's go!"

Gary turned away from the door and sprinted back across the hanger floor, heading for the office. Patrick stood guard at the entrance with the rifle.

Another shot. Gary heard the 'whizz' of the projectile pass by him. It would be stopped by the person running on behind. The route to their escape plane had now been blocked. The pilot had died instantly, a wound the size of a tennis ball in the middle of his chest.

"Leave the rifle; get back in the fucking Land Rover. We won't be flying from here today."

Patrick looked back; noted the unmoving body on the hanger floor, threw the rifle to one side, grabbed the brief-case once more and made speed toward the disheveled four wheel drive vehicle parked up close to the outer office door.

As he grabbed at the driver's door, Gary clambered into the front passenger space.

In an instant, the Rover started and they were charging their way to the gated airfield entrance.

Three shots were fired in the chase after them; two from behind and one from the side.

Fortunately the vehicle and its passengers remained unhurt and within a minute or two they were topping the rise above Abbeyshrule.

"Where are we heading Patrick?"

"We are on our way to Mullingar. I have friends and family there.

I need to keep High Command up to date with what's been happening and the bad news about the

Provo's having become involved.

It's not good Gary.

These guys split from us last year and they really are bloody fanatics. You do not want to be in their clutches for very long my friend ... and from now on we must be extra careful. Do you understand what I'm telling you?"

"I'm sure I do Patrick ... but from my way of looking at it, you don't need me anymore. I can get a helicopter out of here with just one phone call. I have verified the authenticity of the goods, so it might be time for me to go ... don't you think?"

The Irishman turned his face in my direction. It had been overtaken by a dark, forbidding look.

"You, me and these fucking 'chips', or whatever you call them, are staying together until I see the figure we have agreed upon in our numbered overseas account at the Irish Commercial Bank. I hope that's clear Gary ... and I don't want to re-visit the matter again."

So, that was it. No reply required. All done and dusted ... as far as Patrick O'Breian was concerned.

The extensive detached property sitting on its own at the end of a small lane on the outskirts of Mullingar appeared wrapped in darkness when the fugitive couple arrived; not a light in sight. Patrick tapped on the front door. It opened immediately.

The visitors were ushered inside, through a couple of rooms and then, by candle-light, down a set of steps to a basement. Once the door had been closed and curtains drawn across, the place became suddenly lit ... and alive.

Surprisingly, there were possibly twenty or more other people in the rather cavernous space, a place that looked to be well constructed with vaulted brick ceilings and some sort of piped ventilation system. It took less than a minute to fully understand what might be going on here. This was a damn bomb factory.

Gary asked the obvious question.

"Where the hell are we Patrick?"

"If you don't ask, I won't have to kill you!"

The words probably had less effect upon him than the menacing, straight faced delivery. This was no doubt a warning or sorts and one he knew he might need to consider carefully.

Gary mentally studied his situation; at the same time giving thought as to what might be happening back in London. Was everyone playing a 'fair game' over there or would they be quite happy to sacrifice Sergeant Gary Chase ... if it meant getting the bloody micro-chips back without having to pay anyone any money.

"Can I make a phone call Patrick?" Gary asked.

You can call anyone you like Gary as long as it's not a fucking taxi. But before you do, someone back there in Number Ten needs to understand that unless this exchange takes place within the next forty eight hours, then we will be selling to an alternative ... and eager buyer."

"What other buyer might that be?" Gary asked.

"A good try Gary, but one way or another, you will be a long way away from here if I am forced to go such a route."

The person answering the Whitehall number put Gary through to 'the boss' immediately. Although it was late, Brooking sounded bright and attentive.

"What's going on Gary? We hear there are bodies at the airstrip and this is due to an unfortunate intervention by the newly formed Provisional IRA. This has moved everything up a gear. How do you see the situation from over there?"

"It's dire sir. Patrick O'Breian has told me, in no uncertain terms, that if the deal is not done within the next forty eight hours, then he will sell to a third party."

Gary caught the echoes of several sharp intakes of breath and wondered how many ears might be tuned in to this particular conversation.

A long and worrying pause followed.

"Do you believe him Gary?"

"Yes, I do sir."

Another pause ... a few more clicks.

"We will send a helicopter for you and the microchips and once they are back in our hands ... officially, then we will transfer the money."

Gary laughed out loud.

"What is so damned funny?"

"I'm sorry sir, but these guys are not stupid. They trust no one, especially the word of a bunch of British politicians ... and I think they are about to cut me off, so you need to re-think your bloody plan ..."

The loud 'click' followed by a buzzing dialling tone indicated the conversation to be over. Patrick walked over to Gary and placed a hand on his shoulder.

"The clock is ticking Gary and we will not be moving from here until a deal is done."

"I understand that Patrick ... let's hope that they do!"

CHAPTER THIRTEEN

An 'honourable' conspiracy revealed!

The Honourable Sir Tarquin Ludlow left London on Friday afternoon for his country estate at Farnborough Hall. It was the weekend. He had a lot on his mind.

What started out as quite a simple task of hi-jacking the shipment of a small parcel had become complicated. He didn't like 'complicated' and had spent a less than illustrious career avoiding it.

Two days previously it had been confirmed would be promoted to Brigadier in six weeks time. As part of the promotion package, by the end of the following year he would be leaving the Army ... for good. As long as he kept his 'slate' clean between now and then, he would be leaving with his full entitlement.

His final annual pension of more than forty thousand plus and a lump sum of nearly one hundred and thirty thousand would put a smile on the face of most army officers, but not Tarquin Ludlow.

Hung round his neck like the proverbial millstone was the Farnborough Hall Estate, the family seat consisting of the Hall itself, the twenty acres of grounds and the six thousand acres of farm-land split into eight tenancies. All the current tenants had been appointed by his father and, without exception, they planned to hang on tight to their worryingly long leases.

Having been a senior officer within the MoD

purchasing and procurement, section three, technology group for several years had provided many opportunities to 'earn' a bonus or two as provided to him by grateful customers.

It was not a fortune, but over the years it had 'kept the wolf from the damned door' and allowed most of the serious issues with the house to be tackled and resolved.

However, being in receipt of bribes on a regular basis and knowing full well what the consequences might be if discovered, his nerves had suffered as he became addicted to smoking cigarettes and drinking far too much Irish whiskey.

Arriving at Farnborough Hall he found the house bare of wife Martha and children Pricilla and Edwina, all of whom appeared to be 'out and about' shopping in Oxford, as confirmed by his long-time, permanently smiling house keeper, Mrs. Wyatt.

She had been in the family employ for more than thirty years and worked her way up from under-housemaid to house keeper and was much loved by family and estate staff alike.

"There is someone to see you sir," she revealed, "Its Thomas Tandy, head of the tenant farmers committee. I don't think it's really urgent, but he does want to speak with you in private, if that's possible."

"Of course Mrs Wyatt, that's not a problem. If you could rustle up some tea and maybe a crumpet or two, we can talk in the library."

Thomas Tandy had never been seen as someone subservient to 'the master' as his tenants would have happily called someone like Tarquin fifty or so years ago. Farming was now a technical undertaking and required substantial financial investment if it was to succeed as a business.

The two men settled down in cooling leather Chesterfield armchairs sipping at their tea and munching on butter soaked crumpets.

"No matter how you try and eat these bloody wonderful things Thomas, even if they look dry, as soon as you munch on them, butter goes every damn where!"

"That's true sir ... that's very true."

"So Thomas, what brings you here today ahead of our regular meeting in a couple of week's time?"

"Well, as usual, it's about money and investment and what plans you might have for bringing in new machinery. Everyone in the tenant consortium is wondering where their future lies and they wanted me to talk with you before our next meeting to 'get the lay of the land' sort of thing; a bit of a 'heads-up' on what they might expect from you sir."

Tarquin Ludlow moved uneasily in his seat. He lit a cigarette. Martha would go mad if she could smell it when she arrived home.

"We have been here before Thomas and the situation has not changed. As you know, I will be retiring from the Army a year and a few months down the road and then I will receive my pension and a lump sum payment. I expect to invest my capital sum into buying some carefully chosen technology for use by the consortium."

Thomas Tandy did not look that impressed. He had heard it all before.

"I think you'll agree that twelve or more months down the road will not help with this year's harvest on Rosemount Farm or the replacement of milking machinery urgently needed by Bob Wheeler at Green Meadows."

Tarquin wondered if he should reveal the existence of a new form of finance he was depending upon to resolve all the capital investment issues beleaguering the individual farm estates.

Everyone needed to earn a living and there was no-one more aware of that than the Honourable Colonel Sir Tarquin Ludlow.

"All I can tell you Thomas is that I am exploring several avenues of new finance right now and I hope at least one of them will enable us to take a few steps forward within weeks ... although you have to understand, I'm not in a position to give you any more detail. That's the best I can do."

Thomas Tandy left Farnborough Hall half an hour later no wiser than when he arrived. Promises could not be banked in the world of intensive farming and if cows could not be milked and harvests brought home efficiently, then rents due to the landlord might not be paid.

Tarquin checked his watch. He had arranged for someone to visit at six o'clock that evening.

He heard a door slam and some excited voices declare that 'Daddy was home' followed by the noise of two teenage girls running from the kitchen to the library, shouting and laughing as each one tried to outrun the other.

The Master of Farnborough Hall gathered the two animated and energised children in his arms, kissing each one in turn. Pricilla and Edwina put an enormous smile on his face as they related breathlessly what they had been doing in Oxford and how much of his hard earned money they had spent. When he quickly added up the final figure, he winced.

Martha made her entrance, kissing him on the cheek, making a point of 'sniffing' the air surrounding him, letting forth an expletive about smoking and headed back to the kitchen muttering the words 'welcome back' as she went. It looked as if today was going to be one of her 'cool' days.

With the children despatched to their rooms to try on a few new outfits purchased that day, Tarquin sat with his wife in the kitchen discussing the upcoming private dinner and reception to be held at the Hall for the Minister of Defence and a scattering of Generals, Marshalls and Admirals.

All would be well, Martha assured her husband; everything had been taken care of and all he had to do was to turn-up ... sober!

There would be no evening meal for the family she advised, as the girls had eaten out, but she could pull a Pizza out of the freezer if he wanted to eat later.

Tarquin politely declined the offer telling Martha about the impending visitor, due at around six o'clock.

She pulled a face upon hearing the news. The person her husband was expecting was not on her 'favourites' list. She would make sure she kept out of the way.

Major Ewan Magnus McAllister arrived at Farnborough Hall at twenty past six. He apologised to Tarquin for being late but blamed traffic and women drivers.

The two moved into the library, a special place that had been stripped and rebuilt some twenty years previously making it soundproof and bug proof. It also boasted a 'quick exit' feature; a concealed door built into the book-shelves that led to the cellar and then on to an external door next to the old stables. It was all a bit 'James Bondish' but the facility had come in handy on one or two occasions in the past.

Comfortably seated and with a glass of premium blended whiskey each resting on an occasional table filling the space between them, Tarquin kicked off the conversation.

"Speak to me Ewan ... and don't bloody well leave anything out!"

The Major cleared his throat and began. He started with the robbery of the micro-chips at Dublin Airport and the murder of Liam Byrne. He went on to describe the involvement of the Belfast UDA, the recovery of the shipment and the part he personally played in that operation.

He had been in conversation with two members of the IRA High Command. They confirmed the deal to pay out twenty per-cent of whatever the British government was to pay them, was still on.

The news brought a smile to Tarquin's face.

"Don't forget Ewan, our deal still stands for you to receive a fee of twenty per-cent of whatever ends up in my Dubai bank account."

McAllister fell silent.

"What's the problem Ewan?"

"Our contact is a London operator with the code name 'Tommy'. He is our conduit to Patrick O'Breian, someone who has the authority to speak on behalf of the IRA.

He has laid down an ultimatum. If the money is not transferred within forty eight hours, then he will sell to a third party."

"I thought we could trust this guy Ewan. I did the deal with him, through this Tommy character, on your recommendation and as you know, getting the wheels of the treasury moving, especially for such a large amount of money takes time ... quite a lot of time in fact."

"Then of course, there is the matter of the SAS going in Tarquin," Ewan offered. "I did as was asked and it blew up in our face. Now, trust has gone out the damned window and my contact does not want to speak to anyone other than to issue ultimatums."

Tarquin sat contemplating the shimmering gold at the bottom of his whiskey glass, the precious liquid being warmed gently between cupped hands. He knew full well that all forms of skulduggery eventually ended up as a trust issue. Once trust was lost, it would be difficult to recover.

A half hour later, the Major was done, leaving both men in thoughtful mood.

"Do you know where the components are now?"

"No sir." answered McAllister.

"Can you get hold of this Patrick O'Breian ... on the telephone?"

"I'm sure I can. It will be a circuitous route, but it's possible."

"OK. I'm going to have a conversation with the PM and then I want you to get him on the blower. We need to sort this bloody problem out. There are too many damn bodies laying about for this to carry on any longer. He will want to know what has happened to this Air Force Sergeant, Chase. Hopefully he is not one of the bagged-up bodies coming out of this messy and bloody operation."

"He is alive and well as far as I know and I feel sure he wants out of this situation as much as anyone. He's a tough cookie Tarquin. I really don't think you need to worry too much about him."

"Let us hope so Ewan. He is not just a 'face' in this damned game of chess; he has been in front of the PM and is seen as a key element to recovering these damn electronic components."

Two hours later after one phone call to the Treasury and two calls to the PM, Tarquin recovered McAllister from the kitchen. Mrs Wyatt had taken pity on him and 'thrown together' a substantial mushroom omelette with fresh crusty bread and a pat of chilled farm butter. The military Major thanked Mrs.Wyatt with a kiss on the cheek and re-joined the master of the house in the library.

"OK Ewan. It's been a tough gig but the Treasury and the PM have now confirmed that the agreed figure, of three hundred million, will be in the numbered client account at the Caymen Islands branch of the National Irish Bank by nine thirty on Monday morning."

This news brought a smile to Ewan's face.

"Jesus Tarquin, that's a hell of a lot of money right there .... and ..."

"... and you had better make sure that my twenty percent is in my numbered Dubai bank account ... by midday!

"I will speak directly with Patrick. He has your bank details; as I am sure you have mine."

The Major raised an eyebrow, waiting for a response.

"Yes Ewan. I do have your bank details and as soon as my money is cleared ... you will have yours. That is a promise from me ... and I never back down from a promise."

"I hope not Tarquin ... for your sake ... I hope not!"

Tarquin Ludlow finished up his whiskey with a final swallow.

"Right Major, I've done my bit ... now it's time for you to do yours. I'll be waiting in the first floor reception if you need me"

With that he left the room.

Ewan McAllister picked up the phone and dialled a Dublin number.

The 'Protector' answered with a simple 'hello', wanting to know who the caller wished to speak to. Ewan explained he needed to talk with Patrick O'Breian.

The 'Protector' promised to ring him back within fifteen minutes."

Ten long minutes later the phone rang. It was 'The Protector', who, with an on-line click or two made the connection.

"Go ahead Mr. McAllister." confirmed the echoing voice.

"You don't know me Mr. O'Breian but my name is Ewan McAllister and hopefully I am able to pass on some good news for you today."

Silence followed disturbed only by echoing background atmospherics. Then a deep toned, strongly accented voice answered.

"I know of you Major McAllister and I also know of the mad dogs you command who recently murdered some of my men at Ballyshannon. When all this is over my friend, special-forces or no special-forces, I will make sure everyone who pulled a trigger on that day is brought to justice."

Ewan knew quite well he must not lose his cool during these delicate negotiations. The best plan right now was to ignore every comment relating to 'the troubles' and stick to the plan to pay over a ransom and recover these highly valuable components.

"You may be aware that my-self and a well placed partner in this matter, someone who wishes to remain anonymous, have been in contact with your man in London; a man we know only by the codename 'Tommy'."

"Go on ..."

"There appears to be little need to 'beat around the bush'.

You know what my partner has delivered to

Tommy and now we need to finalise the deal."

"Finalise ..?" O'Breian queried.

"Yes. In other words Her Majesties Government will place in a particular offshore bank account the sum of three hundred million pounds sterling by nine-thirty on Monday morning.

As has also been agreed, you will then immediately transfer twenty per-cent of that amount to the account you have details of in the Dubai United Commercial Bank.

When you have done that and my partner receives confirmation from an authorised source, then you will hand over to me the components ... and our man Gary Chase. The meeting will take place at Glassier Lake House Hotel in Killinure at ten thirty. Is that all understood?"

O'Breian reflected on what he had just heard.

"So ... tell me Major, what happens if the money is not there at the time you have specified?"

"Let us not dwell on such a possibility when a much more serious scenario would be if the components, undamaged and in pristine condition ... along with a certain Gary Chase ... undamaged and in pristine condition ... are not received by me at the time and place specified."

Ewan McAllister could feel the heat of emotion and anger surging down the telephone line. Had this been a 'step too far' or had it just been frank enough to ensure O'Breian fully understood the consequences of reneging on the deal.

"I want you to know Major that your man Gary is not being held against his will in any way whatsoever.

He has assured me that wherever these bloody components go ... then he goes as well. If I deliver them to you on Monday, then Gary will go along with them. I hope that provides you with some level of comfort.

Now I must go and report to our High Command. I look forward to meeting with you face to face on Monday."

The line died immediately leaving no more than an echoing dialling tone. Whatever was to happen now would be in the 'lap of the Gods'.

Ewan McAllister found the whiskey bottle and poured him-self a couple of fingers. He sat in one of the Chesterfield's, turning everything over in his mind. It sounded too damn simple. Before he briefed Tarquin, he needed to get his story exactly straight. There could be no room for error. The Colonel was a man who loved to delve into the detail and if he found an issue that looked insecure, then he was likely to want more guarantees.

The trip upstairs in the mansion house known as Farnborough Hall took McAllister to the first floor reception room. Sir Tarquin Ludlow listened intently to what McAllister was saying, analysing each small segment of information as it was being delivered to him.

Finally, he sat back in his chair.

"Well Ewan, it's all about trust at the end of the day. If this all goes 'tits-up' then I remain a Colonel until I die, you end up with a posting to some god-forsaken place in Baluchistan and Mr.

O'Breian ends up with a bullet in the back of the head.

None of these scenarios are particularly attractive but on the other hand, the stakes are high as are the risks and as long as you and I know what the fuck is going on, then that's the best we can hope for I suppose."

He smiled, or certainly made a good attempt to do so.

"When you leave here today, will you be going straight to Ireland?"

"I will Tarquin. I need to be close to everything that's happening. I have a troop of SAS on call and if I need to ... I'll use them."

"Don't screw this one up Ewan. Enough lives have been lost!"

CHAPTER FOURTEEN

A delicate negotiation.

O'Breian took me to one side. He had been speaking to several individuals on the telephone. Whatever the result of such conversations, he remained grim faced.

"These fuckers in the UK seem to think I am somehow holding you captive and that perhaps your release is part of an overall deal with the micro-chips. How could they have cottoned on to such an idea Gary?"

I was quite taken aback. I would need to be careful here.

Everything looked to be balanced on a thin veil of trust and it was essential that Patrick O'Breian had confidence in me and my loyalties.

"Well, the only person I have spoken to is David Brooking, my boss, and he is completely aware of my situation. Is it an issue between us Patrick?"

He thought on the matter for a short while.

"No, I don't really think so. On paper, we represent two different sides but in reality we both want the same ending to this situation ... and hopefully that 'end' is now close."

"So ... tell me, how 'close' is 'close'?"

"Monday morning!"

"... and who will be accepting the handover ...?

"Yer man Major McAllister."

I must have coloured up noticeably when Ewan's name was mentioned.

The very last man on earth I expected to broker this deal would be him.

"No, I'm fine Patrick ... please, tell me the detail."

"The meeting will take place at Glassier Lake House Hotel in Killinure, on Monday at ten thirty. HMG will transfer the three hundred million to our account at the Commercial Irish by nine thirty. Once we have confirmation of that transfer and one further transaction ... then McAllister will arrive at the hotel, collect the micro-chips ... and be on his way."

I picked up on just one thing.

"What 'further transaction' are we talking about here Patrick?"

He looked hesitant.

"We are nearly at the end of this rocky road Gary and as you are fully briefed on everything else, I suppose there can be little harm in telling you about the final piece of this complex puzzle."

"Look my friend, I don't want you to tell me anything that will compromise this operation, or put anyone's life in danger, so the decision is yours."

"The only life in danger Gary will be his if it ever comes out ..."

"His? Who do you mean when you say ... 'his'..?"

"I mean the person who has been giving us information about these bloody components. It is someone high-up in the military, the Army specifically, someone who had the knowledge about the gifting of the micro-chips to the UK. It also needed to be someone who knew of the shipping arrangements in absolute detail, and yet again, someone who had a technical understanding of what he was dealing with. Most telling of all is that this 'someone' knew how to contact us and put the whole deal together."

"... and ... Patrick ...?"

"And ... that person wants twenty per-cent of whatever ends up in our offshore account. It must be transferred directly to a particular Middle East Bank account. We have all the details and payment must be confirmed before the operation can be concluded."

"Hmm ..." I muttered.

"Does anyone know what the consequences will be to you if that figure of twenty percent is not transferred before the handover?"

"The assumption is that we go to war Gary ... us against the mighty SAS I would assume. They will go for everyone in the High Command, including me ... and possibly even you."

He smiled. There would be no more explanation.

Now my mind was left in a state of turmoil, knowing this could all be far from over.

"No doubt when all this is finished Gary, you will be looking for this individual. However, before you jump too hard on any specific name, remember he will have sixty million quid up the bank to pay off, fight off or even fly off to sunnier spots around the world ... but good luck if you want to try."

We spent the next hour or so talking about the plan itself. We agreed we would book into the Glassier Lake House Hotel on the Sunday, have dinner there and be obvious to any observers who may be in place and reporting back to the Major.

Patrick voted to carry a sidearm and he also recommended that I carry one as well. There appeared to be no specific reason for his decision but something told me I would be very grateful to him for making it.

We would drive there in the Range Rover, fully prepared to travel off-road if necessary. There would be no guards or soldiers as back-up. This was something McAllister had insisted on in return for a similar promise from Number Ten.

The handover was meant to be a very low-key affair; no guns on show and no bodies on the floor afterward. I had to admit to being a little nervous knowing who was to be in charge of the activity on behalf of HMG.

I had some level of faith in Patrick. I had been with him for a while now and he appeared to be a brave and committed soul and no one could wish for more than that.

So, now was a time to rest and maybe even spend an hour or two in the local bar where impromptu live Irish Folk music was being dished out most evenings.

A few pints of Guinness and a foot stomping tune or two might be just the thing to lift our spirits. We would be accompanied by one or two 'soldiers' of course but they were local and well known to the pub regulars. I looked forward to it.

Sunday afternoon, Patrick and I set off for the

Glassier Lake House Hotel. The route turned out to be straightforward and untroubled; although I have to admit I kept a hand on my gun for most of the journey.

I took in the surrounding landscape as we approached the hotel. It was relatively flat and very green with what looked like a nine hold golf course to the left and an area of cultivated wetland to the right.

It all looked good. The approaches provided a clear view for about three quarters of the way around the cluster of hotel buildings, and most importantly, an unimpeded view of the paved road covering the short distance from the hotel to the main Killinure road.

It appeared to be a geographically good spot for our particular activity and well chosen by the damned Major. Patrick and I exchanged meaningful glances. We were obviously thinking the same thing.

Dinner turned out to be a quiet affair with Patrick consumed mostly by his own thoughts. Assuming the 'powers that be' in Whitehall perform as required and the money is confirmed in the relevant account at the National Irish, the next big hurdle will be to ensure the required transfer of sixty million pounds to the Dubai Commercial Bank.

All confirmations, exchange of passwords and actual movement of funds would need to be confirmed by Telex, the only secure written communications system recognised by banks for International transfers.

Each bank held a unique and secure identification code that could only be generated on a communication coming from that particular bank. Time between transfers would only be one single hour and that was not a long time in the often slow and unwieldy world banking system. I had my doubts about the inherently variable levels of success and I could see that Patrick carried the weight of it all on his own hopefully capable shoulders. I was glad I had the damned gun!

We met for breakfast at seven o'clock the following morning.

"So, today is the big day Gary." offered Patrick.

"It sure is." I confirmed. "Is this the point at which the 'condemned men ate a hearty breakfast' and then walked to the gallows with a smile?"

Patrick grimaced.

"Whatever goes down here today Gary, some fool, in the future, is going to make a fortune out of writing the fucking book!"

We both laughed out loud.

After consuming a final cup of strong black coffee, Patrick told me he would be going to his room to wait for 'the phone call' and would ring me in my room as soon as he had anything to share. I would have been quite happy to sit with him, but it was obvious he needed some time on his own. So, now it was all about waiting.

The call came at ten minutes past nine o'clock. My room was only three doors down from Patrick's. The instruction was clear.

'Get in here Gary ... it's starting to happen.'

The door to Patrick's room was open and I walked straight in. He smiled at me, as much with relief as with any sense of greeting.

"I need to stay by this phone. Can you collect a Telex message for me from the hotel office?"

"Sure thing Patrick ... I'm on my way."

The flimsy document was handed over to me without any questioning from the busy reception staff. It consisted of one single sheet folded over and so I read it.

It was the verified copy of a Telex sent by the National Irish Bank confirming they had received the sum of three hundred million pounds sterling to the numbered account of 1443-7842-1110.

I smiled. Well, at least the ball was now rolling ... but where would it come to a final stop? That may well end up being a different story.

Back in Patrick's room, I gave him the Telex message.

When he read it, he smiled too.

He studied the wall mounted room clock for a second or two.

"We have just over an hour now to get sixty million quid to Dubai ... and let us hope to God that with the time differences and possible language issues, that this all goes smoothly."

Patrick dialled the number of 'The Protector'. It was answered immediately.

"Put me through to Craig Donnelly, manager of the National Irish Bank and don't drop the line your end. I want you to make sure you record everything that is said. Is that clear?"

"It is Patrick. High Command prepared me and told me to support you in any way necessary. I'm on it now."

"Good. Get him on the line!"

Donnelly needed a series of passwords before he would speak and whatever Patrick mumbled down the line seemed to be satisfactory.

The Dublin based bank manager had been prepared and with Dubai being ahead in time, he had already had a conversation with the manager of the Dubai United Commercial Bank.

They were talking to one another, on-line, over the Telex, and all that was now needed would be confirmation of the fourteen digit account number and the single coded letter at the beginning and end of the number block.

Patrick appeared to have no concerns about Gary being in the room as he read out the necessary codes and account numbers. He was completely focused on getting the job done.

Placing the instrument back in its cradle, Patrick looked up, beads of sweat dripping from his forehead.

"Well it's done now Gary. We are in the lap of the gods, along with the smooth hands of Craig Donnelly and someone known as Mohammed Bhaktir."

I went over and shook his hand.

"So, what happens now?" I asked.

"I think the best thing now is to check out, take

our things and throw them in the Rover, then come back here and have a cup of coffee whilst we wait for the Major …"

He paused …

"That is of course if you are leaving here with me or maybe the Major ..?"

"No Patrick, I will definitely not be leaving with McAllister, but I could do with a lift to Dublin Airport."

"That's not a problem Gary. I'll make sure you get there safe and sound."

With bags in the Range Rover and the reception clock showing a few minutes after ten, we both head to the coffee shop. As we walked back in, one of the receptionists ran up to Patrick.

"Thank God you are still here sir. I have a phone call for you. He says he is your bank manager and needs to speak with you urgently."

Patrick hop skipped it over to the reception desk where a seated female handed him the phone.

"That was Craig Donnelly," an ashen looking Patrick revealed as he returned to our table.

"There is some kind of paperwork issue between our bank and the receiving bank. The transfer is not yet approved but the fucking money has left our account and, due to the vagaries of the BACS inter-banking system … is now seemingly irretrievable."

"Jesus Christ!" I muttered. "So where does that leave us all?"

"In the shit mainly … we are now completely

in the hands of the Arab bankers in Dubai. I hope I can explain that to your Major or else lead is bound to fly!"

I felt down to the brief-case at my feet and touched it ... just to make sure.

"Don't worry. When he gets here I'll talk to him." I offered, though without too much confidence.

As I turned my head to stare thoughtfully out of the picture window, I noticed a liveried florist's van pull up at the front entrance to the hotel. A young girl exited the van with an arm full of flowers. I commented to myself how damned pretty she looked.

My gaze followed her on her short walk from the van through the foyer and eventually ending up at the main reception desk.

My thoughts were obviously very much focused on other events but my idle observation continued.

After a short conversation, the young woman in a bright green branded tee shirt and slim fitting jeans finally handed the flowers over, shook hands with the reception clerk and turned.

It didn't register at first.

Hold on a minute! Where is she going? My casually observing brain expected to see here turn left ... away from the reception counter, back toward the hotel main entrance and the waiting van. This was not to be. She turned right. Maybe she was looking for the toilets.

Then came the give-away; the short skip in her step and anxious look back. This young lady needed to get away from here ... and quickly!

I looked back at the van. What I might have been expecting to see I didn't really know but one thing was for sure ... this was a problem! I quickly checked my watch; the time showed as ten-twenty. This was all going tit's up. We needed to get the hell out of there.

I picked up the case, grabbed Patrick by the shoulder and pushed him out of his seat.

"Come on Patrick ... there's a fucking great bomb literally only yards from us and it could go up at any moment. MOVE!"

I raced the short distance to reception, clutching the all important brief-case and shouted to the surprised clerk. I pointed with my right arm in the direction the girl had fled.

"What's through there?"

"Err ... Err ... that leads to the kitchens and then leads on to the staff car park ... and ... err ..."

"You need to get on to whatever paging system you have and clear this whole damn establishment as quickly as you can. That florist van parked only feet away from this foyer is packed with explosives. You have to get everyone out ... NOW!"

Patrick looked as if he was still attempting to take everything in but he was quickly catching up.

"Follow me!" I shouted as I headed for the kitchens. Pushing past busy prep staff and avoiding the odd collision with a free-wheeling trolley or two, we both found ourselves unexpectedly outside.

The car park area looked to be half full. I scanned the whole site for any movement. I heard the high pitch sounds of a high revving engine in the distance, clocking the red Ford maneuvering at the far side of the car park. I ran and Patrick followed me.

Within seconds the little Ford headed straight toward us, at speed; the face of the young female driver set and determined.

My conscience was clear. This was the florist.

I withdrew my 9mm and took aim ... but I was beaten to it.

As I took that extra second to be sure in my own mind, Patrick, a step or so behind me fired his weapon.

The explosive force left an instantaneous cover of bright red blood over the inside of the wind shield and the car veered immediately to the right.

As a result of the erratic maneuver the now uncontrolled vehicle crashed into two other parked cars.

A numbing silence fell over the scene ... eventually interrupted by an alarm bell screaming out a monotonous warning message somewhere inside the hotel.

The head bomb maker of the Provisional IRA, the Provo's, had set the timer wrongly and instead of going off at twenty five minutes to eleven that morning as planned, it had actually been primed to detonate at twenty five minutes past ten.

Building successful bombs, using large amounts of fertilizer, could be a 'hit' and 'miss' affair, especially if relying upon ammonium nitrate.

The measurement of components for detonation and then fuelling the bomb, needed to be exact.

One thing was for sure, no mistakes had been made with the assembly of the bomb itself, now stationary, hidden in a florist's van, outside the front entrance to the exclusive Glassier Lake House Hotel.

The force of the initial detonation wave lifted the van some fifteen or twenty feet in the air. As the fertilizer content of the bomb began to vaporize, the full energy of the explosive gasses, travelling at two to three miles per second, began to spread outward. The multiplying, unstoppable force would destroy everything in its path.

The twelve foot high picture windows and plate glass entrance doors disintegrated into deathly shards as ignition of the liquid fuel caused massive amounts of oxygen to be released.

It served to feed the combustion, raise the temperature of the fireball and create the bloody horror that was to unfold when the energy of the explosion had finally been spent.

The rumble of death carried on for many seconds after the explosion had finally been exhausted. Then the pain started.

Both Patrick and I had hit the ground hard after seeing the tragically young bomber end her life. What might have been in the car with her ... we didn't know ... another bomb perhaps?

I sat up, my ears ringing, the cries and screams of pain gradually breaking through the barrier of dullness until I shook my head and looked around me.

Patrick looked to be moving now. I went over to help him up. He had a large bruise on his forehead where he had been struck by something travelling at speed. He reached to sooth the spot.

"What the fuck happened?" he said, his voice thick and words barely audible.

"Some bastard has set off a bomb Patrick. Someone, who is not signed up to what we are signed up to, thought they might be getting these damn micro-chips cheap!"

"Jesus Gary, the bloody micro-chips. Do you still have them?"

"Right here Patrick."

"OK. We need to get the hell out of here. We must find the Range Rover and hope it's still in one piece. If the Rover is damaged, then we'll have to steal a car that works. OK?"

"I'm right behind you Patrick. What's the rest of the plan?" I asked.

"We have to find a phone … and bloody quick too. This is all going to rat-shit my friend and yet again, the bloody bodies are piling up!"

We skirted the hotel buildings to our left knowing the car park location of the Rover. There appeared to be little damage to the vehicles but the front of the Hotel was an absolute mess. Sirens could be heard in the distance.

"That'll be the medics and the bloody Garda. We need to be away from here.

Finding the Range Rover was easy, finding the key was not so.

Patrick searched every pocket, becoming more frustrated by the second.

"Where the fuck is it Gary. I had it in my inside

jacket pocket when we booked out. I'm sure it's here somewhere."

"Take you jacket off and shake it." I offered.

"What?"

"Shake the bloody jacket Patrick and see if it caught up somewhere …"

He shook the jacket a couple of times and the key fell to the floor.

"With a smile and the car key in hand, Patrick said.

"Let's go!"

On the narrow road to Killinure there was much activity with blue lights flashing and sirens screaming as the emergency services rushed to the spectacle of horror that was now the Glassier Lake House Hotel.

Once in Killinure, Patrick opted to go south to the town of Athlone. He told me he had a reliable network of 'soldiers' there and some accurate intelligence might be required to settle this current situation.

Whilst Patrick drove the Rover, he remained pensive and silent … as did I. My thoughts were to the operation which had left a popular Irish hotel in ruins along with countless dead and possibly many more injured.

The IRA High Command now had close to three hundred million pounds sterling in their Irish offshore bank account … and no one, not even HMG could take it from them.

As for the 'trade' item, the brief case full of

micro-chips, well that was sitting next to me in a Range Rover currently being piloted at some risk to life by a man who had promised to make a further transfer of funds to a Middle East Bank ... that had seemingly rejected it.

Then, of course, there was the Major, someone who may well have arrived at the hotel at the very moment of the explosion. Did he ... or didn't he? If he did ... did he survive? If he didn't ... where the hell is he now and what might be coming toward us next?

Then, finally, there was the person or persons behind the bomb itself. Who were they? What were they after and what were they about to do next?

It was all a bit of a mess and unfortunately, it looked as if I would not be returning to my nice comfortable bed in my nice comfortable apartment anytime soon.

CHAPTER FIFTEEN

Someone to 'Bank' upon ...

The address Patrick headed to in Athlone appeared to be a poorly maintained building on the northern outskirts of the town. A track at the side of the property gave access to the rear and space for parking several cars.

The IRA Intelligence Chief was greeted warmly by a 'comrade' and ushered into the building.

He introduced his travelling companion to the several other people waiting inside. He also proudly pointed to the brief case Gary Chase was carrying, announcing this was the item that all the fuss was about.

"It doesn't look like much to me!" one of them offered cautiously.

"Well my friend ... sitting right there on that damned kitchen table is three hundred million quid ... and a few lives have been lost along the way getting it here."

This revelation caused something of a stir, part concern and part disbelief.

"Have you heard what happened at the Glassier Lake House Hotel?"

"We have Patrick." said one of the group.

"Well, let me assure you the shit has well and truly hit the fan. I need a telephone and I need one quickly. I can't be sure who is responsible for the bomb attack but I'm pretty sure it was the Provo's ... and I think they got their timing wrong. The target was to get both of us and a British army guy named Major McAllister."

Patrick pointed to Gary as he spoke.

"I don't think they will stop coming; the crazy bastards won't give up with the kind of 'money stakes' in play here. So, we need to be prepared for an attack. It might be the Provo's or even the SAS under instruction from the mad Major.

I hope this is not the case but I want Gary and me to be away from here before someone with a grudge catches up with us. Does everyone understand?"

They all nodded. They knew what had to be done.

In a room at the front of the house sat a telephone and Patrick used it to connect with the 'Protector'. He in turn connected Patrick with Craig Donnelly of the National Irish Bank and the news was not good.

"So, what's the fucking problem Craig? It's a simple trading instruction … take money from your bank … and place it in another."

"The way it has been explained to me Patrick is that the Dubai bank, the DUCB, has received the instruction but the transaction itself must go through its correspondent bank in Pakistan. Such a large amount of money, moving Inter-Bank in one transfer, gives them the opportunity to siphon off a small amount in banking fees."

Patrick would need a moment or two to grasp the significance of what he was being told. He knew nothing about 'correspondent banks' and large sums of money crossing borders. It was a complicated system at best.

"OK Craig ... how much do they want in fees?"

Craig cleared his throat.

"Err ... hmm ... one percent Patrick!"

"One percent ... you must be fucking joking. That's over half a million quid. Where is the money now?"

"It's in the ether my friend. It's not actually anywhere ... it's sort of stuck 'between banks' and the only way it can be released is for the Pakistani correspondent bank of the DUCB to register they have received their claimed commission."

Patrick's heartbeat jumped a few notches. What the hell was he supposed to tell the untrustworthy Major?

He felt sure this was not an issue that could be resolved quickly. The only way for the transaction to be completed was for somebody to take a hit for six hundred thousand pounds.

He couldn't recommend that to his High Command. No doubt Major McAllister would also be quite averse to recommending such a course of action to his client, partner, friend or whatever person he represented in this seemingly complex banking nightmare.

"Tell me Craig, is this position negotiable?"

"Everything in this world is negotiable Patrick ... especially in the world of banking."

"OK. You tell this fucking bank in Dubai to tell their fucking bank in Pakistan that we will offer a commission of one hundred thousand pounds.

That's it. No more chances. The full sixty million must be in the relative Dubai Bank numbered account within the hour.

Failure to do so will cause me to pay every human being involved in this bullshit operation a visit ... and whilst you are having this conversation with whoever it is in Dubai, you better let them know who the fuck they are dealing with!"

Patrick slammed down the telephone and turned to Gary.

"Now ... how do we get hold of this damned Major of yours, in order to avoid world war three breaking out."

As he posed the question, the phone rang. It was the 'Protector'. Major McAllister wanted to speak with him.

"Yes Major. No doubt you have rung me to let me know your world has turned to rat-shit, but ... I can assure you that ..."

"Well Mr. O'Breian, if you are able to describe six dead, eight seriously injured and fifteen other casualties as 'rat shit' then I can do nothing other than agree with you. However, a more pressing issue is sitting with me right now ... the issue of one empty bank account which you were tasked with 'topping up' some hours ago. I have to tell you that the person I represent is disappointed and currently deciding what to do with you Mr. O'Breian."

Patrick felt the flush of insecurity consume him for several seconds, his heart rate running far too high for someone with naturally high blood pressure.

He would need to explain the Middle East banking dilemma as clearly as he could and, more importantly, how he had offered to resolve the issue. He was waiting for an authorized telex to be received from his bank in Dublin, confirming the transfer had been completed.

"That is only one problem I am dealing with right now Patrick. HMG is becoming quite nervous having paid over to you the sum of three hundred million for an agreed number of items we have yet to receive.

Where are the bloody micro-chips?

I need to have them in my hand within the hour or else several hundred horsemen ... of that well known apocalypse ... will descend not only on you as an individual ... but the whole of the fucking IRA. Do you understand me?"

"I do." replied Patrick calmly.

"Is Gary there with you?"

"He is."

"Put him on the line, I need to have a word with him."

Gary took the telephone and waited for Ewan to speak.

"Are you alright Gary?" the voice enquired.

"Yes I am." he replied. "... and I have the microchips with me in good condition and unharmed. Whatever the hell happened at the Hotel I really do not know, but Patrick is sure it was an attack by the Provo's. They are after the shipment and seem to have some good intelligence on our movements."

"Well you know how HMG works. Number Ten is fuming. They want their money or the shipment.

As far as they are concerned this whole business is one hundred percent down to the IRA and they will be looking for a pound or two of flesh very shortly.

If they find you standing in the way, they will cut you down Gary ... have no fear ... they will kill you without a second thought."

Gary Chase looked over to Patrick who appeared to be deep in thought.

"You need to find a way Ewan, a way for me to get the bloody microchips to you ... and soon!"

"Tell me where you are and I'll come and collect them."

"That's not possible. To tell you that would betray a trust ... and I can't do that. We need to be in a public place ... a place like Dublin Airport Departures"

Gary looked over to Patrick once more. He was nodding his head and holding up six fingers.

"Can we say six o'clock this evening Ewan?"

A few clicks on the line and a short segment of heavy breathing later, the Major came back.

"OK Gary. I have to trust you on this one. Six o'clock this evening in the airport departures coffee shop. I will be on my own ... and I hope you will too. If there is any issue at all that hinders the exchange or stops it taking place, then wheels will automatically be set in motion Gary ... wheels I will not be able to stop. Do you understand me?"

Gary replied in the positive.

"I'll see you at six o'clock."

As Gary put down the phone, Patrick breathed a long and meaningful sigh of relief.

Patrick and Gary spent the next hour going over the situation concerning the handover of the 'shipment' at Dublin Airport.

The coffee shop was located at one end of the departures concourse with two entrances leading on to it. Patrick would have three of his more experienced men with him, all carrying 9mm handguns.

There were four entrances to the departure area in total and one man would be in position at each, half an hour before the handover time, checking who might be going in and out.

Gary would enter the coffee shop with briefcase in hand ... on his own and as instructed. He would find a suitable empty table. When Major McAllister appeared he would simply hand over the case, get up and walk away, his hand on his own 9mm tucked inside his jacket.

As some form of insurance, Gary would be carrying a walkie-talkie connecting him to the others on site. It would be left on full display, in his hand, until the handover had been completed. Patrick, Gary and their small team went over the pro's and con's of the operation until all the if's and butt's had been aired and planned for.

It would take about an hour and a half to get to Dublin Airport and the team left in two vehicles, the Range Rover and a black Ford saloon. Each vehicle would take a different route to Dublin. Individuals would communicate through FM Packset radios.

The full crew set off giving them about half an hour before the handover time to observe movements in and out of the departures area.

Patrick and Gary occupied the Range Rover with the other three in the Ford. The worried look had left the Irishman; in fact he now seemed quite at ease.

Gary spoke.

"Do you think this will be the end of it Patrick?" he asked.

The Intelligence chief nodded his head.

"I live in hope Gary ... but once this problem is solved there is an equally pressing one to face ... but fortunately that does not involve you and hopefully we can leave you at the airport so you can make your way home ... unscathed!"

Gary Chase laughed out loud.

"That's a great word Patrick ... 'unscathed' ... I like it a lot and let us hope that every single one of us is able to leave Dublin today ... 'unscathed' ... because we seem to be in the sights of someone who regularly makes a habit of supervising fuck-ups!"

Now it was Patrick's turn to laugh out loud.

Flight Sergeant Gary Chase, serving in Her Majesties Royal Air Force sat at table number six in the Roast & Toast Coffee Shop located at the southern end of the departures concourse at Dublin Airport. The time by the wall mounted clock showed as four minutes to six o'clock.

Chase had one hand on a small brief-case sitting on the seat of the chair next to him and the other tucked inside his close fitting, bomber style jacket. He looked relaxed and expectant, surveying the space around him and clocking anyone who appeared to be going nowhere in particular.

The walkie-talkie set rested on the table, close to him. It was switched on and gave out a steady low volume stream of static.

A petit and rather attractive young woman approached the lone figure at table number six. She had a cigarette in one hand and a handbag in the other. Dressed in a loose fitting coat cut to below the knee she leaned forward over the table and spoke through a thick Irish accent.

"Have you got a light there my friend?" she asked, pushing the unlit cigarette forward and close up to his face; the unexpected action disorienting him for a brief second.

She tapped the handbag now on the table with the zipper opened and the barrel of a heavy caliber handgun poking through.

The words were whispered and only just audible as she inserted her hand to grasp the weapon.

"Give me the case ... NOW ... and don't fuck me about. I've got this whole fucking place covered ... including your little team on the entrances."

She reached over, throwing away the cigarette and grabbing the brief case. Gary let it go without a fight.

"Very sensible my little Air Force Englishman." the girl offered. "Now, I am going to walk out of here with this case in my hand and if anyone tries to stop me ... there is going to be a fucking bloodbath ... do you understand ... Gary?"

Whoever this damn girl might be, she knew he was in the Air Force and she knew his name. This fact alone was disturbing but whatever the situation, he would not be giving up his life for a few microchips anytime soon.

His hand remained inside in his jacket. Would he be pulling it out and revealing whatever he appeared to be holding there.

The girl turned and began to walk away from the Coffee Shop toward the nearest exit route. She looked back, a strange expression on her face; a look possibly betraying the thought that 'this' had been just too damn easy.

As she made her exit to the outside of the terminal, fifty yards away, and heading straight for her, was Major Ewan McAllister. He seemed to recognize her immediately and produced his hand gun. She dropped the bag concealing her stub nosed .44 magnum revolver.

Her first shot release must have been half a second ahead of his as his chest exploded in a mass of bright claret. The second shot finished the job of the first and his decimated body became blown back several feet from the combined powerful impact of the two heavy caliber bullets.

Although the Major had fired his weapon, he was too late. The young girl stood firm and looked to be unharmed. A bewildering silence of three or four seconds surrounded the bloody scene as everyone in the area processed what might be happening ... then, when it was clear this was not a movie set and a life had been lost ... all hell broke loose.

With confused, agitated, screaming passengers

and airport staff running in all directions, Patrick O'Breian, now outside the terminal building, kept his eye on the girl; the cold, calm killer who had just put away a senior UK military intelligence officer. She was not running but walked at a steady pace out onto the pavement area bordering a roadway and a set of drop-off points.

A clean looking green Jaguar saloon car waited in one of the spots; two youthful looking men in the front and the rear passenger door left fully open. The girl took a quick look behind her. She felt the closing presence, the cold chill as Patrick raised his Glock pistol.

The first three bullets pierced her brain and the last two her chest. She hit the floor immediately, but for O'Breian it would be too late. The driver of the waiting Jaguar had him in his sights letting of half a magazine of 9mm ammunition, striking the Irishman several times.

The green saloon, wheels spinning, blue smoke billowing, exited the parking spot at speed, nearly adding further to the casualty list by knocking over an aged gentleman on a crossing. As the powerful getaway vehicle gained grip it began to accelerate, the rear door still gaping open.

Gary Chase heard the 'hullabaloo' outside the terminal but was unaware of the consequences. He simply had to guess that McAllister must now be dead because if not, he would have turned up to collect the micro-chips.

The noise over the radio; the undisciplined comment and query, left Gary feeling something must have happened to O'Breian as well.

His job was to get the hell out of there and back

to England. He picked up his small travel bag and headed for the toilets. He could hear the emergency services sirens in the distance. He would need to be quick.

In one of the cubicles he took the package stuffed inside his jacket and transferred it to the bag. The shipment of micro-chips was safe once more. Now he must get through to departures before they closed down the bloody airport.

In all the confusion the small queue seeking access to the departures lounge was being rushed through without any 'deep' check of luggage. That meant a sigh of relief for Gary having checked the flight departures board confirming his flight was already loading.

As he headed to the gate, the announcement was made that for everyone not yet boarded, the airport will be closed temporarily to allow for the investigation of certain events.

Another large sigh of relief as the airline rep checked his boarding pass and ushered him through to the aircraft.

Flight Sergeant Gary Chase exited the flight from Dublin to be greeted by a cool temperature, a cloudy sky and a drizzle of rain.

Would he be stopped when his luggage was inspected by the ever diligent X-Ray machine? The answer was 'yes' and even with his GCHQ security pass it took a little time and slightly more patience to get past customs.

Stansted Airport was not a particularly pretty

establishment. At any time of day it appeared overcrowded and undermanaged, but it gave shelter to all the usual facilities including a national car hire operator.

Gary hired a standard saloon, filled it up with fuel and set off for Scarborough ... and home! A good night's sleep would no doubt improve his mood.

After everything that had gone down over the last couple of days, Gary felt mentally and physically exhausted. However, tomorrow would be another day and although he had no idea what it had in store for him, he knew it couldn't be any worse than the day he just had.

The early morning phone call did not go down well. However, Gary's boss wished to speak with him and that was a conversation he would not be able to avoid.

CHAPTER SIXTEEN

A necessary meeting of minds ...

"Yes sir ... how can I help you?" I offered when finally put through to the person who acted as my direct superior.

"You can help me by bringing me up to date with what the hell is going on with these damn electronic components. Everyone in Number Ten is nervous, and a nervous politician is a dangerous politician. A lot of jobs are on the line for whatever you tell me next Gary ... including yours and mine ... so it had better be good news!"

"Well if it's the micro-chips you are worried about, I can tell you they are with me and I am looking at them right now."

"Thank God for that. There is all kinds of shit going down back in Ireland but I suppose you know all about that as you seem to have been in the middle of it all."

"I don't know the body count sir ... everything was happening around me. I saw people go down but I have no idea of the state of the casualties."

"Well, on that matter I can definitely be of help. A young girl named Eileen Donahue, the one supposedly carrying the 'chips' taken from you, shot Major McAllister. He died instantly.

Patrick O'Breian shot and killed Donahue seconds later and his personal luck ran out when the driver of the getaway car opened up with a sub-machine pistol, nearly cutting the man in half. As you would imagine, he died on the spot."

"Any more ...?"

"One or two civilians were nicked by stray metal, but no real casualties. The Irish Garda appeared on the scene pretty quickly and as soon as they arrived, all persons of possible interest seem to have disappeared."

I really needed some to time to think about the situation and what might come next because surely, this would never be the end of it.

"Well, there is much to think about now. With McAllister dead I feel sure someone with an official or unofficial interest on behalf of the Army will be looking for a person to blame ... and that might well be me.

The IRA High Command has now received a tactical 'flesh wound'; lost it's highly respected Intelligence Chief and will be wanting to find out who's side the young girl was on.

My guess is the 'Provos' and if that is the case, they will be looking for war ... and, if allowed to start one it would undoubtedly turn into a very violent series of events."

Silence overtook the conversation as both the AVM and I struggled to try and identify all the avenues and exits surrounding the problem.

Finally, David Brooking spoke.

"I think this needs a conversation with Number Ten ... directly with the Prime Minister. If the dogs of war are about to be released then he is the only one who can stop them ... no matter which direction they may well come from."

"I'm sure you will make a splendid job of it sir, and I hope ..."

"Not a cat's chance Sergeant. You are coming

with me. Now, get those bloody micro-chips in a secure place at Irton Moor and then get your backside down here to GCHQ. Understood?"

"Understood sir!"

I knew there would be no use in arguing. If Brooking said something was to done ... then it was to be done."

⋈

By the afternoon of the following day I sat with Air Vice-Marshall Brooking in his adequate but un-palatial office in GCHQ Headquarters, Cheltenham. He opened up to me on several subjects, including some interesting observations about the politics of the IRA and the difficulties encountered in managing the differences in ideology between the IRA and the Provisional IRA.

"So, with O'Breian now gone; the three hundred million in the IRA bank account and the microchips now stored safely inside my office safe ... are we not clear now?" I asked.

"That is exactly the same question the PM is asking of me. With McAllister lying side by side with O'Breian on a cold slab somewhere in Dublin, it appears there are players involved we have yet to consider."

"Such as?"

"Such as ... whoever is feeding the Provisional IRA, the Provo's; who put all this shit together from the point of the chips being robbed in America to a second robbery, but this time by the UDA ... the Ulster Defence Association at Dublin

Airport. No one had a bloody clue that the Ulster boys had somehow become involved.

Think about it Gary. Whoever is pulling the strings here is very well informed and that means connecting at some high level, either in the Military or the Intelligence community ... or both."

I pondered on the matter for some time during which David Brooking ordered more tea. I simply could not understand all the connections and possible motives involved ... the IRA, the Provo's, the UDA, British MI9, British MI6 ... and to a reasonable extent ... GCHQ.

"Do you think that somehow Major McAllister was the witting or unwitting connection here sir, because if so, now he's dead, that particular connection is permanently broken?"

"Well Gary, we may well find out more from the PM. The car will be picking us up in ten minutes."

The Prime Minister did not appear to be in particularly good spirits. Relentless cups of tea and some rather special chocolate cake did nothing to improve his mood.

There would be no small talk. The PM wanted to get stuck straight into it. There was no-one else in the room, just the three of us.

"All recording devices in this room are switched off, so everyone can speak freely. We have a problem that involves the IRA and some as yet unidentified third party ..."

I interrupted.

"Surely we have no issues with the IRA do we sir? They have their 300 million and we have the microchips ... deal done as far as I'm concerned!"

David Brooking looked over at me, his face sending all kinds of mute code, mostly pointing to one simple message ... CAUTION!"

"Listen to me Gary. You do not think for one moment all this ridiculous business has happened by accident do you?"

"Well sir ... I ..."

"Of course it's damn well not. Someone has been orchestrating this whole deal right from the very beginning. You would agree with me on that matter would you not Air Vice-Marshall?"

David looked at me, his expression now pained, the words slipping out reluctantly.

"Yes Prime Minister ... of course!"

"There has been a development since the carnage at Dublin Airport. With the murder of Patrick O'Breian we have lost our singular most sensible line of communication with the IRA. We are now reliant upon just one contact, just one individual left we can talk to as a High Command decision maker."

Silence ...

Brooking fielded the most obvious question.

"Err ... can I ask who that might be Prime Minister?"

The PM hesitated for a second or so, but then revealed the name of the contact to be Nial Sullivan, codename Magpie.

He was known in intelligence quarters as a senior member of the High Command and someone who declared himself to be the most outspoken, anti-British officer of them all. With several hundred well trained and equipped men under his direct command, he was a force to be reckoned with.

"Hmm ..." Brooking commented as he absorbed this new piece of intelligence.

I still could not understand what I was doing there ... and said so.

"In fear of repeating myself Prime Minister, I still don't know what this has to do with me. The money they demanded is in the IRA bank account, and we have the microchips, so what's the issue?"

The PM turned to me.

"You are absolutely right Gary, but an unfortunate circumstance has arisen. The unknown individual, the person who has been feeding the IRA with intelligence is due a commission of twenty percent."

"Twenty percent ..?" I echoed in disbelief.

"Jesus Christ; that's around sixty million quid and that's an awful amount of money sir!"

"It is Gary and someone appears to have stolen it ... or 'lost' it depending upon your point of view. The unknown person is making all kinds of threats to take action against individuals in the IRA High Command if the money is not in a certain Dubai bank account ... within three days."

"And ..?"

"And Gary ... we want you to go to Dubai and find it."

This was not good news. He had heard of Dubai and even knew where it was. The RAF had a base in the small next door enclave of Sharjah. He had never been to anywhere that low down in the Arabian Gulf before but he had spent some time in the rather substantial island air base of Bahrain ... and knew it would be bloody hot!

"Why me ..?" I asked.

"Because Gary, you have been involved with this whole mess of an operation right from the beginning. You have knowledge of all the personalities involved; you appear to have been resourceful and have come out of it all alive ... which cannot be said for either of the two other major players."

I gave the matter some thought. Two pairs of eyes bore down on me. I actually felt quite uncomfortable.

"Do I have any choice?" I asked.

Both men answered with a cool 'of course you do', but the truth behind the eyes told a different story and it looked as if David Brooking might not be fully on my side.

He smiled.

"May we take that as a 'yes' then Gary?" he said, eyes now focused an inch or two above my head. That was the point where I knew for sure I had been well and truly fucked."

"You may sir." I confirmed through a thin smile. "So, what do we do now?"

An hour later I found myself in the back of an armoured Range Rover with a protection officer and driver in the front. I was seemingly on my way to a country estate somewhere near Banbury known as Farnborough Hall.

There, I was to meet with the owner of the estate, the Honourable Sir Tarquin Ludlow.

I had not been told what this person did, or who he reported to, except to say of course he held General Officer rank in the British Army and so must have some knowledge to impart.

A woman, who may well have been past retirement age, opened the door to the impressive property known simply as 'The Hall' and introduced herself as Mrs. Wyatt, the Housekeeper.

I leant forward and offered her a hand, which she avoided skilfully by opening the door wider. I entered a grand hallway with an ornate carved stone staircase at its centre. As I turned back to Mrs. Wyatt, she became startled, her face turning ashen, moving back a step ... as if she had seen a ghost.

"Are you alright my dear ... you appear very pale; would you like to sit down for a second?"

"No thank you sir ... I really am quite well."

Although she was looking at me, our eyes made no connection. Hers appeared focused elsewhere, somewhere above or below my face. My reaction was immediate; cupping my hand over my neck to cover my now exposed birth mark.

It had been some years since I had felt such an emotion, knowing I would colour up as a sign of my embarrassment. Why on earth had I done that?

It had been many years since I had become

defensive over anyone noticing or making comment about my birth mark.

My blood pressure lowered immediately as the housekeeper turned her head away.

"Please follow me sir," Mrs. Wyatt offered as she showed me into an impressive room described as a library and advised that Sir Tarquin would be with me in a moment.

She withdrew, closing the door quietly behind her wearing a confused expression and possibly about to shed a tear.

'What a strange set of events!' I thought to myself as I looked for somewhere comfortable to sit.

It had been a busy day so far and with the light fading fast I knew there must be a lot more to come.

Several minutes later a man of obvious military bearing entered the room. I judged him to be in his early fifties. He had an unexpectedly kindly face and held out his hand to me as he approached. The handshake felt firm and controlled. When he sat down in the green leather Chesterfield opposite me, he smiled and the expression looked to be quite genuine.

"I hope the powers that be have apologised to you for dragging out what has probably been a busy day."

He didn't wait for an answer.

"The reason you are here talking to me is that I hold a very senior position in the MoD and as such I am totally responsible for the activities of the purchasing and procurement, section three, technology group.

Many millions of pounds of government money pass through my hands every day and I have a thorough knowledge of the International banking and BACS transfer system. I also have some excellent contacts at a senior level within most major banking institutions ... and I use them regularly!"

The army officer looked relaxed and comfortable as he spoke and I have to admit to feeling equally relaxed in his company.

"Do you know why I'm here sir ... why it is me sitting in front of you and not someone else?"

"I have no idea Gary ... and please ... call me Tarquin."

The disarming smile underlined the comfort of his words. I could see his natural ability to put people at their ease would have been most useful in his trade. This would be especially pertinent in conversations with bankers; a certain class of individuals with over inflated ego's normally full of their own importance ... and not much else.

The pause in the conversation gave time for thought. How much did this man really know of what had been happening over the past week or so; the events in America and then the catastrophic changes of circumstance in Ireland.

"We do have control of the micro-chips now Tarquin ... you do know that of course. Also I understand that money has exchanged hands and the IRA have received everything they demanded from the Government."

"Yes Gary, I know that ... in fact I know most if not all the detail bringing us up to this very moment in time.

That is why you are here today

By the way, it is so rude of me not to have offered you a drink. I have some excellent ancient whiskey I feel sure you will enjoy. Its Blantyre's best ..."

Half a minute later I nursed half a full measure of the golden liquid, served up in a heavy diamond cut crystal glass.

"If you are in agreement, I am happy to make arrangements for you to stay the night here and send your driver and protection officer back to London. We have a lot to get through and I have to make sure you are on the ten forty flight to Dubai tomorrow morning. Is that OK?"

Yet again, I had the creeping feeling of being corralled into following a path of action I was not that comfortable with.

First it was Brooking twisting my arm to attend a meeting with the PM. Then it was the PM himself pushing me to visit some obscure General in his fancy country seat; a person I had never heard of before. And now, all my choices concerning travel arrangements look to have been removed, leaving me reliant upon a complete stranger to make sure I left the UK for Dubai the following day.

Perhaps my concerns showed in my reluctance to answer immediately.

"Well Tarquin, to be totally honest, I feel a little insecure. I am being expected to travel to some god-forsaken place to discuss god-knows what with a bunch of individuals whose only concern is money ... and the art of hanging on to as much of it as possible. This is simply NOT my kind of work. I am a communications specialist; that is my trade."

My words appeared to have had no effect whatsoever.

"So Gary, shall I send your driver and his friend back to London or ..."

"Send them back Tarquin. I think it's just best to go with the damn flow."

I smiled and Tarquin's face lit up.

"Good Man ...!" he shouted, reaching for my glass, ready for a top-up.

With my minder and driver on their way back to London in the Range Rover and Tarquin and I sipping at our glasses of smooth, warming whiskey, the time was right to find out what might really be going on.

Mick Chatham and Barry Gale, both protection officers with the Metropolitan Police, received the message from the Sir Tarquin that they could now return to London. The person they had driven in their near three hour journey to Farnborough Hall would be staying the night.

That was good news for Mick and Barry who now expected to be home around midnight and would therefore be on a late start for their duties the next day. Insulated flasks had been topped up with fresh coffee, courtesy of Mrs. Wyatt. Now all they had to do was be on their way south.

As they moved through quite heavy traffic toward Oxford, the conversation moved from the latest Bond film, 'Diamonds Are Forever' to the current poor performance of the national football team.

As the Rover pulled east onto the Oxford bypass, an unexpected hissing sound could be heard coming from the rear of the vehicle. Mick turned his head to confirm that the disturbing and unwelcome noise was coming from the inside and not the outside of the vehicle.

The spare wheel, located beneath the rear floor panel, had not been checked before they left the Oxfordshire mansion. Why would they? The Rover had been stationary in the garage block adjacent to the main house.

As Mick and Barry had carried out their quick external check of the vehicle, including a mirror search of the underside, they concluded all was well. The doors were locked and handle latches unmarked.

The car was safe to drive.

How wrong they were!

Mick was about to reveal his concerns to his partner Barry Gale ... but it was to be too late.

Within four seconds both men would be dead.

The explosion itself was driven by two pounds of composition C4 plastic explosive. The trigger had been provided by a radio controlled electrical contact made using a servo.

The action of the servo, cobbled together using a model aeroplane kit, was controlled by a man sitting next to the driver of a white Audi; a vehicle travelling half a mile behind the Rover.

Due to the all-round darkened windows of the black Rover, it was impossible to see how many people were on board.

There were definitely two individuals in the front, and that would be the protection officers for sure. Whoever might be in the back remained unconfirmed, but the Audi driver felt sure it would not be leaving without the passenger it had delivered there earlier.

Both men were confident three people were in the Rover, two protection officers and their target ... named as Gary Chase, some sort of expert in the business of communications.

The fireball from the explosion consumed every gram of oxygen in the vehicle within milliseconds. Desperate to breathe more, it burst from the constricting vacuum and shot upward, lifting the complete vehicle more than six feet into the air. It landed with an almighty 'thump' as the fuel tank exploded and showered burning metal across two carriageways.

No one inside the vehicle could have survived such an unbelievable event. The white Audi began to navigate a way through the burning wreckage trail, attempting to pass and planning to leave the carnage behind them as quickly as possible. A series of crackling explosions confirmed the presence of live ammunition on board.

Once clear, the Audi and its occupants would look to leave the bypass; head back toward Oxford and look out for a telephone box ... one that worked.

With the necessary message passed it confirmed three people were dead ... the target and the protection officers.

The Provo special operations officer in Belfast would receive the message within the hour. He would smile as the information was relayed to him.

It was a job well done!

By the following morning, his own team of field operatives would have arrived in Dubai and they would be seeking the missing sixty million UK pounds. It was not part of his plan to take any prisoners.

With thoughts of getting their hands on all or part of the IRA's three hundred million now dashed, the 'loose' sixty million, supposed to be sitting in a Dubai bank numbered account, was still there for the taking.

Pat Doherty was considered to be number three in the Provo's hierarchy. He was not a man one would normally mess with. Since the split from the IRA High Command the previous year, the Provisional IRA had spread its tentacles all over the world and no crime and certainly no punishment was too egregious for Pat Doherty. He hated the English with a vengeance and gathered around him men and women who would do whatever might be necessary to win the day.

CHAPTER SEVENTEEN

Dubai ... too hot to handle?

I woke at five o'clock. It was not yet fully light but I could hear movement in the house. My weekend bag and personal documents had somehow caught up with me from Cheltenham. After a shower and clean clothes I felt fully refreshed and ready for what might turn out to be a seven hour flight to Dubai.

The envelope of documents contained my passport, driving licence, GCHQ security pass, a gold Amex card with an unlimited financial facility provided by HMG and finally a first class British Airways ticket to Dubai.

Tarquin and I had finished our conversation at around two o'clock in the morning. My head was still buzzing from the knowledge and the detail he needed to instil into me during the short amount of time available to us.

It was a few minutes past six when I heard a light tap at the door and the voice of Mrs. Wyatt telling me breakfast was ready in the dining room and that his host was already downstairs.

"Good morning sir." I announced as I sat at the place laid for me next to Tarquin. Mrs. Wyatt hovered in the background.

"Good morning Gary."

He looked up from his tea settling in a fine bone china cup. He looked distressed.

"I'm afraid there has been a change of plan old chap."

"Change of plan?" I echoed.

"Yes. Last night the two protection officers assigned to you were blown to very small pieces in the vehicle they were driving on the Oxford bypass. It was a well planed and well executed operation. We have no doubt it was you they were after ... whoever 'they' actually might turn out to be."

His voice appeared a little shaky, as if he was taking the matter personally. He looked pale as he sipped at his tea with Mrs. Wyatt delivering some fresh toast to his side plate.

"The whole operation is off Gary ... that's all I can tell you right now."

I needed a few minutes to think.

Eventually I was able to make a decision; one I felt sure I would live to regret somewhere down the damn line.

"Who is it telling you the operation is off?"

"The PM's office Gary ..."

"Well ... get them on the phone and tell them it's NOT off any longer. You told me last night that we would be going to London in a helicopter ... so if that's still on ... we had better get moving. I'll eat on the flight to Dubai."

My offer did not seem to improve his mood but he did react straight away and headed for the nearest phone.

Ten minutes later he came back with the news that we were all set to go. The helicopter had taken off from the nearby army facility at Bicester and would arrive within the half hour. By seven forty-five we were ready to go. Mrs. Wyatt appeared in the hall.

"Now you take some care sir." she said, moving forward, arms opened up, as if to offer me some kind of embrace. There could be little doubt, the focus of her attention was, once more, the small but quite clear 'S' shaped birthmark on my neck.

The hug turned out to be gentle and possibly continuing past politeness. When we separated she turned her head away from us both, avoiding eye contact.

Tarquin looked questioningly confused. He knew Mrs. Wyatt well and also knew that lingering close contact with strangers was completely out of character.

He was about to say something had it not been for the fierce sound of the helicopter settling on the helipad at the rear of the house.

Something very emotional was going on with Mrs. Wyatt; something I had no clue about but something that was obviously connected to me in some way or other. Being in any other situation than the one I was actually in, I would have asked her. However, now was not the time ... or the place!

I was on my way to Heathrow Airport and no matter what kind of adventure this might turn out to be, I hoped to hell I would survive it.

First Class service on the flight to Dubai turned out to be enlightening. I stayed away from alcoholic drinks, not knowing what or who might be greeting me at the other end of the flight. When I exited the aircraft in Dubai the first thing I noticed was the heat; the second thing I noticed was the dust and the third thing I noticed was a very attractive young lady holding up a board with my name scribbled on it.

I caught her attention and seconds later she was with me in the baggage claim area flashing an important looking pass at everyone in a uniform.

"My name is Melissa and I'm here from the Consulate to offer you any assistance that I can."

She held out a hand and I shook it.

"Hi Melissa. My name is Gary and I hope I won't have to impose on your hospitality for too long."

We exchanged smiles and then my luggage appeared. She manoeuvred up close to me as I pulled off my bag.

"As you must know Gary, we are now in the territory of the Trucial Oman States, a British Protectorate.

However, negotiations are in full swing to create the United Arab Emirates, an independent state ruled jointly by the current sheiks.

Tensions are running high and tribal issues creating a certain amount of resentment toward Brits who want the deal done before the end of the year.

So my friend, be on your guard and walk around everywhere with a smile. World war three might break out here at any moment!"

She smiled once more. I think she meant it.

Melissa Winterton, a twenty two year old secretary at the Consulate, was quick on her feet as she navigated a route through the ranks of battered taxis waiting in noisy assembly outside the arrivals building.

We eventually made our way to a waiting black ford car with diplomatic plates and a white uniformed driver.

We piled in and made the short journey to the Ambassador hotel where I was allocated an adequate room overlooking the creek and, judging from the smell, must have been the fish market.

Melissa was first to raise the subject.

"Do you want a drink?"

"You read my mind."

The infectious smile appeared once more.

With two ice cold beers in front of us I felt sure Melissa had something to tell me.

"As I hinted earlier, tensions are running a little high here at the moment with politics ruling all conversations between HMG and the local sheiks. The police, judiciary and military are still managed by Brits and they know you are here. What they don't know is what you are here for."

"Do you know what I'm here for?" I asked.

She hesitated.

"Yes I do."

"And ... do you think I'll find it?"

"No ... I don't!"

That was not what I wanted to hear and my expression probably revealed my disappointment.

"Forgive me for saying so, but you look to be quite young to be working for the security service. So ... which one is it?"

It threw her off her guard but she came back at me firmly.

"I was born here actually, in the Oman and I

speak Arabic. I was educated privately at schools in UK and recruited into military intelligence by my father. That's all I'm going to tell you Gary, but let me just add this. If you are ever in a tight corner, I'm the one you want by your side!"

"I'll drink to that." I said, raising my glass, watching the wonderful smile appear once more.

An appointment had been made for me with a Mr. Kareem, the Head of Operations at the Dubai United Commercial Bank on Maktoum Street.

The Manager of the bank, a Mr. Mohammed Bhaktir would not be available to meet with me and gave no reason why. Maybe this was the way this whole croc of shit was going to go.

The time was nine-thirty and Mr. Abdul Kareem offered me tea which I politely declined. We picked our way through some pleasantries and then finally descended on the reason I was here.

"Not to waste any of your time Abdul but there are sixty million reasons why I am sitting here with you today; sixty million missing reasons and I'm sure we can find them with your help."

I smiled, but behind the eyes burned a dark determination and I felt sure Mr. Kareem knew where I was coming from.

He leaned back in a creaking wooden framed library chair in need of some new upholstery.

"Well Mr. Chase, I would not call these funds 'lost' ... but more like 'resting' somewhere within the International Banking System. Perhaps I can explain."

"I hope so because by this time tomorrow I need to be on a flight back to London with the mystery resolved."

He jiggled the creaking chair back and forth. It was an annoying movement. Then he leaned forward, his elbows planted firmly on his desk top.

"Are you used to 'resolving mysteries' Mr. Chase, for I fear this particular one has gendered interest from several parties, all of whom appear to be quite experienced in this type of task? For example, there is the Bankers Automated Clearing System itself, or BACS as it is commonly referred to. That is a nightmare to negotiate just on its own. Then there is the matter of co-respondent banking agreements requiring commission payments and movement charges."

As he spoke, he looked me straight in the eye, no doubt gauging any sort of reaction to the softly delivered verbal.

"Everyone in the banking system wants a piece of sixty million pounds Mr. Chase, especially when it comes from such a shady source, and some are very practiced at getting their hands on it. So my words to you are 'take care'. You are dealing with some dangerous and highly motivated men who will snuff you out like a damn candle if it suits them!"

He leaned back once more, reaching for his tea; a thin, verging on insolent smile confirming he had no more to say.

"My bank, the DUCB, is an Emirates registered bank with a conditional licence to receive and transmit overseas payments to a maximum of one hundred thousand US Dollars per transaction.

This is normal practice for a start-up bank and as part of the licence conditions, for all greater amounts the transaction must go through a correspondent bank. Each bank within the International BACS system is allocated a Telex code to allow it to receive confirmation of cash movements and that code is unique to each bank and each Telex machine."

The smile remained; the mood defiant. Abdul Kareem looked pleased to be holding the advantage, but everything he told me so far, I already knew. Tarquin had briefed me well and so far everything he told me turned out to be correct.

The DUCB had only been operational for three years and was owned by a family very close to the Dubai ruler. It would be another two years before the bank held a full BACS licence, making it completely independent within the world banking system.

Abdul Kareem leaned forward, becoming even closer; the scent of heavy musk perfume, favoured by many Arab males, prompting me to sit back. He may have taken offence as the narrow smile quickly became a scowl.

He continued the banking lesson. I gave his words my full attention.

"So you see Mr. Chase, the system is relatively fool-proof. If your Dublin bank is telling you they have transmitted sixty million pounds sterling to us and have confirmation of the fact, then we would like to see it, because such a transaction within the BACS system is frankly impossible!"

The more he said, the more sense he made. A phone call to Pat Doherty was needed urgently.

Abdul could no doubt decipher the confusion showing in my expression and the smile returned.

He pushed an envelope across his desk toward me.

"In this envelope you will find all the details of our correspondent bank in Pakistan including Telex codes, all bank and branch addresses, telephone numbers and names of contacts. I feel sure they will welcome you and my advice is to start at the head office in Karachi and speak to Ali Hamza, Head of Operations. He will be expecting your call."

At that point Abdul Kareem lifted himself from his seat and moved to open his office door. It was pretty obvious that our meeting was now over.

"You will need to be quick if you want to book the afternoon flight to Karachi. It's normally pretty full.

Good-day Mr. Chase and I hope you are able to find what you search for, but please take care in Pakistan. Life there is cheap and the taking of one ... even cheaper!"

Outside on the pavement, I took a minute or two to get my mental bearings. Time had slipped by and I appeared to be looking not only in the wrong place, but the wrong fucking country. I grabbed a loitering taxi and made my way back to the hotel.

I hoped to be able to make a telephone call to Craig Donnelly of the National Irish Bank, the original transmitter of the funds. First however, I needed to speak with Melissa ... I needed her help.

I headed to the Creek side and the British Consulate. An enquiry at the gate discovered Melissa's whereabouts and within minutes I found myself sitting in her small but comfortable office relaying a précis of my conversation with Abdul Karim.

She quickly scanned the information in the envelope he had given me and then ordered one of the clerks to book my flight to Karachi and book a hotel room for the night.

There were more words of warning.

"Look Gary, you need to understand that there is not the kind of relationship between Britain and Pakistan that is obvious here between Britain and the Emirates.

People disappear in Pakistan, British people Gary ... and no matter what diplomatic pressure is brought to bear, when it suits them, the Pakistanis will ignore all and any enquiries from the highest levels of government."

Melissa scribbled down a name, address and telephone number of someone who could be trusted in Karachi to provide whatever assistance I needed ... off the book!

"Here, take this. If you are in any kind of trouble ... including needing protection or a firearm, this is the place to go.

This telephone number will be answered round the clock.

Muhammad Attar is completely reliable and if you have to use him do not worry about the costs. He is on our books. Is that all clear Gary?"

"It is Melissa. I only have until tomorrow night to sort this problem out and come up with the sixty million in the correct numbered account at the DUCB."

"Do you know what will happen if you can't do that?"

I paused. No one had ever asked me that question. I didn't know the answer.

"No my dear Melissa ... unfortunately I do not!"

The flight was late; the Taxi journey to the Royal House Hotel hair-raising and the check-in procedure confusing. I was very much aware of the time and any possible meeting with Ali Hamza at the United Habib Bank head office on Daryalal Street.

Once in my room, I rang Mr. Hamza who sounded in very good spirits and advised me not to worry, he would wait for me to appear ... at whatever time.

I thanked him for his kindness and courtesy and for a moment or two, the pressure had been lifted. I might even find time for a cup of coffee and something light to eat.

The head office building of the United Habib Bank was an impressive eleven story building faced with marble and tinted glass. Mr Ali Hamza was also an impressive man who obviously had a good relationship with his tailor.

He stood at over six feet, owned a smile most

professional models would die for and his hands displayed a smooth, artistic quality that was hard to ignore. His handshake felt firm and not over dominant and to anyone in the banking game, this was the kind of man you could do business with.

His office contained the obligatory oversized mahogany desk, the two necessary leather visitor chairs for business visitors and a corner sofa set for less formal visitor events.

He steered me toward the sofa set.

"Tea ... or ... err ... coffee?" he asked after our initial greetings.

"No thank you sir." I offered with a smile.

"OK Mr. Chase ... let us begin ... and maybe see if there is any way I can help you?"

I ran through what I now considered to be a 'script' of what had been labeled as an 'unsettled' transaction of sixty million pounds sterling from the National Irish Bank in Dublin to the Dubai United Commercial Bank in the Emirates.

He listened carefully, his expression fixed, serious looking and giving nothing away.

Finally, I finished and sat back in the uncomfortable sofa expecting to see a glimmer of hope break through the otherwise stern air.

"I can see your dilemma Mr. Chase, but as I have already told our correspondent bank in Dubai, the full amount, less our commission of course, has been sent to the numbered account requested at the Dubai United Commercial Bank.

They have all the relevant details including the telex confirmation of authorisation codes and all that goes along with the transfer of such a large amount."

The disarming smile appeared once more.

"But it is not there Mr. Hamza ... that is what I have been told at the highest level. Mr. Abdul Kareem of the DUCB assures me they do not have it and according to the telex trace back to the National Irish Bank, your banks unique telex code appears as the receiving bank. So where do we go from here?"

The smile remained; the eyes however became immediately dark and threatening.

"That my friend is true. The amount DID arrive in our correspondent general account and was immediately cleared, processed, commissions deducted and sent on to the DUCB. This all happened within an hour of us receiving the initial transfer."

There was one question that simply had to be asked.

"So, perhaps you could tell me what your commission deduction would have been?"

Hamza coughed and reached for a glass of water resting on his desk.

"Err ... our commission structure is quite complex Mr. Chase and explaining it to you in detail means we might be here all day ..."

"Well sir, perhaps we could bypass all of that and you could simply tell me how much commission your bank pared off the original amount?"

The face had returned to a blank, neutral expression as he delivered the words 'ten percent'.

I felt my blood pressure rise.

"Ten percent?" I echoed in disbelief. "You are telling me you took six million pounds from the transfer. That sounds like a hell of a lot of money to me. Can you explain or in any way justify that amount?"

"As I told you before Mr. Chase, the banking system in general is a complex animal and even more so here in the Middle East."

Something was afoot here. Mr. Hamza was beginning to look a little nervous.

"So let me get this straight. The person or persons I represent have transferred what they think is sixty million to their numbered account in a Dubai based bank. However, before it actually get's there, it will have been reduced in value to fifty four million ... is that correct?"

"It is."

"And then ... if we ever find it, this figure will be reduced even more before it is credited to the necessary numbered account as I'm sure the DUCB will want their significant 'commissions' as well!"

"You are correct Mr. Chase."

There could be no doubt about it I had to be staring into the face of an out and out legalised criminal.

This whole damn business was a mess and it was becoming obvious that a major conspiracy was at work here. The big question was ... where in hell was the fucking money?

Time to stop messing about.

"I would like to see your telex machine Hamza."

"For what purpose Mr. Chase?"

"If you are able to show me the transmitted telex confirmation sent to your correspondent bank, the DUCB, then I can check that the codes are genuine, the physical key is un-tampered with and the actual amount of the transfer entered in your ledger."

"The telex machine is a complex piece of equipment Mr. Chase and I really can't allow some unqualified person access to it."

"I can assure you Mr. Hamza, there is no one you can name who is more qualified than me to investigate your machine ... and ..."

The telephone on Hamza's desk rang. He held a short conversation with someone in Arabic, his eyes fixed upon mine throughout the duration. He put the phone down and remained standing obviously reflecting on what had been just said.

He pulled a grey manila file from a desk draw and handed it to me.

"This is the file on the transaction under discussion. All the original paperwork is there and I need your promise there are to be no photocopies please ...!"

"I give you my word Mr. Hamza." I confirmed.

"OK ... I am quite willing to allow you access to our telex machine as long as you have our Senior Maintenance Manager with you at all times. You will appreciate this is a very sensitive piece of equipment and we need to guard its security!"

A Mr. Nair was introduced to me in the 'telex' room. It housed four machines, two of which were chattering away as I entered.

He took my outstretched hand with some

reluctance, the expression on his face best described as wary.

"Right Mr. Nair, let's get started."

This particular printer setup was reserved for financial transactions both internally inside Pakistan and Internationally. The machine, marked 'No 1 International', was on permanent standby to receive instructions.

I removed the cover to give access to the internal workings. The printer was fitted with a mechanical key and the first issue was to be the ease with which I was able to remove it. This device provided the necessary encryption for all 'Tested Telex' messages being received by and sent by this particular serial numbered machine.

I pulled it out of its socket and waved it in front of Mr. Nair.

"There is no lead seal on this key. Where is it?"

He sheepishly pulled open a drawer provided as part of the printer machine stand. It held a small clear plastic bag of half a dozen seals.

"Put them back in the drawer Mr. Nair. This is not looking good and we've only just started!"

For the next hour, I did every check possible on the machine. Things were far from perfect. Either the machine was operating incorrectly due to some error in the operating system, or someone had purposely been tampering with it ... someone with knowledge.

I replaced the original transmission confirmation back in the file, marked up in pencil with a BIC code different than the one shown on the confirmation page.

I copied all the information from the

transmission confirmation onto a clean sheet of printer paper and placed it in my pocket.

"Thank you Mr. Nair. I hope you are not complicit with whatever is going on here, but if you are then you should know that under any normal circumstances you have committed a criminal offence!"

The Senior Maintenance Manager left the room quickly and grabbed the nearest telephone. It looked as if things were about to warm up a little.

༺༻

Back with Hamza, this time I accepted the tea and was invited to sit at one of visitor chairs. I placed the account file carefully on the desk top.

"Our Mr. Nair appears to believe we have an issue with our Telex transfer system. Perhaps you can explain it to me."

I leaned forward and tapped the file with my finger.

"I can explain very easily and very quickly Hamza.

The money you say has been sent to the Dubai United Commercial Bank has physically gone elsewhere despite the DUCB code being correctly quoted in the printed confirmation."

"That is impossible my friend!"

"No Mr. Hamza, I'm afraid it is not and your Mr. Nair will be able to confirm the fact for you.

The encryption key is not locked in with a lead seal ... as it should be and the receiving bank's coded address has been 'cloaked'.

That action, on its own, takes some knowledge

and, dare I say, a lot more knowledge than your Mr. Nair appears to have."

The banker gave nothing away as he reached for the file, opened it and read the scribbled notes on the confirmation sheet.

He then asked one single question; one that revealed to me he was probably not behind this conspiracy to steal over fifty million pounds.

"So, do we know where the money has gone?"

"Judging from the International BICS Code Book, the money, all of it ..., has ended up at a bank somewhere in Peshawar."

He didn't look shocked, he didn't even look surprised. Picking up the phone once more he held a short conversation with someone internally. He looked calm and very controlled prompting me to think of the cruising swan.

"My Manager and deputy chairman of the bank, Mr. Salman Nadeem, would like to speak with you.

CHAPTER EIGHTEEN

A definite conspiracy ...

As I exited the front door of the United Habib Bank the oppressive heat and combined stifling humidity hit me. I stood for a minute before considering hailing a taxi, reflecting seriously on the conversations I had just had. Mr. Nadeem had proven to be a totally differing kettle of fish to the smooth talking Hamza.

I would have categorized him as a 'nasty piece of work' were he not deputy chairman of a major Pakistani banking concern.

The three metre tall plate glass door swung gently closed behind me and as it did so it picked up a reflection of everything that was going on immediately around me.

A flash of light, a glint on polished steel, a hesitant step from someone directly behind dressed in a full black niqab set alarm bells ringing. The light flashed once more on the shiny object and I began to turn in order to face what was to be an attack of some kind.

Adrenalin kicked in. I grabbed the raised arm, the six or seven inch blade now only inches away from my face.

Then, as quickly as the whole event had started ... it ended. I heard two 'pops'. The arm holding the knife became immediately limp as the black robed figure fell to the floor.

For a second or two I simply stood, rooted to the spot, expecting shouts of distress and a clamour of people surrounding the still twitching body.

This however was not to be the case. The throng of people pushing their way up and down the cracked pavement refused to allow a bleeding body to impair their progress.

A voice whispered in my ear in English.

"Follow me but not too close ... and say nothing to anybody. We need to get you away from here. If you understand, nod your head."

I nodded and the European looking man in the open necked shirt and jeans moved quickly away from the deathly scene with me following behind.

Having turned off the main roadway, a car pulled up beside the stranger and he beckoned me to get in the back of the car with him.

"Where are we going?" I asked.

"Well, not back to your hotel, that's for sure. I don't know what went on in there but 'our man' in the personnel department rang the alarm bell on you about half an hour ago. You are lucky to be alive!"

My mind had begun to work overtime. Had I jumped out of the frying pan ... and been somehow dragged into the damn fire?

"Who are you? Did you kill that Arab woman who was about to knife me right outside the bank?"

"My name is of no relevance right now and yes, I did shoot that 'person' who tried to kill you but it was no woman. It was a man, a trained assassin working for an Islamic terrorist group ... and for some unknown reason they want to see you dead."

"Hmm ..." was all I could offer in reply; my mind a whirl in the knowledge of how near I had just been to the call of death.

"We are going to the British Consulate, through the back door of course and then we will need to talk with you about what happens next."

I smiled.

"That should be interesting!"

The quite hum of air conditioning became the welcome background to my conversation with a certain Nigel Devereaux. He didn't look to be a military man, in fact he looked just the opposite; scruffily dressed, smoking a stinking pipe that did little to hide what might have been called a personal hygiene issue.

"Firstly, I need to know if I am within the recognised boundaries of the British Consulate. The answer to that query is either yes ... or no!"

My rescuer stood behind me, out of sight, and quite frankly, I felt insecure.

Devereaux replied calmly, puffing away at the polluting tobacco pipe, his eyes searching mine.

"Yes!" he said.

"Good, so that dispels my original thoughts that we might well be in some un-swept and derelict underground car park for reasons unknown to me."

My rescuer answered; the voice close to my right ear.

"This is indeed a car park and you are right; it is little used. However, it has a secure entrance and exit, has its own power and water supply and is buried ninety feet underground. When the shit hits the fan, this is the place everyone will want to be. Fortunately, until that day comes, we have the keys ... and can do with it as we wish."

Devereaux smiled.

"My second question is who the fuck are you people and how did you become involved in the failed attempt on my life? I hope the answer is a quick one as this bloody place gives me the creeps."

The answer came without hesitation.

"I am Nigel Devereaux, I hold the rank of Major in British Military Intelligence, section Nine."

"So, you are here to replace Ewan McAllister then ..."

Devereaux ignored the comment and continued.

"The person standing behind you; the person who saved your fucking life today is Simon Taggart. He is well known within the British Intelligence Services and usually hangs his hat at Vauxhall Cross. You may, or may not be familiar with that address."

"I am." I confirmed. "... and half the MI6 agents in the whole damn world would no doubt call it home as well Devereaux."

"Please be careful making assumptions Mr Chase. I said that Simon hangs his hat' there on occasion. I did NOT say he was a member of the strange institution you refer to as Military Intelligence Section Six. There is an important difference here, one that will allow us to progress with your search and hopefully bring it to a satisfactory conclusion."

He nodded to Taggart, who moved to my front.

"Let us get away from these dreary surroundings Gary and into the Consulate building itself. Keep your head down and low until we get to my office. We have spies and informers here within our structure, as do most other embassies and consulates in Pakistan. It's simply part of life old chap!"

Simon Taggard occupied a spacious if untidy office space with one wall of window glass giving out to an attractive view of the Boat Basin and Park.

With coffee and tea ordered and the three of us each settled in a chair, I needed to test the temperature of the water.

"So gentlemen, you have told me who you are, therefore can I ask what you know about me and why I am here ... in Pakistan?"

It became quickly obvious they knew quite a lot about me but limited knowledge of the movement of micro-chips from America and the payment by HMG of the three hundred million pound ransom paid to the IRA.

What they did know however, was that a sum of around sixty million sterling was slopping around somewhere within a crooked banking system, and I had been tasked with finding it.

The worry was that the money transfer from the IRA to some mysterious third party 'actor' had not been completed as agreed. HMG had delivered the ransom as requested and received the microchips sent from America.

So, as far as they were concerned, they had no more interest in the matter and to use a well known Americanism, 'what was the beef?'

I explained that although HMG had no real responsibility in how the IRA managed its business, the fact they had been unable to deliver the sixty million 'commission' to whoever had been supplying them with intelligence was of concern to HMG.

The money had somehow disappeared in the International Banking System and that was also of concern to HMG. So, they wanted two answers to two simple questions; where the fuck was the supposedly lost sixty million and what is the identity of the individual providing the IRA with intelligence.

"Let me tell you this. The whole of Ireland is after putting their hands on this missing money; the IRA, the Provo's and now this new completely violent gang of bandits known as the Ulster Defence Association.

Finally, there is the person who was looking to receive it in the first place. Whoever he or she is, they appear to be well placed and their intelligence is completely up to the mark. My Boss, Marshall Brooking believes it is a high ranking military person ... and so does the Prime Minister!"

Direct reference to the PM made both men sit up and take notice. Taggart had a question.

"Are you telling us your current 'adventure' here in sunny Karachi is authorised by the PM? "

"I am ... and much as I would like to thank you for saving my life today, this is the second attempt in a week ... and in the last one, two good men died because of it. Therefore, if you can find a suitable way of getting me the fuck out of here and back to Dubai, I would be forever in your debt."

Taggart and Devereaux exchanged meaningful glances. It was a 'should we or should we not' kind of silent exchange.

"If you have something to say gentlemen, please say it!"

Devereaux pondered on the matter for a while and then spoke but seeming to chose his words carefully.

"We didn't know all the detail of the Irish business. As far as we are concerned, we were advised an extraordinary amount of crooked money was about to pass through the Gulf banking system in one big transfer. We were not told any of the detail except the amount ... sixty million quid."

Taggard nodded his head in agreement.

"We were told to keep an eye on you the minute you left Dubai and cutting through all the bullshit ... that's what we did."

"There must be more to it than that." I said.

"Oh ... there is Gary ... there most certainly is and the big question now, as we fight against the damn clock, is, do you know how the fuck they did it. How did they capture the sixty million ... and where is it now?"

"Oh yes ... I know exactly how they did it but where it actually is right now is not that clear. I know where it should be and as long as no-one has 'cashed in the chips' yet, it can still be recovered."

The two uncomfortable looking intelligence officers exchanged glances once more.

"So, where is it?" asked Taggart.

I pulled the single sheet of Telex paper from my pocket and read from it.

"Right now it's in the branch of a Saudi owned bank in Peshawar ... the home base of a collection of bandits, murderers and fanatical terrorists I understand."

Both men in front of me nodded their heads

"Do you know of a way in there?" I asked innocently.

They both laughed.

"It's not the kind of place you want to spend a weekend Gary. If this money really is sitting on some machine or other in Peshawar, then it will not be long before it's converted into US Dollars ... real US Dollars Gary. It will then be strapped to the back of a camel, over the mountains and on its way to Jalalabad. Once it's physically in Afghanistan ... you can count on it as gone Gary."

"Is it really that bad?"

"Not only is it becoming a major world producer of hard drugs, the aftermath of the worst drought in the country's history has wrecked the economy. Russian interference in political and security affairs has not been welcomed and the whole region is uncomfortable with the current situation; some even fear an eventual invasion by the Soviets. If you thought the bloody IRA could give you some trouble in Ireland ... playing around with this lot could start world war three ... and that's a fact my friend!"

"So how do we get at this money ... if it's still

in Peshawar." I asked. "That's a very good question Gary ... a very good question indeed."

"Well gentlemen ..." offered Simon Taggart. "Let's call in some food and give the matter a serious amount of thought."

The meal arrived in an amazing collection of small aluminium pots and it was surprisingly good. Devereaux conjured up a chilled bottle of white wine from somewhere and when the desk-top was finally cleared, everyone wore a look of complete satisfaction.

Taggart who had spoken little between courses was the first to offer a solution to the problem. To him, it was all quite simple.

"Well guys, if all these fairly devious characters have managed to steal all this money using a standard Telex machine and a little skulduggery, why can't we?"

"Why can't we what?" offered a curious Taggart.

"Why can't we use the same methods, employed by others, to take back the money? All they had to steal it with in the first place was a Telex machine ... and a numbered bank account.

Devereaux and I exchanged thoughtful looks.

"Is that really possible?" he asked.

"Well Nigel, it absolutely should be, but to find out we will need a Telex machine set-up, a blank encryption key and a numbered bank account."

Taggart's face lit up.

"Well if that's all you need then we have a

whole bloody room full of Telex machines downstairs in the basement and the Ministry of Defence has several numbered bank accounts in the Swiss Commercial International Bank based in Zurich.

These accounts are kept 'live' and used by the MoD Purchasing and Procurement Group mainly for money movements connected to military arms transactions.

I'm sure that just one phone call would give us access to something worthwhile"

Devereaux, still buried in thought, began to nod his head. Perhaps ... just perhaps, it might be possible, but time was not on their side. Once the damn money moved outside of Pakistan it would be lost forever.

"So, what's the objective?" I asked.

"To get the money out of Peshawar and into Zurich as quickly as possible ... and before we create some sort of International incident, I really do need to know if you can do it?"

I considered the question for several seconds.

"I can only do my best Nigel."

He turned to Taggart, whose face was now alight with energy. He just wanted to get started.

"Right Simon! You find Gary what he needs downstairs. I'll get on the blower to UK and see if we can get us a numbered Swiss bank account.

There were eleven Telex installations in the basement 'Comms' centre. Nine were used for general day to day communications and two installed in sound-proofed, windowless rooms. They were reserved for 'secure' messaging and fitted with encryption keys.

The Head of Station had approved their use by Taggart, although he didn't have any idea what they might eventually become involved in. There would be no exchange of paperwork, just a shake of the hand and a finger to the lips.

As for Devereaux's phone call to London, this took a little longer until he was able to speak to the PM directly. If what I had told him was true he saw no problem involving the man directly. In other words, someone simply needed to crap ... or get off the damn pot!

Devereaux's request was granted immediately and along with an account number came the name and telephone number of the banking official in Zurich who would provide assistance.

CHAPTER NINETEEN

A diversion ... or another robbery?

The particular abilities and exceptional knowledge of Gary Chase had been sold to Nigel Devereaux by the Prime Minister, over the phone. He certainly appeared to have a lot of faith in someone so young and Nigel hoped he would not be disappointed.

The confused and somewhat affronted Consular official, responsible for all 'comms' systems at the British Consulate in Karach, had handed over installation number ten to the 'intelligence guys' and when asking if they required his assistance, they all politely replied in the negative. However, three cups of tea; milk and two sugar lumps in each, would be most welcome.

"Will you be able to explain to us what you will be doing and how it's done Gary?" Devereaux asked.

"As best I can Nigel." replied Gary. "The first job is to establish communications with the bank in Peshawar and see if the money is still there."

"Is that possible?" asked Taggart.

"Yes it's possible, unless they have moved it from the receiving account to another internal account. Finding that will be much more difficult, but I suspect, not impossible!"

"Right ... let's get down to it!"

Gary Chase had the single sheet of telex paper in front of him. He was carrying out some calculations, scribbling the answers next to lines of typewritten information.

"The first thing I have to do is strip out the authentication code used by the receiving bank and load it on a blank key, a key I have already inserted in this machine. This allows me to talk to the Peshewar based machine and hopefully check the account number used to transfer the money."

Fifteen minutes later, Gary had what he required. However, to get there he had generated over seventy pages of teletype full of numbered and mixed letter code.

The communications specialist read and re-read the code for another hour before declaring he could find no evidence the money might be sitting in a general escrow account. If it was, it might be sitting there alongside several other large amounts. Gary announced

"This is not what I regard as a particularly great piece of luck gents, but if we can crack the code for this escrow account, not only do we stand a chance of stealing our own money back, we might also be able to clean out the whole fucking account."

"How much might that be?" asked an excited Taggart.

"Possibly an extra fifteen or twenty million dollars." said Chase.

Devereaux's normally inscrutable expression turned into a wide, encouraging grin.

"Well, let's damn well go for it!"

Gary Chase became immediately infused. In

the pile of script he had generated were listed a series of account numbers and now would come the laborious job if identifying them. He might need everyone's help in filtering them out.

Once the middle four numbers could be identified, then they would act as a key to all the others. This collection of code would be identified simply by the number of times they appeared on the output sheet taken from the printer.

An hour later, Gary jumped up out of his seat shouting ... 'Gotcha!' The middle code was 2977. Every account must have that configuration of numbers in its title, a title consisting only of numbers. They would also appear in the same place in the numbered account, such as five in from the beginning, or six in from the end depending how many numbers the account code consisted of.

Tracking down the escrow account number took only minutes; it was simply the number that appeared the most amount of times, as money was moved in and out of the account many times a day.

Might it be possible the much searched-for sixty million could still be in there?

Taggart had a question.

"What happens if it's not in this escrow account? What if it's been moved out? Where does that leave us Gary?"

The Royal Air Force communications specialist turned to face the other two directly.

"If we make an attempt to capture all ... or even any of the money in this escrow account ... and there is nothing in there ... then alarm bells will ring throughout the bank and beyond. This interrogating telex identity and the answerback code, will be exposed as being attached to the British Consulate in Karachi. As a result there will be a major fucking International incident ... and heads will roll, including all of ours!"

Silence.

"And if the money IS in there ... what then?"

"The system will treat the instruction as 'competent' as long as the correct 'answerback' codes are received. Then, without any further verification, it should hopefully transfer the amount of money requested.

It will move more or less instantaneously out of escrow in the Peshewar bank and land in the numbered bank account we have nominated.

"Big risk ..." muttered Taggart.

"Big reward ..." commented Devereaux.

Gary explained he would need to send the complete communication by punching it onto a tape feeding an automatic transmitter. This is to ensure the data will travel at a rate of around seventy words a minute and remain uninterrupted for the length of the transmission. The quality of the telephone service used by both machines will dictate everything else.

"We are in your hands Gary. All this is simply gobbledygook to us, so whatever you need to do ... you should do it ... and we will be right behind you if the shit hit's the damn fan!"

Gary Chase cut the tape and after running through a reader, corrected several mistakes and misplaced spaces. Finally, he had a tape he considered to be as perfect as he could make it and he printed out the data for a final read-through.

"Are we set?" asked Nigel Devereaux.

"As we will ever be." confirmed Chase.

The simple pressing of a button kickstarted the whole operation as the Telex machine burst into life and then clattered away for what seemed to be an age.

Finally, after some minutes, the last page of four rotated to the top of the printer carriage. Then the machine fell silent.

Gary Chase ripped off the message and studied the contents, much of it in code.

He smiled, giving his attention to the two anxious faces in front of him.

"It worked. We asked for a transfer of a round sixty million ... and it has sent that complete amount."

"When can we check with the Swiss Commercial International Bank, to see if our money is really there?"

"Give me a few minutes." offered Chase.

The 'few minutes' turned into half an hour but when he entered Devereaux's office waving a piece of telex paper, all three knew it had somehow worked. The money was now under their control, in a Swiss bank account, and they knew it was secure ... or was it?

No doubt, when the managers of the United Habib Bank awoke that morning, all hell would break loose. They would no doubt be starting a search for their money and the only clue they might have would be an answerback code for a community bank in Kerala, South India.

"So, what do we do now?" asked Chase.

"Get some sleep and see what the world looks like when we wake up!"

Taggart smiled.

"I'll second that!" he muttered.

At five o'clock that afternoon 'noise' within the International banking system began to grow louder. There were rumours of a technical robbery having taken place for many millions of dollars and the whole of the Pakistani banking telecoms system had been shut down and de-linked from trading with the rest of the world.

This was causing major problems, both financial and political. However, several hours after the event, no one appeared to know what had really happened. The way the 'robbery' was carried out pointed to a person, or persons, with an awful lot of technical knowledge; in-depth knowledge in fact concerning the way the Teleprinter transmission code system worked.

At five thirty Devereaux received a phone call from Number Ten on a secure line. After a few minutes of discussion, the phone was handed to Gary. The PM wanted to congratulate him on what he called a 'splendid' job. Naturally, he did not want to hear any of the detail. What he didn't know, he didn't need to lie about.

Gary had a question.

"Where do we go from here Prime Minister? We now have the cash back under our control. So, do we give it back to the IRA or back to the numbered account at the DUCB in Dubai?"

The pause was unsettling. Even the fucking Prime Minister did not have a clear plan of what was to happen next?

"I think the best thing to do right now is for you to get back to Dubai whilst I have conversations with Magpie.

We have passed the forty eight hour deadline and he will need to make contact with his 'informant' in order to carry on with the transfer. Ring me when you get back to Dubai.

The Consulate in Karachi will sort out your flight and hotel booking. Stay safe!"

The line disconnected.

Gary briefed the two Intelligence officers about the plan and that the first step would be to get to Dubai and by then, hopefully a decision would have been made about the movement of funds.

A smiling young lady from 'personnel' arrived an hour later with Gary's documents and a ticket to Dubai for the eleven o'clock flight.

"Are they sending you in there on your own?" Devereaux asked; a certain level of concern in his voice.

"Yes they are. All I will need to do, when the money is transmitted, is confirm with the Dubai United Commercial Bank that the money is accounted for electronically ... and then I shall leave. I really don't see too much of an issue with that. It's not as if I'm being sent in there to kill someone ... is it?"

Taggart and Devereaux exchanged worrying looks.

"If you want us to come with you, we have no problem with that. What you don't quite realise is that 'the operation' you have been involved with has pissed off a lot of people over the past couple of weeks ... and the common denominator amongst all of it is ... YOU!

The IRA may not appear outwardly hostile, but they might consider you to have somehow been involved in the murder of several of their top men. There are some who may well be looking for revenge." said Deveraux.

"You have a similar situation with the other side, the UDA ... the Ulster Defence Association. These are all undisciplined young men; thugs and murderers and mostly off the damn leash.

They also want some, if not all, of the money ... and could well see you as either standing in the way ... or being the key to capturing the sixty mil yet again!" confirmed Taggart.

"And then last, but certainly not least, you have just stolen a big lump of money from a bunch of terrorists, probably the Afghan Mujahedeen and these guys do not have forgiveness in their soul.

Included in the 'danger' zone will be whatever criminal gangs are hunting down this money in Dubai. If they get even a sniff of what you are involved in, they will cut your damned throat as easily as shaking your fucking hand.

They have tried once in Karachi ... they will not fail the next time ...!"

Taggart interrupted.

"Then of course there is the small matter of the exploding Range Rover. This shows you are not safe even in the UK. To undertake the manufacture of such a well engineered explosive device, this operator must have resources ... significant resources."

Gary remained thoughtful as he absorbed everything he was hearing. Put to him as it had been made him wonder if this was not really the end game he thought it to be.

Finally, he shared his thoughts.

"Look guys, I see where you are coming from but I'm sure the Consulate in Dubai will be able to offer me some form of viable security, certainly sufficient to keep me safe for a day or so."

Devereaux and Taggart exchanged glances once more. They were not believers but both nodded their head to indicate their tacit agreement.

Nigel Devereaux had a question.

"You talk about 'the money being accounted for electronically' ... but what does that mean? The DUCB cannot receive the funds directly as they still need to physically pass through their commercial correspondent, being the United Habib Bank in Karachi. We know this bank is corrupt and therefore ends up being a dead end."

Gary gave out his explanation.

"By the time I get to Dubai the PM will have spoken to 'Magpie' his most senior source within the IRA High Command. I expect these two gentlemen to have come to an agreement to send the money by Telex transfer to the Foreign Office Emirates Escrow Account at the Gulf British Bank.

Once I am content the money is available and has been transferred electronically, I will authorise its movement to the DUCB in Dubai. This will be an internal 'country' bank to bank transfer. The whole process will be under my control from start to finish. Once done, I'm on my way home!"

"When will you know that all of this routing and re-routing is approved Gary?" asked Taggart.

"By a phone call from the PM either before I leave here or ..."

Devereaux's office telephone rang; the atmosphere in the untidy room tense.

Taggart spoke again.

"And if the answer is initially no, what is the plan 'B' ...?

"There is no plan 'B'." said Gary.

Deveraux handed over the instrument.

"It's the PM for you!"

"I hope you have some good news for me Prime Minister!"

The voice at the other end confirmed the news was indeed good and the transfer of funds, as agreed, was now approved.

Gary Chase asked the one searching question.

"How many people know what's about to happen here in Dubai Prime Minister? Can you assure me that such knowledge is limited?"

"I can", replied the PM "and to keep it that way there must be no more communication between you and me until the job is done. Whatever happens now is down to you and my continuing advice is to take care.

By a quarter to eleven, the PIA flight to Dubai was loaded; doors closed and ready to go. If it managed to pull up the wheels on time, Gary would be in

Dubai in just over two hours; enough to catch up on a few minutes of sleep.

Once inside Dubai arrivals and queuing at immigration, a young man in an open necked shirt and crumpled linen suit told Gary he was from the Consulate. A booking for him had been made at the Ambassador Hotel.

An official car waited outside the airport and after dropping the visitor at the hotel, the young, rather bored looking official informed him he would be collected at eight o'clock the following morning.

Whilst on route to the hotel, the young man handed me a package.

"This is a Makarov 9mm with three spare clips and an ankle holster. I am instructed to hand it to you sir, but do not open the package until you are in your room.

We understand this is a weapon you are familiar with ... but let us hope you do not have to use it. The young man smiled as Gary exited the car. He wondered what the straight faced individual might really do at the Consulate, other than issue undercover weaponry.

Sleep, a long hot shower and a great English breakfast transformed Gary completely. The driver appeared on time to take him to the Gulf British Bank where he was introduced to the senior bank staff. This included the Communications Manager responsible for all electronic communications transmitted and received by the bank. He had with him several of his staff.

Finally, he shook hands with the senior HMG consular official in Dubai, a stern looking individual who did not like 'going off-book' with anything to do with his role as the face of Britain here in the politically sensitive Arabian Gulf.

His name was Cuthbert Brown Whitehaven and he simply introduced himself as 'Whitehaven'. The man responsible for communications and their associated security was a middle aged Asian man named Akshay Bhatia. He carried about him a permanent smile and looked eager to please.

After the introductions, Whitehaven declared he had no interest in any further proceedings except to confirm whatever Mr. Chase needed should be provided by the bank.

He finally confirmed that this unusual working arrangement had the full authority of the British Prime Minister. However, there was to be nothing in writing; no other written instruction of any kind ... and ALL contact with the PM forbidden. Whitehaven left the room and despite the way events were about to unfold, would not be seen again.

CHAPTER TWENTY

A time for delicate negotiations

Mr. Akshay Bhatia guided me to the lower ground floor level where a battery of Telex machines had been installed. Some were chattering away beneath their sound absorbing canopies, some half stripped for maintenance and others rested and waiting for an activation code to wake them up.

He was a very friendly sort of chap; eager to get on with whatever I asked of him. He picked one of the silent machines and typed in a six letter code. The printer clattered into life.

I explained to Akshay that we were about to instigate a 'shake hands' procedure to open a secure, uninterrupted line between this machine and one in the Swiss Commercial International Bank, Zurich branch. An amount of money; a very large amount of money was to be transferred from this particular Swiss bank to the Consulate escrow account here, at the Gulf British Bank.

"What about fees?" Bhatia asked.

"There is an agreement between the two banks that the transfer will be 'clean' of all charges and is to be a round figure of sixty Million Pounds Sterling.

The Communications Manager raised an eyebrow. This was probably the first time he had heard the number!

I waited for a minute to allow the importance of the matter in hand to sink in; then asked the question.

"What do you know about 'cloaking' of dialled numbers; redirecting answerback codes and interrogating file security; mostly achieved by sending information 'packets' or data strippers to a receiving client, through the Telex line connection?"

Mr. Bhatia looked initially surprised at my question, but then couldn't help release a short, slightly self-conscious laugh. The answer came quickly.

"Err ... probably not as much as you ... Mr. Chase."

"Well, our transfer will take place at eleven o'clock our time and when the Swiss bank 'signs on' to the link request, I want you to run a cloaking check of the answerback code before I authorise the release of the money. You will need a second machine of course. Are you with me ... do you know what I want you to do?"

"Yes." confirmed Akshay Bhatia.

"Right then ... I think we have time for a cup of tea. Make sure the two Telex machines we are going to use are secure and kept powered down until we need them."

The two communications specialists moved to Bhatia's office for a refreshing tea and to wait for the hands of the clock to nudge up closer to eleven.

I hoped there would be no complications and Akshay Bhatia expected he might learn something today.

At ten-fifty I rang the Engineering Manager at the Swiss Commercial International Bank to confirm the Telex systems to be used for the transfer were all working and online. After a short conversation I instigated a 'shake hands' procedure to enable one machine to recognise the other on line.

"Keep your wits about you Mr. Bhatia and check the answerback has the right number of letters and numbers ... all in the right sequence."

With the line still open between the two banks, one in Dubai and the other in Zurich, the transfer was initiated. The Telex machine began to chatter. The instruction confirmation came through as a printed page leaving Bhatia to print out pages of code on his system.

The machines stopped; the sudden silence whisper quiet, and quite unsettling. I scanned the printed output. It all looked to be good. The contact in Zurich confirmed the transaction ledger had been updated and Bhatia's quick call to the accounts controller confirmed the amount of sixty million pounds sterling now lay with them in escrow.

Smiles all round. They had done it. Now all that was left was to make a transfer, bank to bank, in-country from the Gulf British Bank to the Dubai United Commercial Bank ... and then ... the job would finally be complete!

"Thank you Mr. Bhatia, you have been most helpful and if I were you, I would keep that fifteen or twenty pages of code you generated ... just in case!"

Both men smiled. They both knew what 'just in case' meant. Because they had hands-on the cash right now did not mean things would stay that way. Bankers, being only slightly less corrupt than lawyers, had a habit of handling money with often quite sticky fingers. As a result, someone, in some bank or other, somewhere down the line, might even have to prove it ever existed in the first place.

Now to deal with the DUCB and with telephone in hand I made the call.

"Can I speak with your Operations Manager, Mr. Abdul Kareem please ... and tell him Mr. Chase is calling."

A minute later a familiar voice came on the line.

"Good afternoon Mr. Chase. How pleasant to hear from you again. It looks as if you have been making a few waves in Pakistan ... and ... if everything I hear is true, you somehow seemed to have just about shut down all banking communications with the outside world. That is so clever of you Mr. Chase ... so clever indeed!"

The tone came across as menacing but I simply had to ignore the jibe. The last part of my job needed to be done and I could not do it without his assistance. I would need to swallow any reservations I might have and just damn well get on with it.

"I would like to meet with you Mr. Kareem, as soon as possible, to finalise the movement of the money your client is expecting in his ... or her ... account."

"My door is always open to you Gary. If you would like to pop along to the office this morning, we can hopefully have this mess cleared up by lunchtime and you can be on your way to sunny Scarborough by this afternoon!"

The line fell to silence. Abdul Kareem had 'left the building.'

I pondered on his final remark for a while. How did Mr. Kareem know I lived in Scarborough? I had never told him that. Perhaps he knew more about me than he should. I would need to be on my guard with him!

I offered my thanks to everyone who had helped me at the GBB and slipped out the side entrance, arm raised hoping to garner the attention of a local taxi. I needed to cross the creek via the bridge and head down a busy Bin Yas Road.

The Operations Manager at the DUCB occupied a 'goldfish bowl' office. It consisted of glass curtain walling lodged in the middle of a sea of desks. They filled one whole floor of the upmarket office building. Each desk appeared to be attended by an Asian man or woman, ploughing through files or attacking a noisy mechanical typewriter.

The walls were lined with dozens of filing cabinets and there appeared to be a substantial traffic of people moving in and out of the busy office space.

I sat inside the glass office, listening to the low hum of air-conditioning and taking in some of the outside activity whilst Kareem organised some tea. He was, as usual, smiling and attentive and had greeted me with an obvious level of enthusiasm. Whilst encapsulated there, idly scanning the occupants of the main office, I noticed a European man, in the distance. He entered the floor from a distant elevator. Strangely, Kareem was with him.

Something niggled in my mind. From such a

distance, the face of the European looked slightly familiar. Abdul Kareem and he were engaged in hot conversation. The stranger suddenly turned his head. He looked in my direction. A bell rang somewhere in my mind; a bell warning of danger. Even from such a distance, our eyes locked for a brief second. I stood up. The European pushed past Abdul and exited through a door next to the elevator. There could be no doubt that Abdul Kareem had not been making tea.

I sat down again as Abdul disappeared into the elevator. The face worried me. I was too far away to be sure but if I had to put money on it ... I would have voted for Tarquin Ludlow.

When Kareem came back, bearing a small tray carrying two glass cups filled with sweet Arabic tea, I asked him the question.

"Who was that European guy you were standing with, near the elevator, just a few minutes ago?"

"European ... elevator? Oh that would have been our British Audit Manager ... Keith."

"Hmm ..." I offered.

That was a lie. The more I thought about it, the more I became convinced the European visitor might well have been Tarquin ... and the big question was ... what the fuck was he doing here?

Abdul Kareem maintained his manufactured smile ... and I maintained my suspicions.

"Well Abdul, perhaps we should get down to business. I have a sum of sixty million sitting in a bank less than a mile away from here and that bank is desperate to move it over to you. So do you think we can do that today?"

"I am sure we can my dear friend. Tell me what you need, other than all the normal wired transfer requirements, and I will arrange it immediately."

An hour later, the transfer had progressed smoothly and each bank had confirmed their ledgers had been updated accordingly. The sum of sixty million pounds sterling now lay with Dubai United Commercial Bank. It would be transferred to a numbered account immediately and with a big sigh of relief, I could now say goodbye to Abdu Kareem.

As we shook hands for what I hoped would be the final time, he muttered his thanks and added a word of warning.

"Be careful my friend. You are still a target. Although this mess now appears to have been sorted out, you are still seen in some way or other as responsible."

"But all I have done Abdul is chase the damn money and bring it all back to where it's supposed to be ... surely no-one can see any wrongdoing in that?" I insisted.

"Well consider this Gary. You have severely annoyed more than one fearsome terrorist group in Ireland who wanted that money to buy arms.

Then you have caused chaos for legitimate banks in Pakistan and Dubai who wanted big chunks of commission to fall their way during the transfers. Finally, there are the 'kin' of all those who lost their lives over the past week or so. Some are wealthy, others are well connected and a small minority are simply full of determined vengeance."

Abdul Kareem smiled now but his eyes had suddenly lost their twinkle.

"You seem to know a lot about this whole business Abdul. In fact an awful amount more than you would have gotten from any briefings by British Intelligence."

He leaned forward.

"If I were you, I would leave by the rear entrance ... and then catch the very first flight out of here ... wherever it's damn well going!"

He picked up his desk phone and spoke to some anonymous individual.

"Get Mr Chase a taxi and have it waiting for him at the rear entrance ... and stay with it until he gets there."

"Goodbye Abdul." I said; resisting the urge to question him further about the identity of the mysterious European. He was far more untrustworthy than he would have me believe.

I took the elevator to the basement and then through a door indicated to me by one of the perspiring staff busy sorting cleaning materials and organising waste into skips.

I entered the bright sunlight, pulling my Polaroid glasses down over my eyes as I turned in the direction of the voice.

"Over here sir." the voice said. "Your taxi is here sir. Where do you want to go?"

Before I could answer, the first shot rang out.

"Get down for God's sake.

Hit the damn floor!" I shouted.

That first shot must have gone over my head and the three following shots looked to have spread out to my right. This was an opportunity.

I dived to my left, landing just behind a heavy steel skip and giving out a protected view of the taxi. 'The voice' was looking for an escape point and had already managed to move several feet away from the Taxi.

I shouted ...

"When I fire ... you move as quickly as you fucking well can towards that door and get yourself inside that building."

He looked terrified.

I recovered the Makarov 9mm from the ankle holster, pulled the safety and checked the magazine.

"Now!" I shouted as loud as I could, at the same time rising up from behind the skip and moving forward, gun in hand, arms fully forward and firing. There were two occupants in the wreck of a car; one driving and one in the rear seat with an AK.

I fired six rounds whilst searching for another clip in my pocket ... moving forward all the time. Two rounds hit the driver. As he slumped forward over the steering wheel, the shooter raised his head.

It was just enough ... and I had only two rounds left in the magazine. I let them both go and the top part of his head disintegrated.

Unfortunately, one of the rounds from the AK had taken down 'the voice' only a few feet away from safety. He had taken the full force of the bullet in his left shoulder; he would survive!

The sound of sirens echoed in the distance as I quickly inspected the car and its two dead occupants. I then moved up to check 'the voice'. He kept saying he was sorry but what for ... I could not quite understand. His wound was nasty but fully survivable ... so thank God for that small mercy.

Four police cars arrived minutes later filled with policemen bearing arms. My gun was taken from me and the spare clips. A softly spoken uniformed Captain ushered me into his car and told me we would be going to Deira Police Station.

CHAPTER TWENTY- ONE

A deathly event ... an untimely end!

No one spoke as the police car transported me on the short journey to the police station. Once there, I was directed to a small room of stifling proportions, containing the all pervading odour of stale sweat ... and cold fear. There was only one small widow opening, high up on what I presumed to be an outside wall, allowing the Arabian energy sucking heat to pour in through it.

The room contained furniture; a small square table bolted to the floor and four cheap plastic chairs of the type one would see on 'special offer' at the local supermarket.

After some time, the Police captain entered the room. He sat down opposite me and officially introduced himself. He held a green file containing no more than a dozen or so loose leaf items, placing it carefully in the space between us.

Handcuffs restricted my movements considerably and without any discussion, the Captain released me from them.

"Thank you sir!" I offered.

He smiled.

"Two people are dead Mr. Chase. Shot to death by a gun you were apparently issued with ... illegally. Eye witnesses state, with absolute certainty, that you were the shooter. So, do you have anything to say to me?"

From Consulate staff briefings I knew Captain Said was a Dubai national. I also knew he was being groomed to be Dubai's first local police chief.

He had been sent away to study English and attended the Police College at Hendon. He held a university degree in criminal law and recently attended the senior leader course at the London Police College.

I had been assured that at the age of thirty two, Said Al Bhani was a switched on police officer with more power in the Emirate of Dubai than even he would care to admit.

The current head of the police force was a Brit, a full Colonel, with complete control of the paramilitary operation dealing with murder, smuggling, white-slaving, corruption and kidnapping on a regular basis.

However, when any mischievousness involved a Brit, Colonel Whitmore-Parker would normally stay clear of it, anxious to ensure no favours were asked for ... or given.

Captain Said looked relaxed and confident as he sat opposite me, perhaps waiting for the obvious question, tapping the file in front of him, in order to focus my attention.

"I would just like to know what's actually happening and if the British Consulate might be aware of my predicament?"

"What's happening ... Mr. Chase ... is that you are being questioned with regard to the act of murder ... The head of the British Consulate is aware we are talking to you and where you are being ... err ... held!"

I was sure he could read the state of confusion showing in my face. I had been told; no ... warned of becoming involved with the police. Historically, the beatings would have begun more or less immediately and diplomatic officials not advised for some time, or even days after incarceration.

"I need you to tell me what you have been up to in order to arrive at a point where you feel you must carry a weapon ... and then kill two people with it ... in broad daylight. I can only advise you to leave nothing out ... you will only have one chance to give me your side of the story."

He tapped the file again. It was worrying; however, I had nothing to loose ... so I gave him the lot!

Over two hours and nearly a bottle or warm water later, I had finished; well finished in terms of some it, the bit that would have been of interest to Captain Said.

"I'll be back in a moment." Said Al Bhani announced, his expression fixed and unrevealing. He took the file with him and I waited anxiously in the oppressive room for fifteen long minutes.

A uniformed sergeant finally collected me and showed me into a large office space with a desk at one end occupied by a uniformed middle aged European showing the rank of Colonel.

This could only have been Whitmore-Parker.

Standing behind him was Captain Said.

"Come in Mr. Chase." commanded the Colonel "Take a seat."

He waved to the two straight backed wooden chairs in front of the desk.

I sat down. Colonel Parker had the green file in front of him. He looked me straight in the eye. This looked to be a man of few words and I knew I would be best advised to listen to every damn one of them.

"You are in a very dangerous situation Mr. Chase. Do you know who the two gunmen were who tried to kill you?"

"No, I'm afraid I don't."

"Well, we do ... and the best advice I can give you right now is to get to the Consulate and stay there until your flight leaves for the UK. We will take you to the Consulate and we will collect you and take you to the airport. Do you understand?"

I needed some thought time. This was all a bit of a rush.

"Do you understand Mr. Chase?"

The words held more emphasis, the delivery more positive.

"Yes sir ... I understand, but I don't know the reason why?"

Captain Said spoke for the first time.

"You have pissed off a lot of people Mr. Chase. These people hold life in very low regard and will therefore keep on sending assassins to hunt you down. You may not want to pick the place and time of your death but what we need to make sure of is that it does NOT happen here. Do we make ourselves clear?"

"It is clear gentlemen." I said having given up the battle to find out more about today's incident.

Colonel Parker closed off the conversation.

"Captain Said will show you out and we have a car and armed officers waiting for you outside.

Goodbye Mr. Chase ... and I do not expect that we will meet again!"

I exited the office with Captain Said holding my arm and guiding me through the mêlée of people in the general reception area.

Heads bobbed up and down and people pushed against one another, some quite violently, in attempts to communicate with barricaded police officers behind a wall of scarred and cracked Perspex.

I saw him only for a second. I shouted out.

"General ... General Ludlow ...!"

The bobbing head turned in my direction. I could see about three quarters of his face ... but it was definitely him.

Said pulled me closer.

"That's him ... that's the General." I shouted once more and within yet another second he had disappeared from view.

"Please don't shout Mr. Chase or else I will have to cuff you again ... do you understand?"

"But that is the General I have been telling you about. What the fuck is he doing here? I saw him at the bank, but wasn't too sure. Now I am sure. It's definitely him!"

The police officer pushed me roughly through the narrow entrance to the packed enquiries area and out onto the street. The calmness had disappeared and the level of frustration revealed as Captain Said delivered me to two police officers waiting by a green and white police car.

"Whatever 'bee' you have in your damned bonnet Mr Chase, my advice to you is to ignore it. Simply get on the flight that is booked for you tomorrow morning and return to the UK. If, for any reason you are still here tomorrow afternoon, I will arrest you. Let me assure you any time spent languishing in our prison system will be a time you will remember for the rest of your damn life. Now ... GO!"

The police car pulled away with spinning wheels and a cloud of dust. Like it or not, it looked as if I would be ending back up at the Consulate again ... and this time the head of station was not particularly pleased to see me.

However, there would be no questions, no interrogation and no investigation. Number Ten had been advised of my predicament and made no comment. David Brooking had also been made aware of the 'incident' outside the DUCB and asked that I be shipped back to the UK ASAP. A room had been made available to me inside the Consular residence and I was asked not to leave it without some form of discussion and approval of the Consulate security team. I agreed of course. I was now completely fed-up with the whole fucking process. Someone seemed to be playing a dirty game here and as Patrick O'Breian had accurately surmised, it was someone with power and influence!

However, As a result of 'fixing' the transfer of funds to the DUCB, I now owned one small but valuable item of information, scribbled in pencil on a piece of scrap paper.

This was the bank's internal interrogation code for the numbered account of the mysterious "twenty per-cent person', man or woman, who knows?

Whoever that person was, they appeared to be at the centre of all this bloody carnage and as a result of all my hard work had ended up sitting on a nice pile of sixty million quid ... a very nice sum indeed!

When I was able to return to my office and sit in front of my own Telex machine, I might very well learn a lot more.

The seven and a half hour flight to Heathrow allowed me to catch up on some much needed sleep. Before settling down, I made one or two trips up and down the aisles checking to see if there were any faces I knew ... or any faces that might look suspicious.

Everything looked good ... and finally I could relax.

Navigating Customs and Immigration turned out to be a standard, smiling affair with no-one raising even a questioning eyebrow.

I headed for the rail station, planning to catch the regular half hourly shuttle to London's Victoria. There I would be able to catch a service to Scarborough.

The journey was cold and uncomfortable and by the time I arrived in Scarborough I was not in the best of moods.

I managed to capture the eye of a miserable looking taxi driver who reluctantly agreed to take me to my address. I could have walked the short distance, but I just wanted to get 'home' and do it as quickly as possible.

Outside the door to my apartment I paused, lowered my hand luggage to the floor and listened. The door had been opened and left slightly ajar, although there was no sign of a forced entry.

I had no phone and no weapon, both of which had been confiscated by a dutiful Captain Said.

I pushed gently at the door, ducking down and ready to spring up at anyone approaching from the inside.

"Is that you Gary?" a familiar voice said.

"Yes it is Sir!" I replied.

"Well, come on in lad ... it's your damn apartment ... not mine."

Marshal Brooking came into view as I nudged the door fully open.

"It's a bloody good job I didn't have my gun with me ... or else you would have been dead by now." I confirmed.

The senior Air Force officer laughed.

"And if I thought for one minute my life would be in danger simply by meeting with you, I would have had you 'lifted' as soon as you got off the damn aircraft."

Now it was my turn to laugh.

"Sit down. I've made some tea and now I need to hear all about it. Don't miss out any detail whatsoever.

The IRA has had their share of good luck in all this mess and it's opened a few doors for us; doors the PM considers to be worth it. However, there is a rotten apple in the barrel Gary. It's rotten to the tune of sixty million ... and we want it back!"

I wondered if he really understood the amount of interest there really was in stealing or 'recovering' the sixty million ... depending upon your viewpoint.

"You sir and many others ..." I confirmed.

Four hours, several cups of tea, a couple of large whiskies and a warm pizza later, Brooking had the full nine yards.

The only item left out was the gaining of valuable knowledge in relation to the internal workings of the Dubai United Commercial Bank and one numbered account in particular.

The 'Boss' voted not to drive back to Cheltenham on a busy Friday and would stay the night in my spare room. This provided time and opportunity to become absolutely plastered together and not boding well for the following morning.

Suffering from tender hangovers and poor eyesight, we were both up at six o'clock the next day.There was work to do at my office and Marshall David Brooking had tasks to tackle at his. He would have to prepare a report for Number Ten and then no doubt sit with the PM and be questioned about the whole affair. This would include the sharp note of protest delivered by the diplomatic representative of the Emirate of Dubai relating to a certain Gary Chase.

Brooking had parked his nearly new Range Rover about a block and a half away due to a shortage of spaces anywhere near to my apartment.

We shook hands as he left and for some unknown reason, when our hands made contact, I felt a distinct shiver run over me, from head to toe. He looked pale ... and I felt it was not necessarily due to an excessive intake of alcohol.

"Are you alright sir?" I asked as our hands disconnected.

"I'm fine Gary, but I am worried about you. From now on, until all this shit blows over and the associated 'back stories' fade into oblivion, you should not travel outside of the UK ... and keep a damn pistol with you at all times. Draw a new one from the RAF Regiment guys when you get back to Irton. Do you understand?"

"I do sir." I confirmed, not knowing that this would be the very last time we would speak to one another.

My eyes followed him until he turned a corner and disappeared from view. He looked back briefly. I was close to running after him but had no real reason to do so; just a hunch that something might possibly be wrong.

Boiling the kettle for yet another cup of tea; kitchen windows half open, encouraging a cooling breeze to circulate and refresh the stale atmosphere, I heard a noise. It was not a particularly loud noise, more of a low frequency rumble as if being played out on a military bass drum.

I knew what it was immediately. I looked out

the kitchen window for any signs of an explosion or rising smoke in the direction of the road running one block away ... the road where David Brooking had parked his car.

There was nothing to be seen.

I ran to the hallway, grabbed a jacket and flew out of the apartment.

I didn't know exactly where the car I was looking for had been parked. There was no sign of anything out of the ordinary having happened. Then in the distance I recognised the dark blue roof line of a Range Rover. It looked to be intact with the only irregular sign being the vehicle sitting at a slight angle in the parking spot as if it had been parked hurriedly.

I made my approach.

From the outside, the Rover looked fine and undamaged. However, every window had been blackened making it impossible to see inside.

I knew immediately the vehicle had not been parked hurriedly, it had been lifted off its wheels with the force of a substantial explosion. I had little doubt; this was an assassination using a sophisticated series of explosive devices planted inside the car. I was tempted to try the driver side door, but something prompted me to move away.

Then the emotion overcame me!

I ran to my apartment, holding back tears, mentally kicking myself for not having checked the fucking car before he got in it. What a damned fool I was. I grabbed my keys spending fifteen minutes checking every square inch of my own car, inside and out until I was finally satisfied it was 'clean' and not carrying any devices, explosives or trackers. However, this did nothing to reassure me ... and I did not feel safe.

From now on, my personal weapon, the Makarov 9mm would travel with me everywhere

On the way to Irton Moor, I stopped at a telephone box and called in the event to the local police headquarters. I only registered the fact that the car looked 'suspicious' rather than being the site of a callous murder; the murder of my long time friend and mentor, David Brooking.

CHAPTER TWENTY-TWO

Back to the 'Bunker' ...

The local 'copper's' caught up with me just before lunchtime. However, the site military police and 'Regiment' guys were holding them at bay and needed to know if I would be coming to speak with them.

Eventually we agreed to meet 'above ground' in the Admin Hut; this being despite the senior police officer amongst them insisting they take me down to the local station for a 'discussion' about a 'delicate' matter.

When I entered the Nissen Hut general briefing room, I was greeted by four policemen; one Chief Inspector, one Sergeant and two uniformed, fresh faced constable's.

I was desperate to find out what had actually happened and how David had died, but I needed to show the minimum of emotion during the interrogation. They called it an 'exchange of useful information', but I knew damn well it was a fucking interrogation!

In the short few hours since the discovery of a body, the police had made only one connection; only one that may be linked to the death of such a senior Air Force Officer. No doubt, they were determined to squeeze it for all it was worth.

Chief Inspector Pryce had lived with the facility at Irton on his patch all his working life as a detective, however, that did not mean he enjoyed the experience.

Military personnel and a major number of civilian operators working there appeared to be immune from police action. Speeding tickets, parking violations and small scale incidents of accidental damage to vehicles had piled up on Pryce's desk during his early years and eventually he had to bin them.

I offered my four visitors a cup of tea or coffee and maybe a chance at a chocolate covered biscuit, but Pryce, speaking on behalf of his 'team' politely declined.

The opening question was always the same.

"Can I ask sir, where were you between seven and eight o'clock this morning?"

The initial game of verbal ping-pong would accelerate the discussion gradually toward a game of chequers and finally end up as a tight standoff chess manoeuvre.

Between Pryce and my-self, interrupted now and again by a very curious Sergeant Deeping, the 'game' lasted just over the hour. At the end of it, neither of us appeared to be any further forward in understanding what happened to David Brooking and the disappointment could be clearly seen on all our faces.

DCI Pryce insisted on having the last word as he raised himself from his chair.

"You will of course understand that no-one seems to know exactly what the hell is going on up here and maybe some of you feel you do not have to answer directly to the law.

However, I am likened to a Jack Russell with a bone Mr Chase and if I feel the effort is worth it, I will pursue anyone ... anywhere ... to get what I want. So, think-on young man ... you are far from holding a clean sheet on this one ... and the next time I see you, you might very well be sitting in front of a Judge. I hope I make myself clear!"

He held out a hand and produced what passed for his very best professional policeman's smile.

"Until we meet again Mr. Chase ..."

"Until then DCI Pryce ..." I echoed.

There were numerous Telex Machine installations scattered around the bunker. Within my direct control I had two; one connected to a standard land-line and one directed through the GCHQ deep code system, something thought to be unbreakable and highly secure.

I planned to use the standard system to start my interrogation of the Dubai United Commercial Bank. Using the 'secure' route meant risking a 'code capture' by the GCHQ and leaving a trail that could not be easily erased from the system memory.

I sat down in front of my machine and prepared to cut a tape. I had with me a scrap of paper, with writing scrawled across the face of it, along with a notepad and pen.

Now I would find out for sure if I was as good as I thought I was.

It took me an hour to write up an interrogation code clean enough to kick start my search for a way into the admin structure of the bank.

I fed the tape though the reader and the machine began to write a load of code; in fact after ten minutes of activity, there were twenty three pages of typewritten script folded on the floor. I would need to study the paperwork with care. Somewhere included in all the script and the digits would be the key to opening up a particular numbered account and the internal bank file linked to it; a file that would give me a name.

At some minutes past eight that evening, it finally happened. The Eureka moment I searched for had arrived. The name and banking details of the person who owned one specific numbered account with the Dubai based DUCB was listed as T. Ludlow. The address appeared to be a Post Office service of some sort and described as Box 83, Banbury Road Post Office.

I moved back into my office, taking the pile of paper folds from the Tele-printer with me. Did I have a result ... or not? That was a particularly difficult question to answer.

The 'cover' address and name was easy to translate to a real human being and I had no doubt the real identity of the real criminal was General Sir Tarquin Ludlow and his real address was Farnborough Hall. I experienced no elation, no celebration of victory and for some strange reason felt emotionally drained. I expected to be jumping around all over the place, completely elated with joy having discovered the identity my shadowy nemesis.

I sat, deep in thought, head in hands staring into the stillness. The steaming black surface of a half consumed cup of coffee stared back at me. Would this be the end? Having thought everything through, it became quite obvious that the man best placed, and someone with guaranteed access to all the information needed to pursue a trail of devastation and destruction, would be none other than the General himself.

But none of it made sense. Here was a man with a distinguished career behind him, due for retirement and remaining master of his substantial Oxfordshire family seat. To be in his position, no one would think he needed money. Surely he must have had a comfortable inheritance handed down to him from his father Lord Avonsbury, so perhaps the motive was not money of necessity, but money due to greed.

I found myself absent-mindedly rubbing my neck. Now and again my birthmark would become inflamed and itchy. It didn't happen often but when it did it was normally an indicator of stress.

There were very few occasions in the past when I could think the dark coloured 'S' shaped mark had bothered me, but I made sure I had it covered with a shirt collar as often as possible.

It was time to grab some sleep and then begin investigating the movements of the itinerant General.

What was I to do with him?

Did I have the courage to take my retribution to the ultimate end; do it quickly and make all the right preparations to leave a scene clean of evidence and short on clues?

What about the family? What about Martha and the children, Pricilla and Edwina? Then of course there was Mrs. Wyatt the housekeeper; what about her?

I moved back to my office, taking the Makarov and ankle holster out of my desk drawer and placing it on the desk-top. I focused on it for a minute or so.

No, this was not the way. Shooting at someone and expecting to kill them with such a light weapon was fraught with danger ... the danger being the target might very well live through it all. The rule was never to hit a big man with a small calibre bullet ... the result would often surprise you! I could of course find myself a heavier weapon, something more powerful, such as the Glock 19, and as a result, more accurate.

One other way to bring this whole dark business to final closure would be to leak the identity of the sixty million pound blackmailer to either Number Ten or the IRA.

Sleep would no doubt provide the answer ... and now I must switch-off and search for some. I had the feeling that tomorrow might end up being a very long day.

I rang Farnborough Hall early the next day. It was a Sunday and all the Ludlow family were at home. Martha, Mrs. Ludlow, answered my call and after consulting with her husband advised I would be most welcome to visit that afternoon. I offered a time of around two thirty and Martha cheerily agreed.

"Yes, that's no problem Gary. Tarquin says he

is looking forward to meeting with you again. Mind you, I don't want you two staying up half the night drinking whiskey. He has an early start at the Ministry tomorrow and will need to leave here at six thirty"

I packed an overnight bag, just in case, making sure the Makarov was firmly strapped into my ankle holster. I had no intention of using it that day, but not knowing what the General might have in store for me, it was a comforting decision to keep it close.

The car journey would take the best part of five hours. I kept an eye on everything going on around me, especially to the rear. Was I being followed? The question niggled at me all the way there.

Was I becoming paranoid?

Mrs. Wyatt answered the door. Yes, I was expected. Yes, the General was waiting for me in the library. Yes, the family were at home. Did I want to stay for dinner?

I thanked Mrs. Wyatt and confirmed I would not be staying for dinner.

She was giving me that damned look again. It showed as piercing and yet curious at the same time. I simply had to comment.

"Is everything alright Mrs. Wyatt ... is there something you want to ask me?"

She remained transfixed for a further few seconds and then her expression suddenly changed to a smile, an unforced smile that nearly became laughter.

"No Sir. Everything is fine and as always, you are welcome here at Farnborough Hall."

She took a step back, taking the door with her and opening up the entrance to let me by. The uncomfortable stare came back, but now, being closer, I could see it was not me in general she was staring at but the birth mark on my neck. It must have been showing, revealed in part just above my collar line.

Sir Tarquin Ludlow sat in one of the comfortable Chesterfields as I was shown into the library. Without turning to look at me, he indicated another leather chair opposite. I sat down.

"More tea I think Mrs. Wyatt ... and maybe a sandwich or two for our visitor?"

"Yes sir." she replied, and left the room.

"I have to say this is somewhat of a surprise Gary, but a welcome one nevertheless. You have come a long way to talk to me today, so I hope you will find it to have been worthwhile."

I smiled. I felt surprisingly comfortable in his presence despite knowing how many murders he had conducted or managed over the past weeks and months ... but now was to be 'confession' time.

"Did you leave your car on the drive or ... err ... by the garages Gary?"

"On the drive ..."

He held out his hand and pushed it toward me.

"Perhaps you give me the keys, my driver will move it to the garage ... it ... hmm ... might be safer there!"

"Safer?" I questioned, leaning forward in my chair.

"How would my car be SAFER on the

driveway General ... please tell me HOW much SAFER it might become?"

The hand hastily with-drawn, the face took on a look of confusion, concern and possibly even a shade or two of fear.

"If I remember correctly, the last time you made any vehicle of mine become SAFER, I ended up with two men dead and bits of their bodies scattered halfway across the Oxford bypass.

Should I scroll through your telephone contacts Tarquin and look for the Provo's Pat Doherty and his gang of murderers to come and do you another favour?"

Tarquin Ludlow coloured up. He moved uneasily in his chair. This was possibly a different kind of conversation than the one he had prepared himself for.

"I'm not sure I really understand what you are getting at Gary. Is there something bothering you, something you need to get of your chest perhaps?"

"Well my dear General, there is the small matter of sixty million quid you stole from a rather disappointed IRA.

Then there is an even bigger role you obviously played in necessitating HMG to excavate national treasury funds to the tune of three hundred million pounds sterling.

This particular 'interest' of yours put in motion a bloody chase extending half way round the world. It left a trail of dead and mutilated bodies with your fucking name attached to every single one of them!"

The atmosphere immediately became cold and forbidding; Tarquin Ludlow appearing as agitated as a storm tossed ship. I waited for his comment; some sort of reply to my accusation that would either make sense or describe the boundaries of a previously rehearsed denial.

He offered neither.

He stood and walked over to a wall mounted button. Pressing on it would summon Mrs. Wyatt.

She tapped the library door gently before entering.

"Yes sir?"

"Can you please cancel the sandwiches Mrs. Wyatt ... our visitor will not be staying long!"

She left without comment; her eyes lingered on me for a second, perhaps looking to transmit some kind of message. Strangely I felt the mark on my neck become uncomfortably hot and itchy. What was it about that damn woman that put me in such a state of unease?

Finally, the General addressed the situation.

"I fear you have been watching too many action and adventure films Flight Sergeant Chase. You should also understand that whatever you THINK you know you are still in the military and bound by the contents of the Official Secrets Act. I am a General Officer and with one single phone call can have you collected from this place and taken to another place ... a place you will find far more uncomfortable.

You are making accusations of treason and murder ... and yet you have no evidence linking me to any singe act, let alone the trail of disaster you appear to have left behind you in pursuing a bag of damned micro-chips."

I needed a minute to think through what the

General had just said. He was right of course. In military terms he could have me arrested on a whole list of charges; isolate me from any form of communications until he had time to organise his next move.

I made a decision and I hoped to God it was the right one.

"I will be leaving you now ... but I will be back and I WILL find ways of exposing you and bringing you to some form of justice."

I stood and made my way out of the library. Mrs. Wyatt waited in the middle of the hallway, her eyes following my every movement as I headed for the door.

I confronted her again.

"Mrs. Wyatt, is there something you really want to say to me?"

Her lips moved and mouthed some words I simply could not hear.

It was time to get the hell out of there."

I checked my car thoroughly for anything out of the ordinary and sped off in the direction of Banbury where I hoped to find a room at the White Horse Hotel.

That evening, a decision had been made. I cared less what happened to me be ... but Ludlow had to die.

I had a telephone number for Finn Sullivan written in my notebook as 'Tommy'. I rang it and after half a minute a female voice answered; a voice difficult to hear over the background noise.

"O'Mally's Pub and Restaurant ... what can I do for yer?"

"I would like to speak with 'Tommy'. You can tell him its Gary Chase calling. It's an important matter."

The line fell silent, the background noise disappeared. Then the female voice spoke again.

"I'm afraid 'Tommy' can't talk to you over the phone. Can you come here ..?"

"No. I'm in a place called Banbury, just north of Oxford and there are about sixty million reasons why its important I speak with 'Tommy'."

More silence. Then ...

"Please ring back on this number straight away and we will ... err ... make a connection for you."

I disconnected and then rang again. A gruff male voice answered with a strong southern Irish accent.

"What do you want Gary?" the voice asked.

"I want what you want 'Tommy'. You have lost a few good men over the past weeks due to the actions, deceit and greed of just one man. I now know who that one man is. We need to talk!"

Some deep breathing appeared to be taking place as Finn Sullivan, codename 'Tommy' considered what I had just told him.

"Have you got evidence?" he asked.

"Yes I have ... and it directly links this person to a bank account in Dubai.

It also links him to the deposit of sixty million big ones.

Are you interested?"

Another pause ... much longer this time.

"Where are you?"

"I'm at the White Hart Hotel in Banbury, room seventeen."

"Will I need a team?"

"Yes, I think so. He seems to have some connection to your favourite British army unit and they might well be here in numbers."

"I'm told we can be there within a couple of hours. We will be in three cars."

"There's plenty of parking at the front of the hotel. I'll be waiting for you!"

CHAPTER TWENTY-THREE

The final reckoning!

Having had something to eat, a glass of wine and two cups of coffee, I felt refreshed and ready to tackle whatever might lie ahead.

The tap on the door came as it was getting dark. Finn Sullivan slipped in when I opened it and accepted my offer of a cup of coffee as he settled into one of the well upholstered armchairs.

"So, tell me what all this is about Gary. From my perspective and probably that of the High Command is that we have a victory on our hands. Despite the fact we now have more than a few million in the bank, we have also scored a massive political victory over the fucking British!"

He sat back in the chair, his face filled to the brim with a massive smile.

"In fact Gary, you may not know this, but you have become something of a folk hero within the IRA. You are the man who doggedly chased this damn opportunity, at the risk of your own life ... for the cause!"

This I did not know. It was a worrying thought.

"No Finn. That is not the reason.

I simply became wrapped up in it as people were dying around me on a near daily basis.

However, strings were being pulled everywhere by the one man we all least suspected.

He also arranged the murder of any individual who looked to be in the way of him getting his hands on what he thought was an untraceable sixty million quid ... but he was wrong."

I took a breath.

"OK. Here is the condensed version of the story and once you know how the whole damn scheme fitted beautifully together, you, like me, will want to kill this bastard."

The question from Finn was unexpected.

"What about the money? Will we be able to get it back if we put this person away?"

My reply was a cautious one.

"It might be possible, but very much depending upon what he could have been doing with it since it arrived in Dubai."

An hour later, I had delivered everything I regarded as highlights in the whole damn business. Finn watched me carefully for any signs of embellishment or discomfort, signs that may prompt him to question what he was being told.

As I was still alive at the end of the delivery, there must have been none.

"I need to make a phone call." Finn announced. "So, if you could leave me alone for a few minutes that would be appreciated."

He smiled but there was no depth to it. It was an expression of politeness.

I left the room and went to the bar; sitting nursing a Jamesons, wondering what was being talked about in my absence.

A quarter of an hour later, Finn joined me and ordered two more drinks.

"OK Gary." Finn whispered. "We are ON. My instructions are that if there is anything 'our man' needs to provide so we can get our hands on the remainder of the sixty million quid, then we are to get it from him, even if strong methods of persuasion are needed!"

I did not need to ask what that meant. We both knew.

"What about the family, Martha and the two girls? They must not be harmed Finn ... I need your assurance on that."

"Don't worry. From what you've told me, he will be leaving the house at six-thirty ... and we will be there to capture him. One of my men will hide his car and we will take him on the half hour journey to a safe house we use in Coventry."

"What happens then?" I asked out of curiosity.

"Once there we can question him to make sure we have the right perpetrator and answer any questions you might have for him."

"And then ..?"

"And then ... we kill him. This whole operation will be tied up and put to bed by ten thirty ... and me and the lads will be on our way to the ferry before anyone really knows he is missing."

"Well, that sounds like a plan to me ... and if the SAS appear somewhere, galloping over the horizon ... what then?"

"We kill them as well!"

He smiled, the eyes remaining alert and intelligent.

"Will you be coming with us?" Finn asked.

"Try and stop me!" I replied.

※

The Honourable Sir Tarquin Ludlow enjoyed a full English breakfast cooked for him by Chef Alex and served at the breakfast table by the ever attentive Mrs. Wyatt.

He checked his watch for time. He would be driving to Banbury to catch the seven o'clock train to London Marylebone Station. He would arrive in the city by nine and be in the office for nine-thirty.

He would be using his own personal transport today, a five year old Jaguar, maintained in pristine condition.

The conversation with Gary Chase the previous day had left him unsettled. He had decided to pick up on some leave; book some time off and get away from the UK with his family. One thing was for sure, he certainly could afford it. So, today he would attend his office and put in place whatever arrangements needed to be made.

He also planned to have lunch at his club and meet up with one of his 'problem solvers', ex-Marine Captain Michael Danvers. The arrogant air-force Sergeant needed to be reminded of one or two simple truths in life ... and maybe even pay some kind price for ignoring them. He had not yet made that very final decision, but planned to have done ... by lunchtime.

The 'capture' was a classic move. As Tarquin guided his car out of the half mile long drive and in the direction of the main highway; Gaydon in one direction and Banbury in the other, he was forced to halt in the middle of the road, narrowly missing the body laying there.

It was a man. His face and the top of his head

looked as if it might be covered in blood. He left the car and approached the 'injured' individual. From literally nowhere, three men appeared, then two cars came screeching to a halt, one behind and one to the front.

The unconscious individual immediately jumped up, showing no signs of injury, and pulled out a 9 mm from beneath a torn and dishevelled looking jacket.

A black cloth bag was pulled roughly over Tarquin's head and wrists cable-tied together. The only words spoken were ... "Get in the fucking car!"

Less than half a minute later the cars were all gone. There would be no sign anything untoward had happened there that day. To Finn and his 'soldiers', this was the easy part. They had carried out what was known as a 'snatch' many times before and everyone involved knew what they had to do.

Less than half an hour later, everyone all gathered at the safe house; a dilapidated looking end terrace with a double size shuttered garage style building to the side. The shutters closed down behind us as our car entered the empty but tidy space.

The Jaguar had been left locked and wiped clean of prints in the back corner of Banbury railway station car park.

As we clambered out of the car, Finn reminded me all that was needed now would be a sensible conversation with the General ... and then we could all go home.

I had to admit that seeing the General hooded

and tied to a chair made me feel a little apprehensive,

"Will you be going the full nine yards?" I asked Finn.

"We go as far as we need to Gary ... and if this looks as if it might turn out to be a bit messy for you, then you should go ... Now!"

"It's not an issue. I've seen bad things before."

"Good ... then you get to ask the first question."

I pulled off the black hood. He blinked, spat on the concrete floor, the central area of which was covered with taped down plastic sheeting.

That alone would be a warning to most men!

Eventually, he looked up to take in the faces of his captors. Everyone in the room wore a mask except me. He knew me. He knew the sound of my voice. There was no use attempting to hide behind any form of mask.

He spoke first.

"What the fuck do you want Gary? Why this childish gangster kidnapping shit? How do you think all of this is going to go down when you finally have to release me?"

He stared at me with wild eyes; eyes that exposed the truth of his fear and underlined the bravado with which he expected to continue.

"Let us talk about money Tarquin; real amounts of money that you have locked up in some dodgy Dubai bank. The gentlemen who are accompanying me on this little exercise feel it belongs to them ... and they would like it back."

The man in the chair glared back at me in silence.

It was obvious at that point, questioning the

General was going to be a little more difficult than first thought.

"Let me help you out here Tarquin. I have access to your account. I know how much is in there and can see all the logged movements made by you since the deposit of your ill-gotten gains. As you know, two passwords are required to operate the account. One allows access and the second one allows the movement of monies in and monies out of the account. Am I right so far?"

No reply.

However, the mention of the 'movement of monies' did strike a chord somewhere. Once again, the eyes gave it away.

I looked toward Finn.

"He obviously has no intention of co-operating with us, so, as I do not specifically wish to witness what is now about to happen, I will leave him your capable hands. I have no doubt he will talk ... eventually, but my worry is ... will he be in any condition to speak to me? Please be careful. Inflicting pain is one thing; destroying a man physically is something else!"

Finn said nothing. He pointed to a door set in the south wall of the garage unit and I headed toward it. One of the soldiers moved over to a workbench and picked up a hammer. Another collected a pair of bolt cutters from the same bench. They moved in on Tarquin.

I had my hand on the door handle. I looked back. He had begun to tremble violently; a white foam exiting his mouth and dribbling down his neck.

This was not good. He might well have a

fucking heart attack before we had a chance at getting anything from him. Then, quite unexpectedly, his lips moved; the dribble now backing up on his chin.

Finn leaned in close, beckoning me to come back. I placed my ear near to our sobbing captive.

"You'll have to say that again General. We can't hear you ..."

He refused to lift his head ... but I understood every damn word.

"Thirty, fifty one, twenty one followed by AGRST in capitals ..."

It was at that point he wet himself.

"Bag him up!" ordered Finn and the hood went on again. We moved away from the General as I scribbled on a scrap piece of paper the password revealed by him.

"What do you think?" Finn asked.

"I don't really know and the only way to find out is to punch what he has just told us into my machine and see what results we get. I think we need to keep him alive until we know what might have happened to the money."

"OK. One of my men will take you back to Banbury. You can collect your car and make your way back to your office. Give me your piece of paper."

He took it and scribbled a phone number on the back.

"We will keep him here until we hear from you ... one way or the other. This is a phone number you can get me on here ... in the garage."

"It will be a four hour road trip, then an hour or so making the bank connection and so you should expect to hear from me late afternoon."

"OK Gary, but drive carefully and keep your damn eyes peeled. If his ex-SAS team have been given the job of finding him, they won't be too worried about leaving a trail. Do you have your gun with you?"

I nodded.

"Good luck then ... and be on your way!"

The young man who took me to Banbury drove the car as if he had stolen it. Therefore I was more than grateful to be alive when we finally pulled up outside the White Hart.

After paying my outstanding bill I checked my car for any unusual additions. Then I watched carefully for any suspicious bodies lurking outside the hotel. Everything looked to be clear but by now I knew the General would have been missed at his office and no doubt an official search would be in progress.

Some hours later I sat in front of my Telex machine looking to log on to Ludlow's numbered account at the Dubai based DUCB. I had been in once and knew the trail. However, when I accessed the account details and authorised movements, I discovered the balance had dropped to fifty-one million and there were payments pending of another six million.

This was the frustrating bit. I could see the

account but could not control any movements in or out.

I typed in the override code and it took me to a password protected script. This was it. What I had scribbled on my scrap of paper would either work ... or not! I took a deep breath and punched it in.

It took a few seconds, but finally, after a scroll of code exited the typed access authority, the single word 'ENTER' appeared. The log showed the date, time and location of the authorised entry event ... and now I knew we were cooking with gas!

I had all the IRA account details at the National Irish Bank and transferred everything in the account, including the reversed 'payments pending' amounts, which I managed to highjack back into the account quite easily. I left one thousand pounds sterling to pay the instruction fees and that looked to be it.

I closed everything down and wiped the facility access log clean. This would make sure no one would be able to trace my use of the system and especially the codes and passwords used to enter the DUCB numbered accounts facility ... illegally.

I returned to my office with a smile on my face. It would not last very long!

I picked up the telephone and rang the number given to me by Finn. It took several rings for him to answer.

"It's done!" I declared.

"How much should we expect?"

"You should be looking for a number of around fifty one million, less a few grand charges at both ends." I confirmed.

I picked up on the sharp intake of breath.

"That sounds very good to me Gary ... I will contact headquarters and let them know the good news. So, is that the end of it?"

"Well Gary ... that depends upon what you want us to do with our ... err ... package." The smile disappeared.

"Is the 'package' in good condition?"

"Possibly one or two internal issues; but alive and breathing."

I did not wear the mantle of God very easily. Deciding whether a man should live or die was not a situation I had ever prepared myself for.

"I can't handle murder just for murder's sake Finn. I think you should return him to Farnborough Hall and then get the hell out of the country and back to Ireland."

"Well my next question has to be ... what about you Gary? Leaving him alive might well put you in jeopardy.

I know you feel those in Number Ten are covering your arse, but they are politicians ... and, as you well know, cannot be trusted in any circumstances.

If power, greed and old school tie association come to the fore, they will turn their back on you at the drop of a damned hat!"

There was no doubt that what Finn was saying was the truth.

"Don't forget who you are dealing with here; a ranking military officer, an ex-Etonian, a father who sat in the Lords, owner of an historical country estate and a wife with family connections to every campaigning General for the past three hundred years. That's what you are up against Gary ... and in any battle between you and them, who do you think will win?"

CHAPTER TWENTY-FOUR

A final revelation

General Sir Tarquin Ludlow was discovered wrapped in an old carpet, hands and feet tied together, in the bottom of a ditch about a mile and a half from Farnborough Hall.

The national search for the General had been urgent but purposely low-key. He had been found as a result of an anonymous phone call to the Metropolitan Police headquarters at Scotland Yard. His body was badly bruised and his ego even more so. He remained silent when questioned as to his recent whereabouts, simply quoting the requirements of the Official Secrets Act.

Martha and the girls were relieved and grateful to still have a father and Mrs. Wyatt offered what she felt sure would be the necessary words of comfort. She had a secret and wondered if now might be the time to reveal it?"

All Tarquin needed to repair him completely was some sleep and time for thought. There had been one or two messages of congratulations from a portion of the few who knew of his circumstances, but nothing from Number Ten.

It was obvious that by now the game was up. The money to finance his retirement and re-invigorate the estate was no more. He had resigned himself to that predicament during the long hour he had spent confined in the dry ditch, not knowing what was to happen next.

Tomorrow would be another day; a new

perspective perhaps and possibly a word of encouragement from someone who might well understand what he had been going through.

At a few minutes past midnight, I received a phone call from the head of MI9, military Intelligence. I had been sleeping. He apologised for the hour but wanted to confirm the missing General had been found and appeared to be fit and well.

I asked why he was telling me?

"Well, Mr. Chase, I thought that as you had been closely involved in the General's recent ... err ... activities, you would like to be kept up to date."

"I don't know what bloody 'activities' you are referring to ... but I think you must have the wrong fucking number!"

I slammed the phone down; very angry at being linked to Tarquin's disappearance and even angrier at having my sleep disturbed. However, this might be a warning sign. I would need to be careful ... it was not all over yet!"

I woke the following morning with a headache and the first two cups of dark coffee didn't help.

'What would today bring' I wondered.

With the horrific murder of my mentor and best friend David Brooking, I felt all at sea. I now had no one to turn to for advice leaving me cautious about where the line between my military responsibilities ended and my civilian ones began.

Whatever was about to happen now, I knew I would need to guard my life with care.

At ten minutes past eight, I turned up at the security gate to CSOS Irton Moor. I immediately noticed the guard room contained not only the expected uniformed military policeman but two sombre looking civilians, both wearing long grey raincoats. This was the uniform of MI5 field officers.

All three heads turned in my direction as I pulled up close to the barrier.

The duty policeman, who normally popped out for a short chat, would be staying inside the guard room today, operating the lifting barrier pole remotely and waving me through.

Three pairs of eyes, decorating blank faces, followed my progress as I navigated my way toward the rear of the Nissan Hut.

My team of technicians were keen to find out what was going on and explain that my frequent absences were now affecting progress on several projects.

I assured all of them we would be back together as a group by the end of the week, but until then, I might have other overriding duties to attend to.

I sat in my office and waited.

The first call came from the PM's private secretary at Number Ten. He wanted to know what the fuck was going on! The second came from Finn. He wanted me to know what had actually gone on. The third came from General Ludlow and the fourth came from some anonymous character whose first language was certainly not English.

The words he used and delivered in a heavy Asian or Middle Eastern accent, were threatening and after listening to the first few seconds of rambling drivel, I slammed the receiver down on its cradle.

The one from Ludlow was the most intriguing. He wanted to meet with me, to tie up a 'myriad' of loose ends ... as he put it. I rang him back. It was a very short conversation and I cautiously agreed to travel down to Farnborough Hall the following day.

I was eager to hear what he had to say.

Mrs. Wyatt opened the door to me, her face strained and pale. The eyes however were sharp as pins and hiding their normal sign of friendliness.

"Come in Mr. Chase." she offered. "Sir Tarquin will see you in the library. He will be with you in a short while."

She looked past my shoulders, left and right.

"Did you come by car sir?" she asked.

"I did Mrs. Wyatt. It's at the end of the drive. I really needed a short walk after my drive down. It's not in anyone's way ... I can assure you."

I delivered my very best 'little boy' smile. She moved to the side and opened the door fully.

"You know your way sir. I'll bring you some tea and sandwiches. By the way, Martha and the children are away for a few days visiting her mother, so you two will have the house to yourselves ... except for the staff of course."

Before I could offer my thanks she was gone. What a curious thing to want to tell me. Perhaps she knew something I didn't. My damn birthmark was itching again. It was as if Mr's Wyatt had some strange effect on me, leaving me to wonder what it could possibly be.

I entered the library. The French windows, leading out to a broad stone terrace, were wide open providing a cool but welcome breeze. I checked for any other open windows and doors or concealed entrances I might not be familiar with. I then took a newspaper from Tarquin's desk and picked a Chesterfield.

Taking my Makarov 9mm from the ankle holster, I placed it inside the folded newspaper. The magazine held nine good reasons why I should reasonably walk away from this place today, alive and in one piece. However, I did not have a crystal ball and no idea what the outcome of today's visit to this wonderful old manor house would be.

The General entered.

He voted to sit at his desk, which meant I would need to turn my body some degrees to the left in order to end up facing him directly.

He raised his head and smiled. It looked to be genuine and well meant.

"Welcome once again Gary. You are truly becoming a regular visitor to me here at Farnborough Hall."

I didn't say anything. I was now eager to find out what the hell he wanted.

"We appear to be coming to the end of this rather sad and complex series of events and now, as far as finances seem to be concerned, everyone has what they expected to be rightfully theirs."

"Well, that would be with only one real

exception General." I confirmed.

"Ah yes Sergeant ... you mean ME of course."

"I do sir."

"We will come to that in a moment, but right now there are issues to be resolved with the authorities; issues that affect the careers and pension of us both!"

I laughed out loud.

"Not from where I'm sitting."

"You may think so right now, but you no longer have a powerful military advocate on your side. You might well find that navigating the Air Force High Command as a mere Flight Sergeant, but soon to be Warrant Officer, has become quite a frustrating procedure. You have blood on your hands my friend ... and it will not wash off easily."

I waited a minute before replying. The words had been spoken with bravado but the outward signs of nervousness told a different story.

"If you are referring to Air Vice-Marshall Brooking, a person whose murder was ordered by YOU, then you are correct. But I have a whole bloody list of murders involving you ... or perpetrated by one of your ex-SAS henchmen."

He looked at me, face darkening, patchwork stress marks growing, hands revealing a slight tremble disguised by the nervous rolling back and forth across the desk of an ornately decorated silver pen.

He lifted his head and our eyes locked together.

Who would blink first?

"Is there something you want to say to me General?"

"Yes Gary. Whatever you stand to accuse me

off, you will need proof. And before it might come anywhere near to being tested in front of a jury, it will have to get past a board of my military peers ... and I wish you good luck on that one!"

I leant forward in the Chesterfield to add a little emphasis to my words.

"Listen to me carefully. You sir, being so full of your own fucking importance, so assured by your 'old public school' connections and your family history as serving military officers, you seem to forget there is a real world out there!"

He turned his head away. He did not want to hear the truth of it.

"The fact is, as far as your 'chum's in high places, military and politically are concerned, you Sir Tarquin Ludlow ... are a dead fucking DUCK!"

The pen manipulation stopped immediately. The General's unoccupied hands disappeared beneath the desk.

"What you seem to have decided to ignore is the situation in Ireland. It could well have exploded into an absolute bloodbath, both in the north and the south, but today remains calm and managed.

That my dear General is due to the fact certain warring factions have found themselves in receipt of monies they had no real right to.

However, in return HMG is now in receipt of some front line inventions; mass produced microelectronics that will, without doubt, change the shape of the world for many centuries to come. The possibilities are immense; the rewards calculated in billions rather than millions.

Due to what has happened over the past weeks,

Britain will become a world leader in a new, wondrous technology. It will compare today's 'down the wire' communications systems with what we will come to see as the Electronic Stone Age!"

He smiled. It was a strange reaction. Perhaps he was not a believer ... and never would be.

"I came here today to listen to you in the hope you would tell me what the hell all this murder and mayhem has been about?

They are coming for you General; maybe not today, maybe not tomorrow but certainly very soon. The wheels are in motion at the highest level inside Downing Street and your Public School connections will be of no use to you there.

As for Military discipline boards, you can forget them. The other Generals, sheep that they are, all deserted you when word came out you had been found in a damn ditch. If you don't believe me, try ringing one of them ... see what result you get!"

The smile became thinner as he considered what I had just said. Maybe it pressed on a nerve. Doubt can be a mile wide but only an inch deep ... and I wondered how deep his doubt was right now.

The General leaned forward.

"I invited you here today Gary to extract a promise from you."

"A promise General?" I questioned.

I was not in the mood for games, so I needed to look the devil in the eye and get to the bottom of what was going on in this man's mind.

"I have no one I can trust Gary.

As you quite rightly say, I can no longer rely

on the colour of my blood."

"... and?"

"You are aware that nine million has been drawn out of the Dubai account, before you gained access to it."

"I am ... and no doubt someone in a black ski mask will be coming for it anytime soon!"

"That money rests in a Channel Island's trust fund. It is to secure the future of my family ... when I'm gone. You, Gary, will be the sole administrator of the fund and I want you to make sure this estate and my family are kept financially secure here. I have no son to pass this responsibility on to and whatever has gone on between us in the past, I know you to be independent and ... honest.

Will you do that one small thing for me?"

I was completely taken aback. There were no words. What the fuck did this man expect of me?"

The thoughtful silence was interrupted by a knock at the library door.

"GO AWAY ... whoever you are ... please GO AWAY!" Ludlow shouted; his face bursting into redness, his hands trembling once more as he slammed them into the desk.

The act shook me out of my deliberations and I suddenly became alive to the noise, the shouting and ... without any doubt ... the answer!

So, here was real evidence that even the blackest heart still beats.

"The answer is 'no' Tarquin ... and I cannot for the life of me think that you would expect anything else. I am much more 'blue collar' than 'blue blood'. In my position within the Royal Air Force I have turned down officer training several times, purely because I do fit that particular 'league' of gentlemen. Perhaps that should tell you something about me!

Your family is YOUR concern ... and you must make whatever arrangements you see fit. At the moment you are driving on a tank-full of empty and when the combined forces of HMG get hold of you, there had better be no talk of offshore trusts. They will want their nine million back ... and you had better be prepared to give it to them!"

This was not the answer he wanted and I wondered if I had now, unknowingly, put my own life on the line. I felt for the Makarov beneath the newspaper.

The General, now close to tears, fidgeted with his hands beneath his desk. With a look of panic mixed with triumph, he produced a powerful Glock handgun. Pulling the slide back, he gripped it firmly, pointing the barrel in my direction.

I didn't need convincing. It was ready to go.

A key scraped in the lock; we both turned our heads to the library door. The handle began to turn and seconds later Mrs. Wyatt stood in the doorway. Her mouth fell open; the sight of the gun in the General's hand completely unexpected.

She had words to deliver and she was determined to deliver them.

"There are two gentlemen to see you sir." she announced, her voice cracked and trembling.

"They insist on seeing you now sir ...!"

The sound was less of a 'crack' or some kind of muted explosion and more of a 'phut', comparable to the sound of a high powered air pistol,

I knew what it was. I had heard that sound many times before. It was unmistakable.

The first .223 high velocity Remington round, probably delivered by an AR-15 rifle, made contact with the side of General Ludlow's head, piercing it and making a neat exit wound on the other side. From that shot alone, he would have died instantly.

This was no doubt a professional hit.

The second pierced his neck as his head rolled back and to the left, a sharp movement caused by the initial energy of the first shot.

The third entered his cheek and travelled upwards, exiting his head above the left eye.

Then there was silence.

The General still had hold of his weapon. Sitting as he was, upright behind the desk, with eyes closed there was very little blood to indicate any form of injury. In fact he gave the impression he might well have just 'nodded off' for a second or two.

Mrs. Wyatt had sensibly 'hit the floor' when the first shot was fired, followed very shortly after by me. Was the gunman looking for just one target today ... or maybe this was a trophy expedition!

I waited one whole minute before cautiously raising my head above the padded arm of the Chesterfield.

In the distance I heard what sounded like a motor cycle starting up. Moving quickly to the open French windows, I looked out beyond the terrace and toward the acre or so of ancient woodland behind. The sound of the racing motor cycle engine could still be heard, fading into the distance.

Was this the end of it then?

I damn well hoped so!

I felt for the birthmark on my neck, attempting to sooth it with my fingers. It had suddenly become inflamed and itching. It had also become very damned annoying. Perhaps it was the stress of the moment or an indicator I should have something done to remove it. I would have to give such an option some thought.

The funeral of General Sir Tarquin Ludlow did not take place for three weeks. The politics remained complex with everyone, including me, trying our best to save Martha and especially her innocent children from the truth of the events surrounding their father's death.

As for Martha, she could never be expected to accept her husband had died, with three sniper bullets in his head, as ... 'death in the line of duty'!

He would be buried in the estate graveyard, next to his father. Would the event attract a wide audience? Martha was asked to keep everything 'low key' and she did just that with very few attendances from distant family aristocracy and no attendances at all from the military and the ministry.

I only attended because I wanted to see closure on the whole bloody business. The church was sadly only half full and Martha and the girls remained silent but tearful in the front pews.

I sat, on my own, amongst the last set of benches at the very back of the church. Mrs. Wyatt came and sat beside me. I turned my head to look at her and immediately my birth-mark began to itch. I put up a hand, covering the spot in an attempt to calm it.

She smiled. Now I really had a feeling, a singularly uncomfortable feeling. The eyes transmitted 'DANGER', the hand that reached out to cover mine felt cold as mountain stone.

Was this to be it? Would I find out today what secret she nurtured, the secret that somehow involved me?

She spoke; her tone calm and controlled.

"What a sad finale to the life of a good man Mr. Chase."

"A good man Mrs. Wyatt ... really? I fear you do not have the full picture of how he came to end up here. If you did, you may well see another side to the man who cared for his family ... and equally cared for his staff Mrs. Wyatt ... staff such as yourself!"

I turned away, needing to break eye contact. I raised myself from the hard wooden bench, preparing to leave. I had become quite uncomfortable talking with Mrs. Wyatt and felt the urge to leave. However, there was just one, possibly awkward question lingering in my mind.

"Tell me Mrs. Wyatt, do you hold on to some secret or other that might involve me? I get the impression that every time we meet there is some kind of barrier between us.

I simply can't think what it might be because until just over a month ago, I had no idea you or the Ludlow family existed on the damn planet!"

I took a step away. Mrs. Wyatt stretched out a hand.

"March 30th, 1946 ... that's your birthday isn't it?"

I was slightly taken aback. How had she come to know my birthday? Surely I never had cause to mention it during the short time we had known one another.

I sat down once more.

"Yes it is ... and I have no idea how you know that, but I feel sure you are about to tell me!"

"Yes Gary ... I can most certainly tell you how I know that ... I was there. At your birth, I was there!"

"There?" I queried, not really understanding how that could have come about.

"Yes ... I was at the private hospital in Oxford and I signed all the necessary paperwork on behalf of Captain the Honourable Tarquin Ludlow and your mother ... Dorothy Beckett. The planned adoption by one of the farm tenants on the estate was cancelled when they saw what was considered to be 'the mark of the devil', an 'S' shaped purple mark on your neck. It was me who signed you over to the damn British Social Care System ... and I have asked for God's forgiveness every single day since."

Now it was beginning to dawn upon me. My colour must have dropped through several shades of pale.

Then, with a tear in her eye she revealed the

truth of it ... a truth that would change the direction of my life, forever!

"You need to know Gary that General Sir Tarquin Ludlow, God rest his soul, was indeed ... your father!"

The word 'stunned' would certainly not be adequate to describe how I felt at that particular moment.

Mrs. Wyatt stood in the mind-shattering silence, ready to leave; trembling with emotion as tears formed. She gently tapped my shoulder as she turned ...

"Did he know?" I asked.

She nodded her head, taking a short step away from me.

"How long Mrs. Wyatt ... how bloody long had he known?"

She didn't pause; she didn't change direction. She took one more step ... and then, as if enveloped by some ethereal shadow, she was gone, leaving my question to drift forever in the wind.

THE END

MECURIAN BOOKS

https://www.mecurianbooks.com

Printed in Great Britain
by Amazon